EXTRAORDINARY TIMES: THE LEGACY

Judith Coates

Library and Archives Canada cataloguing in Publication
Judith Coates.

ISBN Book: 978-1-7751668-7-0
ISBN E-Book: 978-1-7751668-8-7

Cover Design: Free Bing Images
Printed in USA by Kindle

OTHER BOOKS BY THE AUTHOR

Writing as Judith Coates
Be Who You Be
Let Your Light Shine
Extraordinary Time of Good Vs Evil
My life my story (Consulting only)

Writing as J L Coates
Second Chances
The Seer, the Seeker and the Orbs
The Total Equals the Sum of the Parts
A Change of Heart
Journey
When A Door Closes
Two women, Two Loves, Two Stories
Awakening
Shattered
Betrayed

DEDICATION

To my husband Bob
1943-2023
I miss you everyday

ACKNOWLEDGEMENTS

A special thank you to Clarice Nelson who, in spite of being unwell, took the time to read this manuscript and share her opinions. Thank you to the Krooked House Book Club for your encouragement and support.

The names, places and most of the events are fictional and a product of my imagination. The book itself is loosely based upon historical fact. Some of the incidents such as the bombing of the King David Hotel are accurate.

A few years ago, I was sitting in church (supposedly listening to the sermon) when I got an idea, 'What if Jesus and Hitler lived at the same time?' Several years later I published my book Extraordinary Time of Good Vs Evil.

When I was finished, I felt like the story wasn't done, that there was still more to be told. Instead of writing 'the end' I felt I should be writing 'to be continued.' So, two years later you have in your hands the "rest of the story."

During the writing, this manuscript became my break from reality. My husband was dying of Prostate Cancer. I spent my days with him at the hospital and late at night, or early in the morning when I couldn't sleep, I sat up writing. Now I can honestly say "the end" and share this with you.

Thank you to my faithful readers who ask if I have another book coming out. I am also happy when I can say yes. You keep me going and are very special to me.

Yes, there is another coming soon.

Look inward. Be as self-aware as you can possibly be. Life is easier when you know yourself, when you can accept your strengths and desires. When you really know who you are and what you want, and you don't try to be something you are not.

Beyond the Moonlit Sea

PROLOGUE

The two young men, born during the same month, raised in the same village, and educated together were polar opposites. Jesse, a natural born leader, was raised in a loving family, and was well liked. Heinrich, raised by his bitter grandmother, grew up to be a bully. Even as a child Heinrich attempted to intimidate Jesse and failed. Despite his many accomplishments, Heinrich always felt inferior to Jesse.

As a young man Jesse stayed home, worked as a carpenter alongside his father and studied to become a minister. He wasn't aware, until he was older, he was destined to become the spiritual leader of many.

After years of study and personal sacrifice, and on the eve of his ordination, Jesse was shocked to see the corruption and greed among the Elders of his church. Completely disillusioned by what he had been taught and what was actually taking place he left his home and travelled to the city of Bern.

Upon his arrival he joined a group of vagrants living in an alley. There the angry young man began fighting and drinking heavily.

Peter, the informal leader of this group, was drawn to Jesse and became his closest friend and mentor. He took care of Jesse, all the while encouraging him to do better, to be better, and stop wallowing in self-pity.

In the meantime, Heinrich's life followed a different course. After his grandmother died, he joined the Army and suffered a career ending injury in a plane crash. The country was in upheaval after fighting and losing a devastating war. New political parties were struggling for recognition, and Heinrich aligned himself with the Socialist party. He rose quickly through the ranks with the single-minded goal of one day becoming their leader.

The party was betrayed from within and he was sent to jail. While there he wrote a manifesto – a guide he would follow when he became leader of the country. Upon his release he joined the Nationalist party and bullied his way up the ranks until, in a sham election he orchestrated, he was elected leader of the party and of the country.

Jesse, as a favor to Peter, attended a revivalist meeting led by Jean Baptiste. This encounter changed Jesse's life. He sobered up and returned to his ministerial calling eventually becoming the leader of a group known as the Believers. He based his teachings upon "forgive those who hurt you" and "treat others as you would want them to treat you."

While living in the alley. Jesse met and married a young prostitute named Marika, who worked tirelessly by his side.

From his position of power Heinrich felt threatened by Jesse's growing popularity and became determined to destroy him and his group of followers. His one desire was to have Jesse acknowledge him, not only as leader of the country, but also as the leader of the one true church. Naturally Jesse refused.

In an attempt to achieve legitimacy Heinrich authorized the formation of a police group known as the Brown Shirts. They were a brutal group of men whose purpose was to carry out Heinrich's wishes.

On one of Jesse's visits home the Brown Shirts, were sent to capture him. When they failed to find him in the village, they systematically murdered the six hundred residents including Jesse's father, brothers and sisters. His mother Maria, and sister Elizabeth, barely survived the brutality inflicted upon them.

This, and other intentionally cruel acts spurred some of the citizens to form resistance groups focused on usurping Heinrich's rule and deposing him as their leader.

Jesse knew from the beginning of his ministry what his fate would be, yet he plunged ahead in defiance of Heinrich's orders. As the time grew closer, he asked Peter to look after his wife and mother. Jesse was betrayed by Eli, one of his followers and taken to Heinrich. In a fit of rage, he killed Jesse, but he couldn't change Jesse's legacy of forgiveness and love and was unaware of Jesse's pregnant wife carrying the son he hoped would continue his work.

Our story begins when Jesse is captured by the Brown Shirts and taken to Heinrich at Duvanwald prison.

ONE

Maria and Marika watched in horror as several Brown Shirts emerged from the rocks, stepped into Jesse' path and guns drawn, surrounded him. Eli, one of Jesse's disgruntled followers stood with them. Marika started down the path to stop them but one of the guards stepped in front of her pointing his gun at her chest.

"Shut up and stay where you are," he commanded, his sour breath hitting her in the face.

"Marika, comeback, there is nothing we can do right now." Maria called out. They watched as Jesse was hustled away and the sound of a car leaving echoed in the night.

The Brown Shirt, pointing his gun at Marika, turned to the remaining guards. "There are four of us, and two of them, I think we have time for a little party, don't you? The six of us could have a very good time."

One grabbed Marika around the waist and began carrying her to a flat spot in front of the cave She twisted and turned trying to get away, but he was too strong.

"Jesse, help me," she screamed. "Please don't do this" she begged the man who held her but he laughed at her futile efforts.

"I like it when they fight back," he replied, tightening his hold.

"Stop," a new voice called out. "You are to leave those women alone. Jesse made that a condition of going quietly. In return the captain promised they wouldn't be harmed."

"Why?" the first guard asked, "Jesse will never know, and once they are done with him, he won't even care."

"What is more important to you, getting credit for being part of the group that captured Jesse, the leader of the Believers, or being with his whores?"

The Brown Shirt dragging Marika up the path tossed her to the ground. "Filthy whore," he said and spat on her.

The men left but Maria heard them laughing and making crude jokes as they walked away.

Eli scurried up the path towards them. "You have to understand. I had no choice. I had to tell them where he was or they would have continued to torture me."

Maria stared at him. "This was bound to happen one day. If it wasn't you, it would have been someone else"

Holding out his hand Eli said, "here take the money. There are thirty silver kroners here. I don't want it anymore."

Maria answered him sarcastically. "Why do you think I would want your blood money. Keep it, you earned it. If it were me, I would take that money and get as far away as I can. God help you if someone from Jesse's inner circle ever finds you."

She turned to Marika, helped her to her feet and together they stumbled back into the cave Jesse used as his refuge. Aaron was the only follower left; all of the others had fled. When he saw them, he rushed out to their side.

"Where are the others," Maria asked, looking around her.

"Peter told them to leave and they will meet up later. He is following Jesse to see where they take him. You are to stay here until one of them returns. Come, a small fire is still burning in the back and there is still some food left. I was left behind to watch over you. You will be safe here; I don't think those Brown Shirts will return. They have who they came for."

Maria wrapped her arms around a sobbing Marika, "Come inside." she said. She led her to the back of the cave, found a blanket and wrapped it around her shoulders.

"What is going to happen to him? What if I never see him again?" Marika stuttered. "Oh God, what if they take him to Heinrich and he is killed? We need to leave here and find a way to help him," she beseeched Maria, her wild eyes darting around the cave like a trapped animal.

"No Marika, we need to stay here like Peter ordered. Jesse won't want you following him and drawing attention to yourself." Then more quietly she added, "He is in God's hands now."

Maria sat down, her back against a large rock. Pulling Marika to her she held her until her sobs quietened and she fell into an exhausted sleep. Only then did she allow her own tears to fall. After a while, she too fell into a fitful sleep.

Marika woke up first. She nudged Maria and whispered "I have to find a way to get to the prison. Jesse needs me."

Maria instantly woke up. "I don't think that's a good idea. We were told to wait here until Peter returns."

"You can if you want, but I'm leaving. I can't stay here not knowing what is happening."

"How are you going to get to Bern? It is several hours away."

"I will walk. Maybe somebody will see me on the road and offer me a ride."

Maria looked at Marika and saw how determined she was. She stood up and said "I am going with you. Has anybody ever told you how stubborn you are?"

"Yes, Jesse did, all the time."

The two women made their way down the rocky path in the dark. When they came to the road Marika set a brisk pace and it was all Maria could do to keep up with her.

About an hour later the lights of a truck approached from behind. The two women moved to the side of the road. When the driver drew even with them, he stopped and rolled down his window.

"Where are you two beautiful ladies going so early in the morning? I almost didn't see you walking there," the driver asked.

"To Bern." Maria answered, "We wanted to get an early start."

"Hop in. It so happens I am going there myself. I heard Jesse, Leader of the Believers, was captured by the Brown shirts not far from here. I am going to see for myself if it's true or not."

The two women climbed into the cab of the truck beside him. They listened to him chatter the whole way. Other than the occasional nod of their head the women stared out the windshield.

"Some people think this will be the end of Jesse's preaching. Others hope Heinrich is using scare tactics to get his message across and this is another warning. Hard to say what is going to happen. Heinrich goes a little crazy where Jesse is concerned."

Entering the city limits he asked, "Where can I drop you off?"

"We are going to a place not far from the prison. Will that be taking you out of your way?"

"No. I am going there myself. I assume that's where he is being held."

Marika reached over and squeezed Maria's hand. The driver stopped on the outer edge of the people gathered in front of the prison gates. The two women thanked him and got out, waiting until he was out of sight before slowly making their way through the crowd.

As word of Jesse's capture spread the Believers began to gather in front of Duvenwald prison. Helplessly they waited for word about their leader. Although occasional bursts of murmuring were heard, for the most part the crowd was silent.

Peter and Jesse's men joined the crowd maneuvering closer to the front in case Jesse was brought out. They knew Heinrich would use capturing Jesse as a way to show his superiority. If there was even the slightest chance of rescuing Jesse, they wanted to be in a position to try.

Marika was the first to spot Peter. "Come Maria, I see Peter over there, maybe he knows where Jesse is." Pulling Maria through the crowd she made her way over to him.

When Peter saw them, he became angry. "What are you doing here? I thought I told you to stay at the cave until I came and got you. I promised Jesse I would look after you if something happened to him."

"Don't be angry." Placing both hands on her heart she said," I have to be here. Jesse needs me."

"I tried to stop her," Maria added, "but you know when her mind is made up, she doesn't listen to anybody. We were fortunate to get a ride and didn't have to walk very far."

Peter glared at the two frightened women. He put an arm around each of their shoulders and pulled them close. 'Since you are here you might as well wait with me. At least then I know where you are."

Several hours later the prison gates opened and Jesse and two other men were led out. Jesse was bloody, his right arm hanging uselessly at his side and he was dragging his left leg. In spite of this there seemed to be an aura of peace surrounding him. Heinrich, standing in an open jeep, followed behind.

Jesse fell, but the guards stood and watched him struggle to get back on his feet. Marika gasped and began to move toward him, but Peter stopped her.

"No, he will be devastated to know you are here witnessing his humiliation. He thinks you are still at the cave waiting for him."

Jesse and the other men were led to a wall covered in spattered blood. He screamed in pain as one of the guards grabbed his arms and tied them to a hook above his head, then spread his legs and tied each of them to a stake. The other men were forced to stand on either side of him.

"Shoot them," Heinrich commanded.

The two men were shot in the chest and slumped to the ground. Two guards dragged their bodies away, leaving a trail of blood behind.

Heinrich climbed down from the jeep and stood in front of Jesse.

"I am going to give you one more chance to save yourself. Will you declare, in front of your followers, that I am head of the church and you were wrong to preach against me?"

Jesse stared back at him. "I am not going to change my mind."

Heinrich motioned to one of the guards to give him his pistol. Waving it in Jesse's face he screeched "I will shoot you if you don't give me the correct answers."

"Go ahead and do what you plan on doing anyway. I am not afraid."

Heinrich shot him in the shoulder. Jesse screamed in pain.

Heinrich repeated his request three more times and each time Jesse refused Heinrich shot him, first in the other shoulder and then both knees. No longer able to support himself he sagged against the ropes holding him.

By now Heinrich was raving like a mad man waving the gun in Jesse's face. "One last time, will you declare me head of the church?"

Jesse gasped out, "I will not." Heinrich shot him in the stomach.

The crowd watched, in disbelief at the scene taking place in front of them.

As Jesse hung clinging to life Eli spotted Peter. Moving through the crowd to him he said "I didn't know this was going to happen. This is not my fault. Jesse should have given into Heinrich's demands. What would one little lie have cost him?"

Peter fisted his hands at his side. He felt like beating Eli until he couldn't walk any more. "That little lie would have undermined every principal Jesse stood for. Get out of my sight. If I ever see you again, I will kill you with my bare hands wrapped around your scrawny neck. Watch your back Eli because you will never know where or when I will show up." Eli started to say something but, when he saw the look on Peter's face he stumbled backward and melted into the crowd.

Jesse's blood dripped on to the ground and he died several hours later. All this time Heinrich stood in the jeep watching. On his dying breathe he looked at Heinrich and whispered, "I forgive you." Suddenly the sky turned black, thunder rolled and lightening flashed. Jesse was dead.

Peter held Marika as she sobbed. Maria pushed herself away from Peter and made her way through the stunned crowd to Heinrich. "You know who I am. Give me his body so I can bury him."

Heinrich looked at her. "He stays where he is and hangs there until he rots. Nobody is to touch him."

Then signaling his driver to leave the jeep pulled away and went back through the prison gates. The huge doors slammed shut behind him.

Maria climbed the steps to the platform and knelt down in front of her son. Putting both hands around his face she kissed him, his blood soaking into the hem of her dress.

Peter left her there for a while then went and touched her on the shoulder. "Come I need to get you away from here. The crowd is becoming angry and we should leave as quickly as possible."

Reluctantly the two women left with Peter. Twice he had to stop Marika from running back to her husband. Finally, he admonished her. "Let him be. There is nothing more you can do for him. He is at peace with his Father in heaven."

Peter led them through the streets to the alley where he knew they would be safe and would be protected by the men who lived there. Marika backed up to the wall, slid to the ground and buried her face in her hands. Maria sat down beside her. Both women were in shock from the brutality they witnessed.

One of the men offered Maria a blanket and she wrapped it around Marika's shoulders. *How could Jesse's call to serve God end like this? I don't understand. What is going to become of us now?*

TWO

Later that evening Peter joined the group of men warming themselves around the fire in an old steel barrel discussing the demoralizing events of the day. After a short period of time, he left the group and walked over to Maria.

"How is she?" he asked, nodding at Marika.

"She hasn't spoken a word, just sits there and stares."

Peter knelt down in front of Maria. "I am going back to watch over Jesse. After dark some of us are going to try to find a way to move his body. We refuse to allow Heinrich to get away with leaving him hanging like some common criminal. He deserves a decent burial."

Marika looked up. "Where you going to take him?"

"Back to the village, where he will be with his father and family. I'll probably be gone all night and be back some time tomorrow. As we speak several of Jesse's followers are working on making   arrangements. I don't know what the plan is but I need to part of it. If we succeed you will have a place to visit him."

Maria placed her hand on top of Peter's. "Thank you. You have no idea what this means to us. This is very dangerous, please be careful."

"Do not tell Marika where we are taking him. Stay here, the men will keep you safe. When I return, I will find a place for you to stay. Later, after things have settled down, I will take you to live with Mark and Elizabeth like Jesse asked."

Peter gently squeezed each of the women's shoulders, stood up and walked out of the alley. Marika put her head on Maria's shoulder. "I am happy they are doing this for him."

Peter returned to the prison gate and stood in the shadows keeping watch over Jesse's body.

"Peter is that you," a voice whispered behind him.

"Yes, it is me," he whispered back.

Liam and Thomas, two more of Jesse's close followers, emerged from the shadows. "Come, with us, we need to talk to you."

Peter looked around but the two guards Heinrich posted were not to be seen. It was a cold evening and they were staying in the Guard house where it was warm. He followed the two men to the edge of the square; both dressed in black blending into the night around them.

Looking around to make sure nobody could hear him Liam said," we found a way to move Jesse and hide his body. We can't leave him hanging there."

"What are you plans? How are we going to do this?"

"One of our staunchest supporters owns a funeral home. At our signal he is ready to bring his hearse here and we will lay Jesse in the wooden coffin in the back. From there we will take him to Norenburg and bury him with his family."

"What can I do to help?" Peter asked.

"First you must only tell Maria what we have done, but not Marika. It's better she doesn't know in case Heinrich finds and questions her. We will tell her later when the time is right. This is to be our secret for now."

"I agree," Peter replied.

"We will be back in two hours when we are sure the guards are cold and not paying attention. Then you can help cut him down and move him to the hearse."

Peter returned to his vigil.

Two hours later Peter heard the sound of a vehicle arrive in the dark and then the motor was shut off. He heard a door open and Liam and Thomas appeared behind him. The guards hadn't been out of the guard house the whole time he waited.

The three men crept up to the wall and laid a blanket in front of Jesse. One man held his body while the other two cut the ropes. Slowly they lowered him onto the blanket and wrapped it around him. Peter picked up Jesse's body as if he were a child and carried him out into the dark.

Liam walked beside Peter and Thomas went ahead. Peter staggered several times but Liam kept him from falling.

"Peter let me help you, he is too heavy for you to carry."

"No. This is the last thing I can do for him. Jesse was a good friend and I will miss him every day for the rest of my life."

"I know what you mean," Liam replied.

Thomas directed them to the side of the building where the hearse was waiting. The back door was open and the two of them laid Jesse inside the plain wooden coffin. Liam and Thomas drew back the blanket and kissed Jesse on the cheek then got into the front seat of the hearse. Peter chose to stay in the back. He kissed Jesse's forehead and tightened the blanket around him.

"Do you think the authorities will stop us?" he whispered loudly to the two men in the front.

"No, it's a common occurrence to see a hearse on the street any time of the day or night."

Liam pulled away and began the long journey to Jesse's final resting place. In the back Peter lifted the lid and closed the coffin, and then, wracked with guilt, cried deep heart wrenching sobs. *I am sorry Jesse. I failed to protect you from Heinrich. I should have forced you to leave while you still had a chance. Can you ever forgive me?*

The sun was up when they arrived at Jesse's village. The burnt shells of the buildings stood in contrast to the bright blue sky. Six hundred men women and children had died here slaughtered by the Brown shirts.

They drove through the town to the large mound of dirt in the cemetery. The villagers were buried in a mass grave and an unknown person had placed a large wooden cross on top. The men dug a hole along one edge and buried Jesse besides his father, brothers and sisters.

"What if they come here looking for him. they will see where the ground has been disturbed." Thomas asked.

"We will dig around all sides of the grave making it look like someone has already looked here." Each of the men grabbed a shovel and set to work. When finished, they took off their hats and stood quietly each whispering a silent prayer.

As he was leaving Peter whispered "I swear I will do everything in my power to keep them safe, even if I die trying."

"What's going to happen now Peter?" Liam asked.

"I don't know," he replied.

Although tired and hungry they drove back to Bern. Liam returned the hearse and Peter went in search of a place for Maria and Marika to live. They couldn't stay in the alley. He had to keep them out of sight until he could move them away from the city. He knew Heinrich would be enraged when he discovered Jesse's body was gone and would stop at nothing to try and find it.

THREE

.

, Heinrich was livid when he was told Jesse's body had disappeared during the night. He had the guards who were supposed to be watching brought to him.

"How did this happen?" he screamed at them.

"We don't know sir. He was there when we went into the guard house to get warm and when we came back, he was gone."

"Did you see or hear anything. Corpses don't untie themselves and walk away."

"No sir," they replied in unison.

"Do you know what you have done? You have made me look stupid and incompetent. Even dead Jesse makes me look like a fool."

Heinrich looked like a wild man. His face was red and saliva was running down his chin as he berated the two guards. Reaching across his desk he pushed a buzzer. When another guard appeared, he said "shoot them. There is no room for idiots in my army."

The third guard pulled out his pistol and pointed it at the men.

"Not here stupid. Take them someplace else. I don't want their blood staining the floor. "The guard marched the men out at gun point.

Heinrich then issued an order for the Brown Shirts to spread throughout the city and, using whatever force was necessary, find out who had taken Jesse and where they had put him.

Rumors were already flying. Jesse was still alive and taken to a hospital. Others believed he had undone his ropes, healed himself and walked away.

Before Peter returned to the alley, he located a small two room apartment for Maria and Marika. Located not far from the alley it was a second story walk up, consisting of a bedroom and kitchen. A common bathroom was down the hallway. He heard the Brown Shirts were questioning everybody in an attempt to find out who was responsible for moving Jesse's body and expected them to show up at the alley as one of the first places to look,

Upon his return he said to Maria," we have to get you out of here. Heinrich is in a rage because Jesse's body disappeared. I have no doubt it is only a matter of time before the Brown shirts show up here and I don't want them to find you."

Pulling Peter aside Maria asked," were you able to …"

"Yes, he is beside his family. I will explain more later, but in the mean time we must leave. I found a small apartment for the two of you not far from here. It's not much, but the best I could do on short notice."

"All of our belongings are still back at the cave."

"I'll make sure somebody brings them to you. Maria, stop talking. We need to go now, before the Brown Shirts show up."

Maria urged Marika to her feet and the two women followed Peter out of the alley. "Like I said, it isn't much, but you will be safe for now and, as soon as I am able to I'll bring you some food. Stay inside. Don't let any of the neighbors see you."

When they got to the door of the apartment Peter handed Maria the key. "Lock the door and don't open it for anyone except me."

Peter waited outside the door until he heard the lock click then took a different route back to the alley in case he had been followed.

Maria was exhausted. She led Marika into the bedroom, helped her lay down on the bare, stained mattress and then laid down beside her.

"He is really dead," Marika quietly said.

"Yes," Maria replied.

"I heard you talking with Peter. Is it true they stole Jesse's body from in front of the prison and took it away? Do you know where he is?"

"Yes," Maria replied. She was glad Marika didn't ask where they had taken him.

Marika began to cry. "I don't know how I am going to live without him Maria. I don't know how to go on from here."

Maria put her arms around her. "I felt the same way when Joe was killed." Tears fell from her eyes. "We will find a way. Jesse won't want us to give up."

* * *

Peter had no sooner returned to the alley when a group of Brown Shirts stormed in. At gun point the men were forced to line up against one of the walls.

One of them spotted Peter. "I recognize you. You are one of Jesse's followers. I saw you with him the night he was captured."

"You must be mistaken" Peter replied. Too late he remembered Jesse's words; *you will not acknowledge me.*

The Brown Shirt moved closer, pointing his gun at Peter's chest. "Jesse's body has disappeared. Do you know anything about it?"

The men standing along the wall began talking among themselves. *How can this be? Who would have taken it?*

"What do you mean disappeared?" Peter asked, his heart pounding in his chest felt so loud he thought the Brown Shirt would hear it.

"Just what I said! Somebody came in the night and stole him. The guards saw and heard nothing and paid with their lives. We are positive the Believers were behind this."

Looking at the men backed up against the wall the Brown shirt shouted at them. "If you know something you better tell us."

Peter spoke up. "How could they know; they have been here with me all night. I assure you it wasn't one of them." The men nodded their heads and murmured their assent.

The Brown Shirt said to Peter. "I don't believe you. If you know who was responsible it would be best to tell me now."

Peter drew himself to his full height. "Go look someplace else. We had nothing to do with that, but I congratulate who ever did. They have more guts than I do."

The Brown Shirt turned to his men. "Move out, we will keep looking. Somebody has to know."

Turning back, he glared at Peter. "I think you know more than you are telling me. I think you know where Jesse's body is."

Peter stared back at him. "Even if I did, I wouldn't tell you."

After the Brown Shirts left, the men crowded around the fire again. They had come to the same conclusion. Each assumed Peter knew more than what he was saying but they didn't want to know the name of the person responsible. This way, if questioned a second time, they could honestly say they didn't know.

FOUR

Something woke Maria from a sound sleep. She turned over to check on Marika and saw she was awake, staring into space. She slipped her arm under the child's shoulders and Marika cuddled into her. They lay there in silence, both grieving for the man who had so cruelly been snatched from them.

"Try not to worry Marika. Jesse may be gone but Peter will take care of us."

Quietly Marika said "I often wondered what it would be like to be held like this, a mother comforting her child."

"Where is your mother?" Maria asked gently.

"Gone, I was a little girl when she left. There was only my father and me for as far back as I can remember. He did his best to look after me but eventually his drinking and gambling got the best of him."

"I love you as if you were my own daughter. You don't need to tell me anything you don't want to."

Marika kept on talking as though she hadn't heard Maria's words. "I clearly remember the last time I saw him. He promised to come back for me but never did." Her mind drifted back to that fateful day

Marika, get out of stinking bed right now," my dad hollered at me as he staggered into the house. I remember thinking oh no, he is drunk again. I pulled the covers over my head, curled into a ball trying to make myself as small as possible and ignored him. I hoped he would pass out on the couch as usual. He had been gone for two days leaving me to fend for myself with no money and no food. I was eleven years old. As I cowered under the blanket, I wished my mother would come back and take me away.

Suddenly my bedroom door flew open and bounced off the wall. I held my breath wondering what was going to happen. I never knew what mood he was going to be in when he came home. This time he yanked the blanket off me and hollered, "Get you skinny ass out of bed and get dressed. You are coming with me."

"Did he beat you?" Maria asked.

"No, mostly he yelled and called me names."

I had never seen him like this. I got out of bed, pulled my well-worn dress over my head. I reached down the side of the bed and put on my shoes and socks. I was so scared.

"Where are we going this late at night father?" I asked. "Maybe we should wait until morning."

He grabbed me by my arm pulled me to my feet and yanked me toward the door. "You are coming with me – can't keep people waiting."

He held my wrist in a tight grip as he staggered down the street and it was all I could do to keep up with him. I was sure I would have bruises in the morning.

He stopped in front of faded dilapidated gray house and looked down at me. "You do as you are told, don't embarrass me."

We went up three steps to the door and my father knocked. When the door opened, he shoved me inside and a large beefy man closed the door behind us. He looked me over from head to toe. I remember he stunk of garlic and body odors.

"Kind of skinny, isn't she," he said to my father, "how old did you say she was?"

"I am eleven," I told him, "My birthday was last month."

"She will do," he said and handed my father a handful of bills.

Taking the money my father bent down to me." you live here now" and then lurched toward the door.

"Father, don't leave me." I screamed and tried to run behind him but the man grabbed my arm. "I promise I will do better. I will keep the house clean. I am sorry for all the bad things I said to you. Please take me with you."

My father stopped with his hand on the door knob. He looked at me. "I promise to come back for you when I can repay this money." Closing his fist around the bills, he opened the door and walked out of my life.

The man sneered at me. I will never forget his words. "You are mine, bought and paid for and I can do whatever I want with you. Get into the bedroom and take off your clothes."

"No, I won't." I yelled back at him and ran to the door trying to open it. "Daddy, don't leave me here. Please come back. I am sorry," I screamed.

The man grabbed me, slapped me across the face, picked me up and carried me into the bedroom. He ripped off my clothes, took his off and lay on the bed beside me. He hurt me.

I tried to fight but he punched me in the face and told me to shut up. He kept me in that room for two days using me three or four times a day. At first, I cried and fought, but then I stopped. I never cried again when he came to me.

Several days later he came in and said "You stink. Go have a bath and then get dressed. Other men are coming tonight and you will do as they say." I was numb, in pain and had no fight left in me.

That became my life, one or more men during the night and the man during the day. All I wanted to do was die. When I got bigger and began developing as a woman, he put me out on the street and took the money men gave me.

After a while he got tired of me and brought other little girls into the house. I tried to help them the best I could. I heard later he was killed and I am glad he is dead."

"Oh, you poor child," Maria said, stroking Maria's hair, tears running down her face, "Did you ever see your father again?"

"No. All I know is that he never came back for me. He could be dead for all I care."

"How did you meet Jesse?" Maria sked.

"I heard some of the other women talking about him and how he talked about forgiveness. I went to where he lived in the alley and asked him if I could be forgiven for what I was doing. He told me yes, but I would have to stop. I wanted to but didn't know how I could survive. I needed money for food and a place to live. He was so kind. He never judged me for what I was or what I did,

Several weeks later the Brown shirts attacked the men living in the alley. I was on my way to see Jesse and five of them attacked me. I don't remember much except a man carrying me into the alley. I was badly hurt and because Mark, a man who lived there used to be a doctor they thought he could help me.

Peter, Jesse and the other men let me stay with them and Jesse and I became good friends. One evening, while we were sitting by the river talking, he asked me to marry him and I said Yes. I loved him and he loved me enough to overlook my past. We found Jean Baptiste and he married us but we forgot to register our marriage at the court house. I'm not sure if we were legally married or not. Jesse said we were in the eyes of God and that was all that mattered. There is only one thing I wish for."

"What is that Marika?"

"That I could have given Jesse a child. I was too young and the men hurt me inside."

"Did Jesse know?"

"Yes, I told him."

Maria hugged Marika closer. *What a terrible life she has had. I'm glad she found the love a good man like Jesse.*

Maria was always the first up in the morning. She used this time to pray, relive happy memories of her family and spend the time alone, but his morning Marika's story haunted her. *How could a man do that to his own daughter?*

It wasn't that she didn't enjoy Marika's company but, because they were confined in such a small space, it was difficult for either of them to spend time alone. They felt uneasy because they didn't know what was happening on the streets. There were so many rumors it was difficult to know what was true and what wasn't.

"Good morning, Maria," Marika said sleepily. "You are up early. Didn't you sleep well last night?"

"Nothing to worry about Marika, some nights are better than others. Come, I made some fresh coffee and I will cook each of us one of the eggs Peter brought yesterday."

Marika sat down at the table. Maria poured her a cup of coffee and then turned back to the stove to fry the eggs.

Suddenly, she heard Marika gasp. The apartment door flew open and Marika was running down the hall way to the communal bath room.

She returned about ten minutes later, her face as white as a ghost. "I don't know what is wrong with me. This is the third morning in a row I have felt ill as soon as I smelled the coffee, but is the first time I felt the need to vomit"

Maria smiled. She remembered Jesse's words, "Tonight Marika and I conceived a son whom you will name after me."

"Do you think you could be with child?" Maria asked.

"No, I cannot have children. I am too damaged." Then she paused, "Maria, do you think it is possible the last time Jesse and I were together I could have conceived?"

"If you don't mind me asking Marika, when was that?"

"The night he was taken away."

"Do you have any other signs?"

"I missed my monthly time but that's not unusual."

"Sit down Marika I have something to tell you. Before he was taken Jesse came to me and said you had conceived a son, but that you weren't aware yet."

Marika put her hand on her stomach. Could this be true? The only thing I ever wanted was to have Jesse's child but we thought it was impossible."

Tears filled her eyes, "I only wish Jesse could be here to see his son."

Maria grinned. "Nothing is impossible my child. Come, eat your egg, you are eating for two now."

FIVE

A month of horror followed Jesse's death. Heinrich was determined to eradicate the Believers. Terror filled the streets; people hid in their houses afraid to answer their doors.

Rotter stayed away from the city and used Heinrich's anger as an opportunity to turn the Brown Shirts loose to expunge the Believers. Nobody was safe. They roamed the streets in gangs, looting the stores, and shooting anyone who tried to stop them. Those suspected of following Jesse were dragged from their homes, tortured or killed in public. Women and girls were openly abused while others were forced to watch.

Then, as suddenly as it started, the killing stopped, as if a giant voice shouted. "That is enough."

Jesse's death and Heinrich's subsequent rampage left Peter and the remainder of Jesse's closest followers with broken spirits. For some unknown reason Heinrich decimated his army by having all of the top commanders executed. The resistance was, for all intents and purposes destroyed and the country was in ruins.

Peter was sitting on a park bench trying to make sense out of what had taken place since Jesse's death. Two Brown Shirts wandered into the park, noticed him sitting there and approached. Standing in front of Peter the younger one asked, "Aren't you Peter, the man who hung around with Jesse and the Believers?"

Peter started to say no, but then remembered Jesse's statement "You will deny me."

"Yes, he replied and stood up. "Why do you want to know?" Peter's hands were balled into fists at his side. He would fight both of them if he had to.

"Heinrich wants to see you. Come with us now."

Against his better judgement and, not wanting to draw attention, he went with them. *What choice do I have, there were two of them and one of me?*

He was escorted out of the park, a Brown Shirt on each side. They walked to the road and then he was put into the back seat of an open-air jeep and driven to the police station. From there he was escorted directly to Heinrich's office.

Heinrich was a mess. There were food stains on his uniform, his eyes were red, he needed a shave and smelled like he hadn't bathed for days.

Heinrich looked at him. "Where is Jesse's body?" he demanded.

Peter knew better, but he looked at Heinrich and quipped "I don't know, did you lose him?"

Heinrich walked over to and slapped him across the face. "What did you do with him?"

"I don't know what you are talking about," Peter lied.

Heinrich slapped him again. "You know," he shouted. "What did you do with him? You were seen there after everybody else left. It had to be you."

Petr straightened up and stared back at him, "You had guards posted all night, they should be able to tell you if I was there or not. I commend who ever came up with the plan and executed it, but I have no idea of where Jesse's body is.

Besides," he continued, "what difference does it make? By shooting him in public the way you did, you signed your own death warrant. Did you honestly think killing Jesse was going to stop the movement he started and the effects of his teaching? In reality your actions made him a martyr and will end up making the Believers stronger."

Peter stepped toward Heinrich and poked a finger into his chest. "You have made yourself the most despised man that ever lived."

Heinrich began cursing and screaming at Peter. "Get out of my sight before I have you thrown into a cell."

Peter turned, let himself out through the door and walked as calmly as he could down the hallway. All the while he was waiting for a guard to come behind him and drag him away. When he was outside, he ran up alleys and down streets in order to get as far away as fast as he could.

SIX

Peter had just returned to the alley after delivering what bread, eggs and cheese he could find to Maria and Marika. Food was getting harder to come by as produce in the market was becoming scarcer. He was standing by the fire warming his hands when George, one of the men who lived there, ran into the alley.

"What's your hurry George," he asked as the breathless man stopped in front of him.

"I came to find you. They are rioting in the streets and Heinrich is trapped in the building beside his office. The leaders are determined to force him out."

Without hesitation Peter left with George. They had just arrived and were standing at the back of the crowd when a cheer went up. Peter pushed his way closer to the front.

Heinrich, his hands handcuffed behind his back, was kneeling on the front step. Four guards surrounded him. Heinrich was speaking. Peter watched as one of the guards removed his handcuffs.

"Please forgive me. I beg you for a second chance and I will rectify what I have done. I had nothing to do with the despicable acts carried out in my name by the Brown shirts."

"You expect us to believe that?" somebody shouted from the crowd.

"My family was in one of your camps. They are all dead," another shouted.

"You shot and killed our beloved Jesse. I was there. I saw what happened that day. Can you bring him back to us?" a woman called out.

The crowd began to shout and shake their fists.

Then, in one swift movement, Heinrich pulled himself to his feet, grabbed a pistol from the holster of the closest guard, opened the door and backed inside the building.

A cry went up from the crowd. "Somebody go after him. Don't let him get away"

. One of the leaders hurried up the stairs. "I'll stop him," he said, opening the door just wide enough to slip through closing it behind him. The crowd was silent. Minutes later he came out. "He is dead. The coward shot himself in the head."

Speaking to the two men who followed him to the door he said "Go drag his worthless body out here so we can see for ourselves."

At the same time Rotter pushed through the crowd and walked up the steps. *Finally, my time has come. What a perfect opportunity to step in and take Heinrich's place.*

"I will step in and take Heinrich's place as your leader. He was a cruel vindictive man, concerned only about what was good for him. I can rectify all he did and bring our country a new prosperity."

Again, someone shouted out from the crowd "You worked for him. Your hands are as dirty as his,"

"Only because he made me." Rotter tried to explain. "You can't hold me responsible for the acts of a mad man. I was only doing what he commanded me to do. I had no choice."

The four guards standing on the step disappeared and left Rotter standing alone. Three men rushed up the stairs and dragged him down into the crowd. In a frenzy, the onlookers began hitting and kicking him. Rotter begged for his life, but his pleas fell upon deaf ears.

"Stop," one of the leaders cried out. The people backed away and Rotter lay in a bloody heap on the street. The leader walked down the stairs and felt his neck for a pulse. "He's dead." he declared.

Peter shook his head. *How had a childhood rivalry come to this? Thousands died and for what? This is insane and never should have gone this far. I wish they were still alive and forced to defend themselves in court.*

A man appeared with two lengths of rope. One was tied around Rotter's neck and his body was dragged to the street and hung from a lamp post. Somebody went inside, tied the other rope around Heinrich's neck and dragged him outside. A trail of blood followed his body down the stairs and out into the street. His body was hung beside Rotter's.

The crowd began to break up. Some left laughing and singing a victory song. Some quietly went back to their homes. Still others walked past and spit on the two hanging bodies.

Peter walked back to the alley. For the first time in ages, he felt truly happy and at peace. *Finally, this nightmare is over. So many lives lost for nothing. Maybe now, with both Heinrich and Rotter gone, this country will find a way to heal.*

SEVEN

Maria was on edge. All day the streets bustled with activity. People gathered in large groups. shouting and talking. Several fistfights broke out. There was a feeling of anticipation in the air that something was about to happen. She wanted to hear what was being said but wasn't brave enough to go out into the street to find out.

Marika was tired and had gone to bed early. Maria was restless and, instead of going to bed, sat in the kitchen looking out the window. She jumped when she heard a knock on her door. Nothing good ever came from someone coming so late in the evening.

"Who is there?" she asked. "What do you want?"

"Maria, open the door. It is me, Peter."

Maria opened the door and Peter stepped into the small apartment.

"What is it? she asked. "What is wrong? Why have you come so late?"

Peter was laughing. He picked her up and swung her around. "I have wonderful news to share and I wanted to be the first to tell you."

"Put me down and tell me what? I have never seen you so happy. Hurry up before I burst."

"Heinrich and Rotter are both dead. They died earlier this evening."

Maria was stunned by his announcement. "Is this finally over?"

"Yes," Peter exclaimed.

"Are you sure? Tell me what happened."

"There was a riot and his guards tricked him into coming to them, then they handcuffed him and brought him outside. He begged for his life and the people jeered him. Somehow, he took a gun from one of the guards, went back inside the building and shot himself in the head.

Sig Rotter arrived and tried to appeal to the crowd to let him take Heinrich's place. He tried to appease the crowd, begging for forgiveness and telling them he was only following orders but he was attacked and killed. Both bodies are hanging from a lamp post for all to see.

They are dead Maria. I saw them myself. When Jesse was alive, he asked me to take you and Marika to live with Mathew and Elizabeth where he knew you would be safe. I think this is a good time for us to leave while the city is celebrating."

"I agree. After you leave, I will awaken Marika and tell her the good news, then we will begin packing our few belongings. Peter, do you think this what Jesse's death was meant to accomplish?"

"We will never know for sure, but I would like to think his death played a big part. How soon can you be ready? I want to leave as soon as the sun is up. The city is going to be in turmoil for a long time and I don't want you to be here. "

"We will be ready whenever you get here. Marika went to be bed early because she hasn't been feeling well lately." *This is not the time to tell him Marika is expecting Jesse's baby. Later when life is more settled, she can share her good news.*

Peter walked to the door, opened it, then turned and kissed Maria on the cheek. "I will see you tomorrow then. Now I am going to go back to the alley to celebrate with my friends. What a wonderful day this is."

The women were ready and waiting when Peter arrived. Each had a small suitcase and Maria carried an extra bundle.

"I brought what food we had. There was no sense in leaving it to spoil" she said. "I left everything else for the next person who will live in the apartment. You look tired this morning."

Peter laughed. "I was up late. I've secured a ride for us for most of the way, the rest we will have to walk."

The two women carrying their suitcases followed Peter down the stairs to the street. The shops were opening for the day. The sun was shining and a festive air hung over the city.

Three blocks later they met Jacques Monet who had borrowed his brother's old truck. Maria and Marika sat in the cab and Peter crawled into the back and slept most of the way.

Three hours later Jacques dropped them off in Norenburg, their burned-out village. Peter handed him some money.

"Thank you, Jacques, you have done us a great service today. I appreciate the fact that you went out of your way to bring us here."

When Jacque was out of sight he turned to the two women. "Come, I will show you where Jesse's body is buried."

Marika turned to Maria, a surprised look on her face. "You didn't tell me he was buried here."

"Please forgive us" Maria replied. "We didn't know what was going to happen and we thought it best if you didn't know in case Heinrich found you."

"I forgive you," Marika smiled. "You were right to do that. If I had known I would have found a way to come here."

Peter led the two women to the cemetery. Marika tried to hold her emotions in, but as soon as Peter pointed to the spot where Jesse's body lay, she threw herself face down on the grave and wept. Maria and Peter waited patiently, giving her all of the time she needed.

Eventually Peter touched her on the shoulder. "We have to go now Marika. From here we have to walk. We still need to be careful about being here" he cautioned. "You never know who will see us and we don't want to draw attention to Jesse's grave site.".

A somber trio arrived at Mark's late that afternoon. Maria and Marika were both tired. Mark and Elizabeth were at the hospital when they arrived.

Peter opened the front door and shouted, "Guess who's here?"

Elizabeth came running from the back but stopped short when she saw them. "Mother is it really you? I didn't know you were coming." She ran to her mother and hugged her, then hugged Peter.

"Who is the young lady with you?" she asked, motioning to Marika.

Maria smiled. "I would like you to meet Jesse's wife Marika."

Elizabeth was stunned. "Jesse married? How come I wasn't told?"

"We needed to keep this a secret." Turning to Marika she introduced the two women. "This is Elizabeth, Jesse's only surviving sister and the man talking to Peter is her husband, Mark."

Marika recognized Mark right away. She went up to him, "I am happy to see you again. You were good to me when we lived in the alley. Thank you."

Mark smiled, "I am glad you are safe. We had no idea what happened to you after you left the cave."

"We were in the crowd and watched Jesse die. Although he may not have seen us, I am sure he felt our presence."

Elizabeth grabbed her mother's hand. "Come, we will go to the house I will make us some tea. We'll leave the two men to talk." Turning to Marika she said, "tell me all about you and Jesse. How did you meet? Why did you keep this a secret from us? How long were you married?"

When they were alone Peter told Mark about the chain of events that brought them there. "I have fulfilled the promise I made to Jesse. I know they will be safe here."

"What are you going to do now Peter," Mark asked.

"I don't know."

"You are welcome to stay as long as you wish. Thank you for bringing them back to us."

EIGHT

Peter stayed for several more days until he was sure Maria and Marika were settled. One evening he pulled Mark aside. "I am leaving in the morning. I want to thank you for your hospitality, but my job here is done. I have fulfilled Jesse's wishes."

"What are your plans?" Mark asked.

"I don't have any. To tell you the truth, I feel kind of lost. Now I know how Jesse felt when he came to live with us in the alley. I didn't picture a life beyond serving Jesse, but now all I feel is his disappointment in me."

"Why do you think that?"

"I should have stood up for him, fought the Brown Shirts and stopped them from taking him. I should have done something to stop Heinrich from torturing him instead of standing by and watching him die. Maybe if I had done that, he would still be alive. Did you know he wanted me to take over the leadership of the Believers and I don't even know where they are?"

"Peter you are being too hard on yourself. You had no control over anything that transpired with Jesse capture or Heinrich's actions."

"At least I got one thing right, I got Maria and Marika here safely."

"Yes, and we are grateful. Elizabeth was worried when we didn't hear from them. You know you don't have to leave. Stay here with us, there is lots of work available in the village."

"No, I think it's best if I go. I need time to figure out what I am going to do with the rest of my life. I intended to serve Jesse for as long as he needed me."

"I can understand that, but know you are welcome here anytime."

"Thank you, my friend. I feel good leaving knowing Maria and Marika here with you."

"Do you have any idea where you are going from here?"

"I was thinking about finding the main group of Believers and spending time with them, but now I'm not sure I have anything to offer them."

"Have you any idea where they are? The last I heard they were in the southern part of the country, but that was quite a while ago and may have been a rumor."

"Don't worry, I'll find them. I am sure that if I ask enough people, I will locate them."

After breakfast the next morning Peter hugged and kissed Maria and Marika good bye. Like Mark, they tried to talk him into staying.

"Maria I must go. I will write to you when I find a place to settle down. This is not good bye but simply until we meet again."

The four of them watched Peter trudge down the road. His shoulders were stooped, an air of despondency hung around him.

"I am worried about him," Maria commented. Do you think he will ever find peace?"

"I don't know" Mark replied. "He is a very troubled man. He thinks he let Jesse down and is responsible for his death, but I told him he was being too hard on himself but, I don't think he heard me."

"I think you are right, but I wonder why he feels that way? Did he say anything to you?"

"No not really. I guess he has his reasons."

From where they stood Mark and Maria couldn't see the tears streaming down Peter's face. For the first time since Jesse's death, he felt free to let them flow. Until now he held them back in an attempt to be strong for those looking to him for guidance. Now that he was alone, he gave himself permission to cry.

I am sorry I let you down Jesse. Instead of standing and fighting I took the easy way out standing with Maria and Marika watching what Heinrich did to you. I hope you can forgive me. I know you asked me to take care of Maria and Marika and I have done what you asked.

It is my fault you were captured. I knew Eli was unstable and I should have stopped him. I swear to you I will find him and make him pay even if it is the last thing I do.

You also told me I was the person who will unite your followers after your death, that they will follow me because they trust me. You can see for yourself what a good job I am doing of that. Please forgive me because you put your trust in the wrong person. What a failure I turned out to be.

Peter walked for three days, stopping only to sleep for a few hours in the trees along the side of the road. When he came to a town, he stopped long enough to buy a little food to carry with him. At each place he cautiously asked if anybody knew where the Believes were, but nobody seemed to know. If they did, they chose not to share their knowledge with a stranger. The longer he walked, the more he thought, the deeper the blackness of despair settled over him.

NINE

The further he walked, the more depressed he became. He also was a man who despised people who drank heavily. He knew firsthand the effects alcoholism had on families and swore to himself he would always abstain.

He stopped at a tavern in a small town for supper and had no intention of taking that first drink. The day had been scorching hot and he was thirsty. For some unknown reason he ordered a cold beer with his meal. That one tasted good, so he ordered a second, and then a third. By the time he left he felt better than he had for a long time. The alcohol removed that voice of regret echoing in his head and, for the first time since Jesse's death, he had an untroubled sleep.

Unconsciously he began stopping at a tavern in every town he visited. He kept telling himself *I am only stopping at the taverns to ask for information about the location of the Believers.* While there he had several drinks. Slowly he kept walking south in the direction he was told.

His journey, which should have taken a week stretched into months. Rarely sober he stumbled along the road. Sometimes he woke up in the morning not remembering what had transpired the day before or where he was. He stopped eating and drank his evenings away. Almost by accident he learned that by telling stories about his time with Jesse and watching Heinrich and Rotter die others, eager to hear his firsthand account, bought him drinks.

He had very little money when he left Mark's and he quickly drank that away. When he couldn't get free drinks, he sat outside the tavern begging for coins.

His hair became unkempt, his beard ragged and dirty and his clothes unwashed. Some took pity on him and gave him enough to for a meal but, instead of eating, he used the money to buy more beer. At every tavern he came to he asked the same question, "do you know where the Believers are."

One evening he was surprised when he was told "I saw their camp yesterday, about five miles from here, along the Eula River. A sorry looking sight they are. It's no wonder people want nothing to do with them."

Peter was elated to hear the news. Early the next morning, he began walking in the direction of the camp. On the way he stopped and bathed in a stream, combed his hair with his fingers and changed into the clean clothes he saved for this day.

He wasn't sure what to expect when he arrived, but wasn't prepared for what he saw when he crested the top of a hill. A ramshackle tent city was spread out along the river bank. A pall of heavy gray smoke hung in the air from the cooking fires. The stench of a nearby latrines assaulted his nostrils. He stood and watched as children laughed and played. He spotted a group of women washing clothes further down the river.

His hands were shaking and his stomach was rolling from drinking too much the previous night. Instead of feeling relived at finding the Believers he was filled with despair. *How did this great wonderful movement Jesse gave his life for be reduced to this? What happened to these people to make them choose to live this way?* A wave of guilt washed over him. *If I had done what Jesse asked, I could have prevented most of this.*

Gathering up his courage he walked toward the camp. *I wish I had something to drink before I walk in there. That would steady my nerves.*

At the edge of the camp, he immediately spotted a large white tent with a cross on the front. *That must be the church. I'm sure the leaders will be close by.*

Moving toward the tent, he felt people watching him and whispering among themselves. Soon a large, black-haired, heavy-set man came out through the tent flap. The man studied Peter for several seconds and then began walking toward him.

When they were closer Peter put out his hand. "I am Peter, a follower and friend of Jesse." The two men shook hands.

"I know who you are," the man replied. "I am Saul Rothenburger, the leader of the people in this camp. We have been waiting for you. We have always known one day somebody would come to take Jesse's place. Follow me and we will go into my tent where we can talk."

. Once inside, Saul walked over to a small wooden stand and withdrew a bottle of whiskey and two glasses. "Let's have a drink to celebrate your arrival."

He poured two shot glasses of whiskey and handed one to Peter. "To a new beginning."

They raised their glasses to each other and tossed back their drinks. As soon as the alcohol reached Peter's stomach he began to relax. Saul poured them each a second drink then sat down beside a small table and motioned Peter to join him.

"What is this place," Peter asked. "How did you end up here?"

"Most of us are camp survivors with no place to call home. Most are alone, because their friends and family didn't survive the camps."

Peter sat quietly and listened while Saul told him about the camp and the people who lived there. The more he heard the more, guilt he piled upon himself. They talked and drank until late in the night.

This is my fault. If I had done what Jesse wanted none of this would have happened. These people will hate me when they find out.

"What about you Peter? Do you have some place to go? If not, you are welcome to stay here, there is much you can teach us."

Peter thought for a moment. "Yes, I'll stay with you. That's what Jesse would expect me to do."

"Come it is late and we should find you a place to sleep. There is an extra cot in the tent next door we use for visitors."

When Peter was alone in the tent, he thought *now I can finally fulfill my promise to Jesse. I will quit drinking and do what I can to help these people.*

* * *

On the surface Peter appeared calm. Each evening, he met with the camp leaders and they formed a plan to resettle the inhabitants. During this time, they usually shared several drinks and Peter drank with them. His promise of quitting long forgotten.

"Have you seen Peter today?" Saul asked a small boy standing nearby. "I've been looking for him."

"He went to town yesterday and hasn't come back yet," the boy replied.

Three days later Peter staggered back into the camp. His clothes were torn and his eye was swollen and black. When Saul approached him, he recognized the stench of alcohol and sour reek of vomit.

"Let's get you cleaned up then you can sleep it off," he told Peter.

When he awoke, Peter was sick and embarrassed. He wanted to apologize to Saul but couldn't find the words. He was grateful that Saul didn't comment on his actions.

Once turned into twice, and then into three times. Sometimes, in a drunken haze, he roamed the streets of the camp shouting about becoming their leader and taking Jesses' place. Other times he approached people begging for their forgiveness for letting Jesse down. Soon those in the camp began avoiding him and others complained to Saul and the other leaders about his behavior.

Finally, left with no choice, Saul called a special meeting of the camp officials. One man wanted Peter to stay so he could lead them in Jesse's ways. Another argued what good would he be if he was always drunk. After a spirited discussion they decided to ask Peter to leave. Saul was given the task of being their spokesperson.

The next morning, he approached Peter. "I have to tell you something that you are not going to like. Last night the officials met, we took a vote and decided it is in our best interest and yours if you leave."

Peter was taken by surprise, "leave? Oh no, I can't. I am here to take Jesse's place. He wanted me to."

"Maybe that's what you tell yourself, but the truth is you are a drunk and have become a nuisance. Even the children shy away from you when you come back to camp drunk and raving.

What happened to you Peter? The man I remember walking beside Jesse was strong, confident and caring. My heart breaks to see what you have become.

Jesse taught about forgiveness which is all good, but not only do we need to forgive others, we also need to forgive ourselves. Nobody is perfect Peter. We all make mistakes, but we have to live with them and move forward. I am sure you will find other ways you to live up to your promise to Jesse, just not here."

He didn't argue. He knew Saul was right. "I'll leave today. I couldn't even do this right for Jesse. I have failed him again."

"No Peter," Saul replied sadly, "the only person you have failed is yourself. When you get yourself right you will find what you are supposed to do."

An hour later Peter was seen slowly walking back up the hill, his knapsack on his back, his head hung in shame.

Saul watched him walk away. *He is a good man but just as lost as the rest of us.*

TEN

Unlocking the door of the jail cell the guard said, "You are free to go, but take my advice, start walking and keep going. We don't want your kind around here. Next time you are going to get yourself killed."

Pete sat on the edge of the stained cot, bleary eyed and sick to his stomach. He could taste the blood and vomit in his mouth. He ran his tongue over his teeth. *Thank goodness they are all still there.*

The guard handed him a cup of hot bitter black coffee, "Here, drink this and then get out."

Peter looked at him. "What happened? How did I get here?"

"Don't you remember? You took on three ex-Brown Shirts in the pub last night."

"I don't remember anything after I sat down to have a beer?"

"They seemed to know who you were, although I don't know how they recognized you under that long dirty hair and scraggly beard."

"What happened? Why did I do that?"

"They started taunting you, calling you names and talking about your friend Jesse and how useless you were as you watched Heinrich kill him. For a long time, you seemed to ignore them, then next thing we knew you walked over to their table tipped it over and called them out?"

"How did I get in here?"

"Three against one didn't seem fair so a couple of the town guys decided to help you out. When the fight was over, they carried you here for safe keeping. Lucky for you the other guys were as drunk as you or else you would have been killed. I'll probably have to fumigate that cell before I can put anybody else in there."

Peter looked at him and grinned "did we win?"

"Well in this case, it is safe to say you should see the other guys." The two men laughed.

Peter finished his coffee and handed the cup back to the guard. When he stood up dizziness washed over him and he clutched a bar of the cell door until it passed. Carefully putting one foot in front of the other to keep from falling, he made his way from the cell to the door.

"Peter what happened to you?" the guard asked. "Jesse gave his life for all of us and this is how you repay him? I'm sure if he saw you, and the rest of his Believers today, he would be very disappointed. Probably he would shake his head and wonder if the price he paid was worth it?"

The guard's words cut through the fog in Peter's brain and the pain they caused nearly doubled him over. Without saying a word, he opened the door and walked out on to the sidewalk. The bright morning light hurt his eyes.

Behind him the guard called out," turn left, follow the road and soon you will be out of town. If you know what is good for you, keep going."

Peter turned left as he was told and, using the buildings for support, staggered down the street. He shrugged his shoulders, shaking off the guard's questions. *I wish they would have killed me last night and then this torment will be over. The world would be better off without me.*

ELEVEN

"Marika," Maria called out while knocking on the bedroom door, "I saw your face when you came back from shopping. Did something happen?"

"Go away" Marika called back, "Leave me alone."

"Why are you crying? I heard your sobs down the hallway."

"I'm fine, just go away."

Maria didn't know what to do. *Something is seriously wrong. Do I go in or do I leave her alone?*

When she heard another sob, she quietly opened the door and stepped into the room. Marika was lying on her bed, and curled in a fetal position, a blanket covering her shaking shoulders.

Maria walked to the side of the bed and sat down. Gently she began to rub Marika's back, just like her mother did when she was a child.

"Do you want to tell me what's bothering you?"

Marika rolled on to her back. "Every time I walk down the street they call me names. Jesse's whore, slut or any other derisive name they can think of. When I go into the shops the clerks sometimes refuse to serve me. If they do, they look down on me. Today some of the bigger boys called me names and threw rocks at me. I don't know what I've done to deserve this?"

"Oh Marika, why didn't you say something before now? How long has this been going on?"

"It started a few days after we moved here, as soon as they found out I lived with Jesse. I want to scream at them to leave me alone that we were man and wife, but I can't. I don't know why this still has to be kept secret, Heinrich is dead. Can you tell me why they are acting this way?"

"I don't know Marika. For some I think putting others down elevates themselves in their own eyes."

"Maria, do we have to stay here? Can we start over in a new place where no one knows us and we can live in peace? Do you think there is such a place?'"

Maria thought for several seconds. *Marika is right. As much as I enjoy living here with Mark and Elizabeth, this is their home. What is happening isn't good for Marika or the baby. One thing for sure, people will continue to harass her as long as we stay here.*

She reached over, picked up the blanket and covered Marika. "Rest now. I'll talk to Mark about finding our own place."

Marika smiled, "Thank you."

That evening, when supper had ended, Maria found Mark sitting outside on the front door step. "Mark, can I speak to you for a minute?"

"Sure Maria, you know you don't have to ask. This is your home too." He moved over making room for her.

"Mark, Marika and I are thinking about finding a place of our own in another town."

"What brought his on? I thought you were happy here."

"We are, and please don't take this the wrong way. We appreciate all you have done for us but some the town folk are bullying Marika and making her life miserable. Today some boys threw rocks at her and called her names and she came home in tears."

"Tell me more," Mark said. Maria went on to explain what Marika told her.

After hearing the story Mark said, "I agree with you. As long as she is here the bullying will continue. Leave it with me. I will see what I can do, but it may take some time."

Several days later he called Maria and Marika to him. "I found a two-bedroom apartment in Eidelberg. It's a large town where I think you can live as quietly as you wish."

Speaking to Marika he added "It's not that far away and I can still come and check on you. When you get close to your delivery time, I will bring you back here until you are fully recovered."

The two women agreed with him. "But we have no furniture to take with us and we can't afford to buy any."

"Let me ask my patients, I'm sure some will have items they can spare."

Mark's patients came through. Within days Maria and Marika were ready to move to their new apartment. Friends of Mark's offered to help them move and within a week they were settled.

Word quickly spread among the Believers living in the area that Maria and Marika had moved to Eidelberg. Many came, introduced themselves and brought gifts of food. Mark and Elizabeth came by once a week with groceries and newspapers. The first question Maria always asked was "have you heard from Peter?" but each time the answer was no.

Then one day everything changed. When Mark and Elizabeth were going on their weekly visit, they found a wall of razor-sharp barbed wire fence strung across the highway extending as far as they could see on either side. A new guard tower with two security guards stood at the side of the road. None could enter, nor could anybody leave. Maria and Marika were trapped on the other side.

"Wait here," he said to Elizabeth.

He got out of the car and walked toward the fence. "I am a doctor. I have a sick patient I have to see today."

One of the guards walked toward him. "Go away, you are no longer allowed to cross."

"But my patient may die. I have the medicine he needs with me. I have to get it to him."

The guard raised his gun. "If you don't get back into your car I will shoot you."

Mark went back to the car, turned it around and drove away. "Elizabeth there is nothing we can do to help them now."

TWELVE

Lost in his alcoholic haze and apathy Peter was unaware that the world around him was changing. After Heinrich's death events in the small country evolved rapidly. Within hours Otto Rohm and his shadow government, with the help of the resistance and the Believers, moved to replace Heinrich's regime. Quickly they commanded his office, the police station, the newspaper and the radio station.

Their intention was to bring stability and peace to a country ravaged by death and hate. In his last days Heinrich decimated the country. Food was scarce, jobs were scarcer, businesses remained closed, children cried from hunger and mothers wept. The indoctrination camps left a legacy of shattered lives and destroyed families.

The people breathed a sigh of relief under this new regime and began the task of rebuilding what was lost. They buried their dead, built monuments to their heroes, picked up their broken lives and carried on. Short of money and resources Rhom's government appealed for international help which went largely unheeded.

The Brown Shirts were hunted down like common criminals. Some were captured and sent to Duvenwald prison. Many were killed. Others left the country to escape being held accountable for their actions. Still others, forced into hiding, regrouped and began to regain their strength.

The Believers hoped and prayed that they would be left alone, free to worship and practice Jesse teachings, but that was not the result. Word began to filter from one person to another of a place known as the Promise Land where they would be welcomed and able to live in peace. The problem was few Believers were allowed to immigrate legally. Those who tried to sneak into the Promise Land were jailed and eventually returned back to where they came from. Many waited a short period of time and tried again.

Rebels, opposed to Rohm's government, joined forces with the regrouped Brown Shirts. This group blamed the Believers for Heinrich's death and once again they were forced to live in fear and, without Jesse's leadership, became silent.

Attacks were launched against Rohm's government. People disappeared in the night; others were assassinated in broad day light and Rohm's control slowly disintegrated.

While Rohm fought to survive Brussia, a large country to the north, began moving against its neighbors, first encircling them, then absorbing them. First their ideology crossed the borders infiltrating the lives of the people and spread like a cancer. Next came a massive relief effort plying the people with badly needed money and food. Finally, without warning, tanks and soldiers appeared taking their land from them.

This new ideology was about a political and social economic system ruled by a single party without formal opposition. Property was confiscated, the productivity and distribution of goods was controlled and finally freedom of religion and social life were curtailed.

By the time Rohm's government realized what was happening Brussia was poised along their northern border. The rebels quickly negotiated a treaty and, with their help, Brussia began claiming parts of the land under Rohm's jurisdiction. The roads to Bern became clogged with refugees trying to escape. Food became scarcer, jobs disappeared and people became more afraid.

Nobody was prepared for what happened next. One morning the country awoke to find that during the night thousands of men had erected a barbed wire fence along vast stretches of the northern border. Armed guards protected the workers as they toiled through the coming days Essentially the country was divided in half.

Farms were divided, people cut off from their fields and cattle. Children were separated from their parents. Some people, on both sides of the fence, were unable to return to their homes and families. Roads became armed crossings guarded by tall wooden towers Desperate to cross the border some were shot and killed for not obeying orders.

Rohm attempted to negotiate with the Brussian leaders but was unsuccessful. The once proud country was finally defeated.

THIRTEEN

When Peter woke up, he was lying inside a hedge growing along the side of the road. The sun was beating down on his face. He felt disoriented, and couldn't remember where he was or how he got there.

He tried to get up to his feet but the world was spinning so he lay back down. He was cold and hungry, every bone in his body ached but, most of all he wanted a drink. He put his hand into his pocket but the few coins he had were gone.

Lying there he tried to remember what he had done the previous evening. Slowly it came back to him and a wave of guilt and revulsion stole over him. *Not again. This is happening too often and each time it gets harder to remember. The days and events all seem the same. I am such a failure I would be better off dead. I have nothing left to contribute to this world.*

He remembered going into a tavern and ordering a drink but when the bar keeper brought it, he didn't have enough money. First, they argued, then he drew back his fist and punched the man in the face. Other men drinking in the bar rushed to the bartender's aid and, after a brief scuffle, Peter was thrown out the door landing face first on the street. He had gone from tavern to tavern drinking all day until he ran out of money.

He also remembered the bar keeper yelling at him, "You no good piece of trash, don't ever come back. You are the poorest excuse for a man I have ever seen."

Shouting at the closed-door Peter said "I was good enough when I had a few coins in my pocket."

He remembered struggling to his feet and staggering down the middle of the road out of town. At one point a car honked behind him and he lurched to the side muttering to himself.

He recalled that he stumbled and fell to his knees. After several attempts, and with great difficulty, he managed to get back on his feet, thinking if he could get to the hedge of trees ahead of him, he could stay there until morning.

Then he had fallen to his hands and knees again and vomited in the middle of the road. Once more he managed to get back on his feet, but fell again. He crawled down into the ditch, up the other side and lay in the grass. He was almost there when he vomited again. He tried to stand but this time but he couldn't. After what seemed hours, he managed to get onto his hands and knees and crawl to the trees ahead of him. Once there, he wiggled under the branches and passed out.

Many hours later he awoke feeling much better. Stumbling he made his way to the road and began walking. Each time he heard a vehicle approaching he stopped and put out his thumb, hoping to get a ride, but nobody stopped.

Suddenly he heard a voice call out his name, but when he looked around, he was alone.

"Peter, it's me, Jesse."

He looked around again but there was nobody in sight. "No way," he muttered," I must be hallucinating, you are dead."

"Oh Peter, look at you. What have you done to yourself?"

"Go away. You are a figment of my imagination and I am not talking to you."

If a car had driven past at this point the driver would have seen a man in dirty tattered clothes, broken run-down boots, long hair and matted beard wildly gesticulating with his hands, talking to himself.

Suddenly he was angry. Standing at the side of the road he shouted," I let you down that's what happened. You entrusted me with the lives of Maria and Marika and I don't even know where they are. You told me to continue being a voice for the Believers and I couldn't even do that. You expected too much from me.

Things are different now. There is a new government persecuting the Believers and they are no better off than before. I have failed you and I am so sorry. Go away and leave me alone. The best thing that can happen is that I kill myself. Did you know that I denied knowing you twice just like you said I would? Nobody will miss a coward like me."

Peter began walking down the road again, tears of self-loathing and self-pity streaming down his face.

Once again, the voice called out "I need you now more than ever.".

"Yeah, for what," Peter shouted, "so I can disappoint you down again. You died and left me alone and I didn't even try to save you. I tried to do what you asked but I couldn't. I am good for nothing. Ask any bartender along this road, they know the truth."

"Peter you are only a day's walk from the town where Mark and Elizabeth live. Go to them, they know you are coming. Stay with them until you are healed. The task I gave you is not finished yet. There is much more that needs to be done, in my name."

Peter shook his head. *I must be going crazy. How can a sane man be walking down the road talking to Jesse? It's not possible*

Peter kept walking and by evening he realized he was on the outskirts of the town where Mark and Elizabeth lived. After that it was easy to find the hospital. When he walked through the door Mark moved toward him, his arms out stretched to hug his old friend.

"I have been expecting you. A friend of mine spotted you walking into town. Come let's get some food into you, get you cleaned up and into a bed. After that we will talk."

Peter turned and began walking away but Mark grabbed his arm. "Don't turn away my friend. Let us help you."

Peter stayed in the hospital for ten days, the first three the worst he ever experienced in his life. Small unseen creatures' bit him and he couldn't make them stop. He heard Jesse screaming for his help but couldn't reach him. Fire lapped at his body and everywhere he turned, blood and gore surrounded him.

He carried on like a mad man, begging for a drink. At times Mark tied him to the bed so he wouldn't hurt himself or others. Elizabeth cleaned him when he soiled himself. Yet, each time he opened his eyes, one or the other was sitting in a chair beside his bed.

On the fourth day he opened his eyes and looked around. Elizabeth was asleep in the chair beside him. His mind was clear, his thoughts vivid for the first time since he had left Maria and Marika here.

Elizabeth stirred. "I see you are awake. How do you feel today?" she asked.

Peter looked at her and replied, "Hungry."

Elizabeth laughed, "That's a good sign. I'll go fix you a tray. Do you know where you are?"

"Yes," he replied.

Peter spent one more day in the hospital and then Elizabeth took him home to recuperate. "What happened Peter? When you left here you were going to find the Believers and join them."

"I was numb from Jesse's death and overwhelmed by everything that happened. Jesse was an integral part of my life and I couldn't find a way to function without him. People recognized me and wanted to talk about him, but I couldn't.

I started going into taverns to hide, nobody discussed religion there. After a while I simply stopped caring. I found the Believers but, because I was always drunk, they didn't want anything to do with me. I was of no use to them and broke another promise to Jesse.

They sat quietly for a few minutes each lost in their own thoughts. Finally, Elizabeth spoke up "how is it you came to us?"

"You aren't going to believe this. I was thrown out of yet another tavern and ended up sleeping in a hedge of trees. The next morning, I was cold, sick and hungry walking down the road wondering where I could get a drink. Suddenly I heard Jesse talking to me. I thought I was hallucinating. He wanted answers about how my life had taken this turn.

I became angry and shouted at him for leaving me and how disappointed I was because I had let him down. After I calmed down, he told me to come to you. He told me that my work is not yet finished, so here I am."

"I believe you. Maybe you had to go through this to get to where you need to be and what you need to do. Jesse's spirit is still here even if his body is gone, Sometimes God works in mysterious ways."

"I didn't think of that. Surely there was an easier way to get my attention."

She smiled at him. "Have you thought about what you are going to do now?"

"First of all, I plan to visit Maria and Marika. Are they still here?" He felt as though a heavy weight had settled in his stomach.

"No, they moved away several weeks ago."

"Are they okay? Tell me where they live and I will surprise them with a visit."

"You can't."

"What do you mean I can't? Has something happened to them?"

"They moved to the village of Eidelberg and are now trapped behind the wall which divides our country. They can't come to us and we can't go to them. To try is to be killed."

Peter put his head in his hands. "This is my fault. I assumed they were here with you. I heard about a wall being built but never paid much attention. Have you heard how they are?"

"We heard they are in dire straits. The authorities know who they are and watch every move they make. Marika is worried about her baby. Somehow, they managed to get a message to us asking for help."

Peter lifted his head, "Baby? Marika is pregnant? Is Jesse the child's father?"

"Yes."

"That is wonderful news. Did Jesse know before he died?"

Elisabeth smiled, "yes he knew."

Peter sat there staring at the floor and heard Jesse's voice in his head. "I need you now more than ever."

Mark had joined them while they were talking. Peter looked at his two friends. "I promised Jesse I would look after them so I guess it's time I stepped up."

"What are you going to do?"

"I am going to get them out of there."

Peter, now, clean, sober had a new mission in life. *This time I will not let Jesse down.*

Elizabeth smiled at him. "Sometimes we need to go through our own dark times before we can be of use to others."

FOURTEEN

The next morning Mark drove Peter to the border. A six-foot barbed wire fence still blocked the road the elevated guard tower still stood on the other side. As soon as Mark approached the barrier two men with guns came out of the small shed beside the tower.

Peter studied what was in front of him. Through the fence he saw a hundred-foot slash of earth had been cleared along the fence line. All of the trees had been removed. and a ditch had been dug on the other side of that. Signs hung from the fence: "Crossing Prohibited. Stop. Come any further and you will be shot."

Peter looked at Mark. "Is the fence to keep them in or us out? "

Mark chuckled. "I think it is to keep them in. Nobody in their right mind would want to go there. Many have tried to cross near here and a few actually made it by cutting holes in the wire, but most were shot or stepped on a mine and were blown to bits."

"Is there some way we can get a message to Maria and Marika?"

"Why? What are you thinking?"

"I'm not sure, but there has to be a way to get across and bring them back."

"I personally don't know of a way but I can put you in contact with some of the Believers who may. I heard of a clandestine group who are not letting the fence stop their activities."

"Then what are we waiting for, let's get started. Jesse would want us to try."

As they got back in Mark's car Peter turned and waved at the guards. "I'll be back," he called out. One of the men raised his middle finger at him.

He stayed with Mark and Elizabeth for several more weeks. During this time, he walked miles every day, read newspapers, and studied maps trying to learn all he could about getting over the wall. He knew getting across the border would be fairly easy but getting back with the two women appeared to be impossible.

He talked to people, asked questions and quickly learned that certain suppliers had permits allowing them to deliver fresh fruit and vegetables to a market on the outskirts of Eidelberg. They were allowed to stay ten hours to sell their goods but had to return that same day,

Peter began to develop a plan. He knew how he could get across to Maria and Marika but bringing them back presented a bigger problem, especially if they were being closely watched. One man he spoke to was able to tell him where they lived and gave him directions. Another mentioned he heard they were in dire straits and that Maria had slowly been selling off their furnishings for food but she was not well. Believers who were in contact with people who lived close to them told him that the secret police are watching the two women and anybody who went to their apartment building was brought in and questioned.

The more Peter heard, the more concerned he became. Every day there were rumors of people starving to death, or being taken from their homes, never to return. Time was of the essence.

FIFTEEN

A loud pounding on the door startled Maria and Marika who were enjoying a cup of tea after their supper of potato soup and bread.

"Open up immediately, it's the police," a deep voice bellowed.

Unconsciously patting her hair and smoothing the front of her apron Maria opened the door. Although she appeared calm, she was terrified. Other Believers had told them of visits from the police.

Two men in black trench coats and black hats glared back at her. Before she could say anything, they pushed way their way into the room. One stood by the door, his arms crossed over his chest, the other spoke to the frightened women.

"Who else lives here?" he demanded.

"Nobody, there is only the two of us" Marika replied, wrapping her arm protectively around her stomach.

"Sit down," he shouted at Marika. "You too," he commanded Maria.

He walked around the small apartment checking out the two tiny bedrooms, looking under the beds and peering into the closet. When he was satisfied, he stood in front of the women. "Who are you? Where did you come from?"

Maria stared him down. "We will not answer your question until you tell us who you are and why you are here. We have done nothing wrong."

"I am Detective Olaf Rudinski of the local police. My partner is Detective Gunther Grosinski. We heard reports that Believers have been seen coming and going from this apartment. All religions, other than those sanctioned by the state, are forbidden"

"Whoever told you that is wrong," Maria replied, "Certainly friends have come to visit but I don't make it a point of asking their religious affiliations. I could care less what their beliefs are."

"Are you one of those Believers?" Olaf asked.

"We have no religious affiliation." Marika lied. "My name is Marika and this is my mother-in-law, Maria. My husband was away and got caught on the other side of the wall when it went up. We are here waiting for him to return."

Olaf walked over and grabbed Maria by the arm. "You are coming with me."

Maria tried to protest and looked at Marika for help

"Leave her alone," Marika demanded, but when she saw the look in Rudinski's face she stopped talking. "Where are you taking her? "Can't you see she is a frightened old lady?"

Maria shot her a disapproving look as if to say I'm not that old.

Marika looked at Maria. "Go with them. As soon as our neighbor gets home from his truck driving job, I will have him come and get you."

Maria grasped the idea of what Marika was saying. Marika was going to seek out one of the Believers for help.

.   "Take your hands off me," Maria said, "I'll come with you.".

With as much dignity as she could muster Maria walked into the first small bedroom and retrieved her coat and purse. She stopped in front of the mirror and combed her hair.

"Now we can go," she said to Olaf.

As soon as the men were gone Marika ran to the door and locked it. She was shaking so hard she could barely stand. *What if they find out that we are the wife and mother of Jesse, the leader of the Believers. What will happen to us then?*

She sat down on a chair, wrapped her arms around her middle and rocked back and forth. *Jesse, I need your help. I am so afraid.*

Hours later Maria returned home. Her left eye and cheek were swollen, her eyes red from crying.

Marika ran to her. "Are you okay? What did they do to you?"

"I am fine," Maria replied.

"But your eye…?"

"That one, Gunther, slapped me across the face, The other became angry and sent him out of the room. That was after I told him that if he hit me again, I would have no control over where my foot was going to land. He got my message."

"What did they want?'

"It was more of the same as when they were here. This was meant to scare us, but from now on everything we do and everybody we see will be under suspicion."

"Do they know who we are?"

"Not yet, but it is only a matter of time until they find out we were close to Jesse. We have two weeks to apply for residency papers and need to report to the police station to pick them up."

" I'm afraid Maria. What if someone there recognizes us? What will we do then?"

"We don't have any choice," Maria answered. "It's either that or have the police at our door every day. Somehow, I will try to get word to Mark that we need help."

Marika started to giggle. "Did you really tell him you would kick him?"

"I did and would have too," Maria replied. Then she also started to giggle. That little Maria would kick big Gunther was too funny to think about.

Early the next morning they walked to the police station and waited in line for hours to speak to somebody who could tell them about the residency requirements and give them the necessary forms. When they got them, they sat on a bench and read them over. "We don't have all of the information they require."

"Then we will lie," Maria said, "hopefully they will never find out."

As they were leaving one of the police officers approached them. "I have seen you before," he said," but I can't remember where. Have you ever been to Bern?"

Marika looked him straight in the eye. "No, we have never been there. Why do you ask?"

"I could have sworn I saw you there. Good day ladies," he said and walked away. The two women left the building and walked down the sidewalk as quickly as they could.

Three days later Detective Olaf knocked on their door again. "I demand to see your residency papers."

Marika picked them up off the table. "As you can see, we haven't quite finished filling them out. My mother-in-law has been quite ill and I have been looking after her. She has a heart condition and being hauled down to the police station upset her. You said we had two weeks and that time isn't up yet."

Olaf looked at them, "Get them done and, if they are not filed by next Monday, you will be arrested. I will be back to check on your progress." Then looking at Maria he said, "You know what we are capable of already. I would hate to see your pregnant daughter-in-law have to go through that."

Marika was shaking when she closed the door. She said to Maria, "now what do we do? He is not going to leave us alone."

* * *

Mark was walking home from the hospital when a man stepped out of an alley and spoke to him," I have a message from Maria. The police are hassling her and she is afraid they will find out who they are. They are afraid and begging for help."

"Thank you," Mark replied. "I will see if there is anything I can do."

When he returned home, he took Peter aside and told him about the message. Peter looked at him. "Don't worry. I'll find a way to bring them back home."

SIXTEEN

Mark and Peter were sitting on the front step talking as they did most evenings. It had been a hot day and a cool breeze was blowing on them. "Mark, do you know any of the men who drive produce over the border?" Peter asked.

"Why do you ask?" Mark replied.

"I have a plan to cross the border but I'm not sure how to bring Maria and Marika back."

"What are you thinking?"

"I thought if I could get a job with one of those men and travel back and forth with them a few times the guards will remember my face. Then, one time I could go with them but not return in the evening. I could find Maria and Marika, check on them and work on a way to bring them back."

Mark stared straight ahead and then turned to Peter. "I received word they are not well, possibly starving. Some of the Believers are taking them what little food they can spare. I was also told the police are watching them closely. One woman who visited them was stopped on a street corner and questioned after she was seen leaving their building. The two of them never leave their apartment because they are afraid of being arrested. If need be, as a doctor, I might be able to cross the border if they have an emergency, but I'm not sure. I haven' told Elizabeth any of these new developments because she worries enough about them as it is."

"Sounds like a good idea but best we wait. If too many strangers are seen going in and out the police may become suspicious and watch them closer."

Mark looked at his watch. "It's getting late and I have another busy day tomorrow. There is an outbreak of measles in the community and some of the children are very ill."

Peter went to bed but couldn't sleep. Suddenly it dawned on him. *Measles is contagious.* An idea began to take shape in his mind. The next morning, he outlined his plan to Mark.

"I will need somebody we can trust with a truck and two wooden coffins. I can bring back Maria and Marika in the coffins."

"What if the guards want to look at the bodies?"

"I will tell them they died from a virulent form of Measles and must be buried as quickly as possible. Even though they are dead, they are still contagious."

"Do you think that will work?"

"I can be very convincing when I need to be. I am sure I could make it sound that if the coffins were opened the guards get sick and possibly die."

They spent the next hour going over the details. "Now all we need is a truck and somebody we can trust. That person must understand how dangerous this will be if we are caught."

"I know just the man," Mark said. "Igor Sigurdson. He is a farmer who crosses the border to sell his produce every day. We could put the coffins in the bottom and then fill the truck with produce. The guards are used to him coming and going. You could be his new hired helper. I could talk to him. He is a Believer and hates what has happened to his people and his country. I'm not sure, but I think at one time he was part of the resistance."

Later that evening Mark knocked on Peter's bedroom door. "It is set for the day after tomorrow. We are to meet him at five in the morning. Wear your oldest clothes so that you look like a farm hand."

"Can we trust him, Mark? Does he know our plan and who we are going to rescue?"

"Yes. I only told him they were two women who needed our help. With the rumors floating around he may figure who they are by himself."

Two days later Mark and Peter arrived at the farm. Mark introduced Peter to Igor and then returned home and Peter stayed to help load the truck. Igor was a tall brawny man with a booming voice and liked to give orders.

First, they drilled holes around the sides of each coffin to allow for air. Then they stacked wooden crates filled with vegetable on top and around them. When finished no one would have guessed what they were actually transporting.

The truck was old and slow and it took sometime before they joined the others lined up at the border. When it was their turn to cross Igor rolled down his window. "Good morning, Gustave, how are you this fine day. See what I have for you," and produced two long cucumbers.

Gustav slipped the cucumbers under his shirt then loudly announced "you may pass."

As they drove away Igor explained that border guards were poorly paid and one of the cucumbers would be a treat for his family and he would probably sell the other.

Peter explained his plan to Igor. "When we get to where you unload your produce I will slip away. I have an address and an idea of where to go. I will bring the two women there and hopefully we can get them into your truck without being seen. Once we are out of town we will stop and put them into the coffins."

"Usually, I am in a hurry to get back but today I think I will be slow and visit with the other drivers. Be as quick as you can. If I hang around too long the patrol may stop and ask questions."

"How long do I have?" Peter asked.

"I would say about three hours" Reaching down to the floor of his truck he grinned. "I brought extra cucumbers just in case."

While Igor waited in line to unload his truck Peter slipped out the side door. He needn't have worried about being seen by the other drivers because they were more interested in a shouting match taking place between two of them. Others were standing in a group talking about the day's low prices. He sauntered across the street disappearing into the nearest alley.

He had to stop for a few seconds his heart was pounding so hard. When he felt more in control he headed north. Mark had also been told the authorities forced the women to move into a smaller apartment in the slum area of the town.

Eidelberg wasn't a big town but the further he walked, the more decrepit the area and buildings became. Peter's fear for Maria and Marika's safety increased. It wasn't long before he found himself in front of a shabby building. The front steps were broken, some of the windows were boarded up, most of the others were also broken. Graffiti in red paint covered the walls.

He looked around to see if anybody was watching then, when he was sure it was safe, he entered the building and climbed the stairs to the second floor. The inside reeked of poverty and decay. Outside of apartment twenty-four he listened and heard the murmuring of voices. He knocked on the door and waited. When nobody answered he knocked again, louder this time.

"Who is there?" a timid voice asked.

"I am looking for two women, I was told they live here."

Then door opened slightly and he heard a gasp. "Peter? Is that you?" The door opened wider and a hand reached out and pulled him in.

"Maria, come quickly Peter is here. He has found us; our prayers have been answered." Marika whispered loudly.

Peter was shocked when he went inside. The two women were mere shadows of themselves. Marika looked like she had a small football where her stomach should be. He didn't know what to say. *How had they come to this? They both look like they are starving.*

Both women, laughing and crying at the same time, launched themselves into his arms. He led them to the thread bare sofa and sat down, one on either side of him.

"How did you find us?"

Peter grinned. "I have my ways. And what is this?" he said waving his hand at Marika's stomach. "Mark told me you were pregnant and having Jesse's baby? This is wonderful news."

"Yes, it's our miracle baby".

At that moment Peter understood why Jesse had come to him on the road and told him there was still much to do.

"Did anybody see you?" Maria whispered. "If the officials find out you are here, we will be in trouble."

"I will explain all to you later. Right now, I have come to take you home. We need to move as quickly as possible because we don't have much time. Go get your coats and purses and take only what you can carry in your pockets. You will have to leave the rest here."

The women did as they were told. Each covered their hair with a kerchief and carried a small bag. Peter looked at them.

"If we are supposed to look like we are going shopping we need something to carry our purchases in."

"Smart thinking. I will go ahead and wait for you at the corner. Wait a few minutes and then come out behind me. Maria, lean on Marika as though you need help walking."

"What if the police are watching and we are stopped?"

"You will need to convince them you are going to the market."

"The neighbors will wonder. We rarely go out and they will be worried when we don't come back. They have been very good to us."

"You have to leave without saying goodbye. We can't take a chance that one might turn you in. Besides if all goes well, you will be across the border before they notice. We will send them a message later. Come, we need to get going."

"Where are we going?" Maria asked.

"My friend is waiting for us at the produce unloading station by the market. Do you know where that is?"

"Yes," Marika answered. "We went there one time to buy some fresh potatoes."

"Don't cross the street but go into the alley and wait If we get separated you must continue on your way and ask for Igor Sigurdson's truck and tell him that you heard he has good cucumbers for sale at a low price. He will know the message is from me."

Peter opened the door, checked to make sure the hallway was empty then made his way down the stairs. Once outside he pulled his hat low over his eyes and walked to the corner. Several minutes later Maria and Marika came out the door and walked toward him. Maria leaned heavily of Marika's arm. Peter then realized how weak the women were.

They hurried down the street, Peter followed a short distance behind them. In their urgency they failed to notice a young policeman step out of the shadows.

"Good morning, ladies. Where are you off to in such a hurry?"

They stopped in their tracks. "We are going to the market. We want to get there early before everything is sold out. My daughter is pregnant and we want some fresh milk and cheese for her," Maria answered.

The policeman looked the women up and down. Marika's hand rested on her stomach. "Is this your first?" he asked.

"Yes."

"Let me see what's in your bags."

Maria looked up at him. "We have very little money and are hoping to trade these few items for food. If we wait too long others will have the same idea."

He paused for several seconds. "Go then but as soon as you are done go straight home. Women are not safe in this part of town." He watched them walk away but still had an uneasy feeling. Shrugging his shoulders, he lit a cigarette, turned and walked in the other direction.

Peter crossed the street and stood watching the exchange. He had picked up a rock from the road and was prepared to hit the policeman over the head if necessary. He breathed a sigh of relief when the two women began to walk away. He watched the policeman until he turned a corner and disappeared from sight.

Life is not safe on this side of the wall. I wonder if that young man knows he made the biggest mistake of his career.

Upon their arrival Peter noticed Igor had moved the truck and it was now parked on the other side of the street near the entrance to the alley. He noticed Igor talking to some of the men. Instead of rolling up the tarp as most drivers did once they were unloaded Igor's was down.

"Get into the back and crouch down. We don't want anyone to see you," he said to the women.

Peter staggered across the street.

"Where have you been?" Igor roared. "I was just about ready to leave without you. I see you are drunk again? This is the last time I am bringing you with me. Do you want to get us arrested for staying here too long? Get into the truck so we can leave, I am already late."

With his head hung down Peter lurched back to the truck and climbed in the passenger's side. Igor followed behind him continuing to shout. Peter ignored him and rested his head against the window.

Igor got in started the truck, honked the horn, waved at his friends and began driving down the street. "I was getting worried," he said to Peter.

"The apartment was farther than I thought it would be. The women are weak and unable to walk quickly."

A few miles out of town Igor pulled off the road. "I gotta take a piss," he said to nobody in particular and made a big show of standing on the side of the road. In the meantime, Peter sneaked out the other side and climbed into the back of the truck.

"You must hide in the coffins until we are safely on the other side. We drilled extra air holes so you should be okay. When we stop at the border you must be very quiet. I am hoping I can convince the guards not to open them." Peter helped them get as comfortable as possible and then he put the lids on and scattered the crates as though they had been haphazardly tossed into the back.

Fifteen minutes later Igor pulled up to the border. A different guard was on duty. He walked around the truck and peeked into the back noticing the two coffins.

"Open them," he commanded "I want to see what's inside."

"Are you sure? These people died from a virulent form of measles, even though they are dead, they are still contagious.

The guard got a strange look in his face, "I'm supposed to look to make sure you aren't smuggling somebody out."

"Go ahead," Peter replied, "but don't say I didn't warn you about what could happen. In two days, you will have a fever, then itchy red pustules will cover your body and, if it gets into your eyes, you will go blind. Go ahead, open them but you are taking your life in your hands."

The guard looked at Peter and then at Igor and said "get out of here now."

Igor drove slowly through the checkpoint so as not to raise any suspicion, and once on the other side he sped home and parked the truck where it couldn't be seen from the road. Peter helped Maria and Marika out of the coffins while Igor went into the house and brought out two glasses of water.

"You are safe now." he told them. "Drink this and then I will take you to Mark's." Winking at them he added "I think being dead must make one thirsty." Turning to Peter he said, "I know who these women are and I am honored to be the one who helped bring them to safety."

"You mustn't tell anybody what we did today."

"Don't worry about me, your secret is safe, although I may spread a rumor that I heard the women are safe on this side."

Mark and Elizabeth were waiting for them when they arrived. When Elizabeth saw how emaciated they were she told Igor to take them directly to the hospital.

Once they were settled Peter said to Mark, "I'm leaving in the morning."

"Where are you going?"

"I have heard talk of a place called the Promise Land. I need to find out if there is such a place and if there is, I want to take Maria and Marika there."

"It will be some time before they are ready to travel," Mark replied. "They need to build up their strength. You do realize Marika is going to have a baby and a long journey may be too dangerous for her."

"That's what made me decide. They need some place where they can live in peace and a safe place to raise Jesse's baby.

SEVENTEEN

. From the shadows Peter stood watching a group of men standing around a fire. He didn't see anyone he knew and cautiously approached. He was tired, hungry, cold and needed a place to stay for the night.

"Have your room for one more? It's getting cold and I need a place to rest tonight," he asked.

"Strangers are welcome here," one of the men replied.

As Peter moved closer to the fire a man stepped out of the darkness and approached him. "Peter is that you? Where have you been all this time?"

Peter recognized the voice as that of his good friend Liam. The two men shook hands, then Liam pulled him into a hug.

"Maria and Marika…?" he questioned.

"Safe with Mark."

"Thank God. We were worried. Nobody seemed to know what happened to them after Jesse was killed."

Before Peter could answer Liam announced to the men watching. "Look who is here, Peter, one of Jesse's most ardent followers and my good friend."

The men crowded around Peter, all of them seeming to ask questions at the same time, others wanting to shake his hand.

Finally, Liam stepped in, "leave him for now, he is probably tired and hungry. When did you eat last?"

"I'm not sure, yesterday I think."

Liam chuckled, "You never were very good about looking after yourself."

The men drifted back to what they were doing and Liam led Peter to a back corner of the alley. He dug in his knapsack pulled out an apple and a piece of cheese and handed them to Peter.

"No, you keep it. This is probably all you have."

"Go ahead. I can find more tomorrow. Tell me what has happened between now and the last time I saw you."

They talked well into the night but Peter was too ashamed to tell Liam what he had become and his feelings about letting Jesse down. They reminisced about their time with Jesse and the Believers and laughed about the joke they had played on Heinrich by moving Jesse's body and burying it. Then their talk turned to politics.

"Not much has changed Peter. Rohm is failing as he tries desperately to rebuild what Heinrich destroyed. It is almost an impossible task for one man. Some of the Brown Shirts regrouped and are still beating and killing Jesse's followers. Without Jesse's leadership the Believers stay in their homes and hide.

Now there is the fear of Brussia taking over the country as they have our neighbors. Rohm will do his best to stop them but he doesn't have the man power nor the full support of all the members of his government. Some see Brussia as the answer to their problems, but don't realize their doctrine is completely different. The state controls everything and everyone."

"I haven't been paying much attention to politics lately and didn't realize how bad things were getting. I have been behind the fence along the border and it is nearly impossible to get across."

"Maybe you should," Liam stated, "If Brussia succeeds, our way of life is once again threatened and it will be almost as bad if not worse than living under Heinrich. But enough catching up for tonight. Maybe we should get some rest. You are probably tired and have travelled a long way today."

He wanted to ask Peter more but he didn't. Digging into his knapsack and he handed Peter his spare blanket. "I will wake you when it is time to go to the soup kitchen for breakfast."

The next time Liam looked over at Peter he was already asleep. He lay awake for a long time. *This is not the Peter I used to know. Something has changed him and not for the better. This man is deeply troubled and afraid to talk about what is bothering him.*

Liam woke Peter up early the next morning and they walked to the Soup Kitchen. The lineup was twice as long than it had been before. Those who recognized Peter shook his hand as he walked past. He stopped and spoke to those he recognized.

"Is it always like this?" he asked.

"Yes "Lam replied. "Not much has changed. Men are still poor and hungry and there isn't enough work to go around."

A man left the line and walked over to Peter. "Are you the Peter, who was one of Jesse's followers?"

"Yes, why are you asking?" Peter felt embarrassed and ashamed. He alone knew how undeserving he was of the man's respect.

"There is a man who is very ill and asks every day if we have seen you."

"What is this man's name?" Peter asked.

"Jean. Jean Baptiste."

Peter's heart slammed into his chest. Could it be the same Jean Baptiste? He had been told that Jean was tortured to death in the camps.

"You must take me to him," Peter said. Then turning to Liam he added, "I am going with this man. If it is our friend Jean Baptiste I don't know when I'll be back."

"Go with God," Liam replied pulling him into a hug. "It was good to see you again my friend."

The young man led Peter through the streets to a squalid old shack in the poorest part of the city. Peter was shocked when he went inside. John Baptiste was lying on a filthy cot in a dark room. The rank smell of dirt and decay made his eyes water.

When Jean heard people talking in the door way he called out, "Who is here, come closer where I can see you."

"It is I, Peter."

He sensed the emaciated man was near death. When he moved closer, he saw Jean's hands were deformed, reminiscent of an animal's claws.

"I knew you would come," Jean said, his voice barely above a whisper. "I am happy to see you again my friend."

"Jean, what happened to your hands?"

"I was tortured. They broke my fingers one at a time when I refused to denounce Jesse. Life in the camps was hard. I am lucky to have survived at all."

"We heard you had been tortured and killed by the guards."

Jean chuckled. "It takes more than those feeble efforts to get rid of me. They tried, but as you can see, were unsuccessful."

Peter looked around, took in the filthy conditions and made a decision. "I am going to stay with you. A little tender loving care and I will have you back on your feet in no time."

Turning to the young man waiting in the doorway, Peter said to him "bring me warm water so I can bathe him and wash his bedding and clothes. Find someone to help you clean up this room. It is filthy and it stinks. How is a man supposed to get better if he is living in this?"

The young man scurried away. Soon Jean was clean and two young girls had swept and washed the floor and the lone window above Jean's bed. Jean tried to sit on a chair while this was going on but Peter saw how exhausted he was.

"Rest while I go and find you some food to help you get your strength back."

"Thank you, Peter, but you are wasting your time. I am dying and not long for this world."

. For the next several days Peter watched over him. He coaxed him to eat, tended to his bodily functions and changed his bed. He watched Jean's life ebb away and vowed to stay with him until the end.

At one point he whispered to Jean "I will not let you die alone. You deserved better than this. Damn Heinrich. He took so much from all of us and for what? We got nothing but misery in return."

Late one night Jean woke up. "I sense something is bothering you. Will you tell me what it is?"

Peter looked into his red rimmed eyes. "You are right. I am a failure Jean, and I let Jesse down. I betrayed his faith and trust in me."

Once Peter began talking his feelings of guilt, self-loathing and fear spilled out. He didn't stop talking until he told him everything. Jean listened attentively.

When he finished talking Jean looked at him. "Don't you think it is time for you to stop feeling sorry for yourself and start doing what you have been called to do?"

"You think I am feeling sorry for myself?' Peter shouted, "How do you figure that?

"Did you listen to what you were saying. I...I.. me....me... Do you think you are the only person who feels they let Jesse down? We all did. Jesse knew the plan for his life and embraced it, death and all. Most of us didn't try to hide in a bottle and drink ourselves to death.

Can't you see that this is a small part of a bigger plan? Yes, he meant for you to look after Maria and Marika for the short term, but also the long term. They are two women alone in an unsavory world and they will need your guidance for a long time. That is why Jesse entrusted you with the lives of two people he loved the most. Forget what happened in the past, you can't change a thing. Now, more than ever, is the time to step up and be the man Jesse needs you to be. You have been given a second chance to prove yourself."

Jean was exhausted from talking, Taking Peter's hand he slowly drifted back to sleep. Later, in the early morning hours he took his last breath. Peter was alone again.

* * *

Liam was the first to spot Peter when he returned to the alley. "Jean..."

"He left this world this morning my friend. He was a truly great man."

"Yes, he was," Liam agreed.

The two men walked over and stood by the fire warming their hands. The days were getting colder and Peter didn't have any warm clothes.

"Liam, have you ever heard of the Promise land?" Peter asked.

"I have heard it mentioned, but don't know much about it."

"Supposedly it's a place where Believers can live in peace and harmony with people of the same beliefs."

"Do you think there could be such a place Peter?"

"I don't know, but I am going to find out. If there is, I am going to take Maria and Marika there."

EIGHTEEN

After Maria and Marika's rescue and Jean's death, Peter felt more alone and confused than ever. *What exactly did Jean mean when he said more was needed from me in regards to Maria and Marika? I wish I had a crystal ball to see what lies ahead.*

Each time he entered a town he was tempted to go to a tavern and have a drink yet, he knew if he gave into his craving, everything he worked so hard to accomplish be would be lost. Now that he had promised Mark he was going to move the two women to the Promise land, if there was such a place, he had to follow through. Because of Marika's pregnancy it needed to be sooner rather than later.

Frequently he met up with fellow travelers who were as lost and alone as he. Sometimes he stayed with them for a day or two, others for just a few hours. Each group he met he questioned about the Promise Land. Some had vague answers, other didn't know what he was talking about.

He was walking down the road and noticed a group of men standing off to one side talking. He could tell from their raised voices and excited hand gestures something of great importance had happened.

As he approached, he slowed down trying to hear what they were talking about, but too many were talking at one time. More men came from a side road and joined the group. Suddenly he heard someone call out his name. "Peter, is that you?"

A short skeletal man detached himself from the group and began walking toward him. Peter turned at the sound of his name but the sun was in his eyes and he couldn't see. He began walking faster. There were many of them and only one of him.

"Peter, wait," the man called out again. "It's me, Jacobus from the alley in Bern."

Pete stood there; his hands turned into fists ready to fight. The man, stopped in front of Peter breathing hard.

Peter looked at him for a time and then began to smile. "Jacobus you old reprobate. How are you?" the two men hugged, and slapped each other on the back, each pleased to see an old friend.

"Come, join me and my friends," Jacobus said. "I'm sure they will be pleased to meet you."

Peter hesitated for a moment then walked back with Jacobus to join the group. As they approached Jacobus shouted out "come and meet my friend Peter. Once he was a close friend and follower of Jesse of the Believers."

Turning to Peter he added "I told them I knew you but I don't think they believed me."

Peter walked up to the group. Many shook hands with him and told him their name. Others simply nodded. Peter noticed an older man leaning on a walking stick standing off to the side watching closely.

After a few minutes the men returned to their discussion. Peter asked Jacobus. "Who is that man standing over there?"

'That is our leader, Leonard Tremblay. If he wants to know more about you, he will come over and ask. Since he returned from the camps, he is very cautious and wary of strangers. He doesn't trust anybody, even those of us who have been with him for a long time."

"I heard you talking when I was passing and you all seemed to be excited about something."

"Oh, you don't know then," Jacobus stated. The Brussians put a barbed wire fence across the northern part of the country and claimed the land and people for themselves.

We heard they were turning people back and they aren't allowed across. We also heard some tried to climb the fence and were shot and killed. This is unbelievable. After all we have been through with Heinrich. This doesn't make any sense to me."

"Unfortunately, what you've heard is true. I have seen it for myself. Do you remember Mark? He tried to get across to see some of his patients but has been refused each time."

Peter hadn't noticed that the man called Leonard approaching them "There is nothing you can do for them if they are the other side," he continued." Brussian policy is "nobody leaves, nobody enters." For people who live on this side of the wall life goes on as normal."

Leonard studied Peter for a moment then asked, "Are you really Jesse's friend Peter?"

"I was until the day he died."

"Come walk with me, "Leonard said. "I wish to speak to you in private. Our camp is just down the road aways."

As they walked Leonard told Peter about his time in the camps and questioned him about Jesse. Later sitting outside of Leonard's tent Peter felt apprehensive.

"What is your plan, Peter? Where are you going from here?

"I'm not sure. Have you ever heard of a place called the Promise Land?"

"Yes, it is actually a country known as Disreal by the Red Sea, and currently under British control. They are trying desperately to keep the Believers out but some are getting through."

"I want to go there and see for myself if the rumors are true and that it is actually a place where Believers can live in Peace."

"I would like to go there also," Leonard said. "Ultimately this band of travelers will get there; at least that is the purpose of our journey. If you are serious, I can give you the name of a man to contact and tell him I sent you, He will help you get across the border. One man alone is easier to move than a group. The British are known to deal harshly with anybody they catch entering the country illegally."

At supper that evening one of the men told him how some of them hitched rides in empty freight cars to get from one place to another. Trouble was you had to get in while the train was moving.

"Sounds easy."

"It is, if you don't kill yourself trying," the man replied.

Peter stayed the night with Leonard and left before sunrise the next morning. He was now more determined than ever to find this place called the Promised Land and move Maria and Marika there.

NINETEEN

Peter made his way to the railway station located on the edge of town. He didn't have enough money to purchase a ticket but other men told him how they jumped on a moving train and hid in an empty freight car. They also told him stories of those who fell under the train, many of whom who lost their lives trying.

The train was forced to slow down when it entered the town and he hoped this would work to his advantage. He also hoped to get into an open freight car without being seen.

He walked down the tracks until he came to a stand of trees bordering the tracks and waited. Within an hour he heard the whistle of the train entering the town and began to slow. Cautiously he moved to the edge of the trees and watched the train approach. There was a slight bend in the tracks and he saw an open door in one of the freight cars approaching. He heard the engine began to pick up speed. It was now or never.

When the freight car was in front of him Peter grabbed the handle on the outside and held on. He was lifted off his feet and dangled precariously from one hand. He swung his legs up and managed to hook his foot on the side of the open door. At first, he thought he was going to have to let go but found a way to steady himself. Using his free hand, he clutched the door frame and slowly inched his body into the car until he was lying flat, then let go of the handle. Now all he had to do was hope he didn't get caught.

He travelled this way for three days. Sometimes he was alone, other times others travelled with him. During these times Peter kept to himself. Whenever the train slowed down to enter a large town he jumped off and then followed the tracks to the other edge of town. Several times he was challenged by the track inspectors who watched for people like himself. Both times he was let off with a warning. "If you get caught hitching a ride on the train you will be arrested and automatically put in jail for seven days."

On the fourth morning he jumped off the train in the town of Supora. One of his fellow travelers told him that when he arrived he was three miles from the border of the Promise Land there.

He found a cheap hotel room, bathed, put on clean clothes and headed for the nearest tavern. This was usually a good place to get information and something to eat. He ordered coffee with his meal surprised that he felt no inclination to have a drink. His mission was too important to go down that road again. He listened to talking men around him hoping to get information about how to cross the border but what he heard made him nervous.

The British had a heavy guard presence along the border. As well search lights continually swept the area at night and during the day the patrols walked with dogs.

For several days Peter followed this routine but didn't learn the exact information he wanted. As he was getting ready to leave one evening a big man with a scar running down the side of his face approached his table.

"Do you mind if I join you?"

"I was just leaving so you are welcome to my table." Peter answered.

"Are you waiting for someone?" the man asked. "I noticed you sitting here the last two evenings."

"I am merely visiting," Peter replied.

The man ordered a beer and then asked "what brings you here stranger?"

Peter was unsure what to say but then decided to tell the truth. "I am looking for a way into the Promise Land."

Instead of laughing the man said. "Everybody believes there is such a place but the British stop anyone who wants to enter. Many Believers come here with the same idea. They try, but most don't make it. Those who are caught are kept in a prison camp for several months and then returned home."

"I will make it," Peter announced.

The two men talked for a short time and then Peter returned to his room. He had enough money for two more nights and one more meal at the tavern. After that he would have to come up with a new plan.

The next evening when he returned the man was already there. He motioned Peter to come and sit with him. "My name is Noah and I know that you are Peter, one of Jesse's followers and closest friends." he said.

"How do you know who I am?" Peter was shocked.

"I received a message telling me to watch for you."

"What now?" Peter asked.

"I am to help you cross the border safely, a Believer on the other side will be waiting for you."

"How did they know I was here. I was careful not to let anybody know who I was and where I was going." Peter felt uneasy, still not sure if he should trust this man or not.

"Word travels fast in these parts. Meet me outside the post office at three o'clock tomorrow afternoon ready to travel. We will have to be walk in the dark tomorrow night."

"We are going to cross here?"

"No, further down, through the hills where there are fewer guards."

Peter was waiting for Noah at the designated spot and they went to a nearby café. where Noah outlined his plan. "If you are caught," he told Peter, "You don't know me. Go with the authorities and I will find a way to slip away.

The last half a mile you will be on your own. The British are always on the lookout for me and would like nothing better than to catch me and throw me in jail. Tell me Peter, what is so important that you are willing to take this risk?"

"There are two women I am responsible for. I cannot tell you their full story but I swore an oath to look after them. One is older and not well, the other is pregnant. Neither one is safe at the present time."

He went on to explain how he had found them starving and rescued them from behind the wall. "I want them to be in a safe place. Both have suffered greatly for the cause of the Believers and deserve to live in peace. Once I see how things are I plan on returning home and bringing them back."

"Two women, eh? The safest way is to take them is by ship. I don't think they will be able to hop on freight trains like you did. When you know what you are doing send word to me and I will make arrangements for them to board a ship at Ludlow. We have a long-rugged coast line which we use to unload ships, but it is still dangerous. I hope they will be up to the voyage."

Noah looked at his watch. "It's time to go. We have to meet somebody." Noah placed a few bills on the table and they left.

I hope I can trust him. The last thing I want is to *end up in a British prison.*

A farm truck was waiting for them on the edge of town. Noah motioned for Peter to climb in the back. As soon as they were settled the truck drove off. Noah's friend drove for twenty minutes toward the high hills in the distance, then pulled over and the two men got out.

"Meet me back here in six hours "Noah said to the driver.

"Six hours?" Peter questioned.

"That gives us plenty of time if the patrols are in the area and we are forced to wait."

Noah began walking through the trees. Peter walked behind him. After a while he noticed they were following a barely discernable path upward.

About an hour later they crested the top of a hill and Peter could see for miles. There was a town in the distance.

"That is where you need to go," Noah explained. "Once you arrive look for a place called Armistead's Tailor Shop and go inside. The code word is Nightingale. Someone will take you from here. Now we wait until the sun sets and the night patrol has passed."

After waiting for what seemed forever Peter noticed lights in the distance. They lay on the ground so as not to be seen. Peter heard the voices of the men talking, the hill side was bathed in light from the search lights on a vehicle.

They waited until the vehicle was out of sight then made their way down the steep embankment. As they neared the bottom Noah said, "I must leave you now." He pulled a flash light out of his pocket, blinked it three times and a man came out of the shadows. "He will take you the rest of the way. Go directly to the tailors, they are expecting you."

The two men spoke quietly to each other but Peter was unable to hear what they were saying then Noah turned and left. "Go with God," he whispered, disappearing into the darkness.

The man turned to Peter and introduced himself. "My name is Chaim. We must hurry and leave before the patrol comes back."

Peter had no choice but to follow him, but he still felt uneasy. He didn't like the idea of his life being in the hands of a man he didn't know.

They walked until they came to a road with deep ditches on each side. "We must follow the road and hide in the ditches if someone comes. We should be safe for a while. It's too early for the day patrols to leave the garrison and the night to return."

Chaim set a blistering pace and it was all Peter could do keep up with him. Less than an hour later they were on the edge of town.

"I will be leaving you here," Chaim said. "Cross the road and follow it to the next alley, turn left and follow the alleys for three blocks and then turn right. Armistead's Tailors is in the middle of the street. Watch out for the soldiers patrolling the streets. Knock three times, stop and then four times. Someone will open the door for you".

Peter did as he was told. He stayed close to the side of the buildings, and when he was sure nobody was watching, crossed the street. He moved cautiously walking close to the buildings down the next three alleys until he came to the tailor's shop. A small sign was placed on the side of the door. He knocked as he was directed.

The door opened and a man said "we have been waiting for you Peter."

"You know who I am?" he asked. All he received in return was a grunt. He followed the man up the stairs to a small apartment.

"You can rest here for today. I must open my shop and get my employees started then I will return. There is fresh coffee and biscuits if you are hungry. Help yourself."

TWENTY

Peter was asleep when the man returned hours later. The sound of a door opening woke him up.

"Allow me to introduce myself. I am Job the tailor and I have been told you are Peter, who was a close friend of Jesse. Why are you here? I have a feeling you aren't here to immigrate."

"You are right," Peter replied. "I wish to bring two women here. One is pregnant with Jesse's child and the other is his mother."

"I didn't know Jesse was married."

"Most people don't and since his death she has learned she is expecting his child. I fear they are in grave danger if anybody finds out. There are those who are still persecuting the Believers and, if they should find out, I don't know what will happen to her or the baby.

I'm also afraid she will be in danger here if the Believers find out. They would herald the baby as the second coming of Jesse and make her life miserable." he added.

"You don't need to say any more. I understand. I won't tell anybody who these women are. I will call a meeting for tomorrow night to make plans to see what we can do to help you. Until then you must stay hidden and wait. Nobody knows you are here and I prefer to keep it that way."

Peter looked at Job. "Can I trust you? This is far too important for anything to go wrong."

"Yes, you can," Job replied. He put out his hand and the two men shook hands.

When the shop closed that evening Job came back to the apartment, made supper and they talked late into the night.

Peter remained hidden the next day until Job closed his shop. After a quick supper they left to go to the meeting he had arranged. When they arrived eight men were gathered in a room behind a noisy tavern filled with British soldiers.

"Aren't you afraid of getting caught?" Peter asked.

"No. they would never suspect what we are doing. Many of those men are sympathetic to our cause but only following orders."

"I have heard that before. Heinrich's men used to say the same thing after his death."

"Yes, but this is different. Most of them are not our enemy and they are simply doing what is required of them."

Job introduced the men to Peter, then he addressed the group. "This is Peter, a good friend and follower of Jesse. He has come to ask for our help."

'How do we know he is not a spy?" a large swarthy looking man asked. The other men murmured in assent.

"Noah vouched for him. He would have made sure who he was before smuggling him across the border. Peter, tell them what you told me last night."

Peter told them Maria and Marika's remarkable story. "I need to find a safe haven for them, a place where they can heal and live in peace. I let them down before and I promised Jesse I would watch over them. I want his child to be born here among the people who loved and revered his father.

The men were silent. Turning their backs to Peter and Job they discussed what they had heard.

"How long before the baby is born?'

"I'm not sure, my guess is three or four months."

"Are they well enough to travel?"

"Yes, I believe so. Maria isn't well but I know she won't stay behind. This will be her one and only grandson. The rest of her family was killed in the Norenburg massacre."

"Why I am asking is that a mercy ship is leaving Ludlow in one months' time. Do you think you can be there by then? We will arrange your passage, but if you are late, the captain will leave without you. The name of the ship is the Lucy Mae."

"How long does it take?"

"Three or four days. The captain needs to get into international waters at night and then find a way to avoid capture by the British. For some reason they frown upon us smuggling refugees into their country." The other men laughed.

"Once they are on our soil, we will move them inland. We will arrange for you to meet up with Noah tomorrow evening so you can begin your journey home.

"The same way I came?"

"No, by a different route. Chaim will meet you at the Tailors at eight tomorrow evening. He will be our guide again."

As they were preparing to leave the large man stepped in front of Peter and said, "you better not by lying. We have our own way of dealing with traitors and spies."

TWENTY-ONE

Chaim and Peter travelled out of town in a jeep which could easily be mistaken for a British one. They followed the highway for a time then turned north "The moon is bright," Chaim said, "I would have preferred a cloudy night."

"You seem anxious. Are you expecting trouble?"

"No, but a person never knows where the British are hiding."

Suddenly he stopped. "Did you see that?" he whispered.

"I didn't see anything." Peter replied.

"I am sure I saw a flash of light in the rocks."

"Could it be Noah?"

"No, it is too early for him to be here. There, did you see it this time?"

"Yes, what do you think it is?"

"I think it is the moonlight reflecting off something, I think we have company. Hang on." Chaim stepped on the gas and hurtled down the road.

"When I slow down jump out and hide in a pile of rocks"

"But Noah…"

"He knows to come here. I have no doubt he is watching from the top of the hill."

Suddenly there was the sound of a ping on the rocks behind them.

"They are shooting at us," Peter exclaimed ducking his head.

A second shot sounded even closer. "They aren't quite sure where we are. Get out now and run. I will turn on my headlights to distract them. By the time they come after you I will be far away."

Peter touched the man on the arm. "Thank you, my friend."

Chaim slowed the jeep and he jumped out, ducked down and ran toward the rocks. Chaim had already turned on the headlights and was driving in the opposite direction as fast as he could, spewing dust and sand behind him. Almost immediately Peter saw a second set of headlights come on, turn in a circle and begin chasing Chaim.

I hope he gets away. I wouldn't want him to suffer on my account.

He moved deeper into the rocks trying not to make a sound. He saw a path ahead and was trying to decide if he should follow it when he heard a noise off to his right. He crouched down, waiting to see if he heard the noise again.

Then he heard a whisper. "Peter is that you?"

"Noah?"

"Yes. Follow the path upwards and I will meet you. The British will soon return with their spotlights and will be able to see you. I'll find us a way out of here."

The moonlight made it easier for Peter to see where he was going.

"Hurry, they are coming. Lay down among the rocks and I will come to you."

Seconds later Peter felt Noah lay down beside him. He looked over his right shoulder and saw the searchlight hovering over the rocks below. He heard two men talking.

"I'm sure it stopped here." The search light slowly scanned the hillside.

"I don't see anything. Besides if somebody was here, they would be long gone. We'll keep looking."

The two men lay still until the jeep was out of sight.

"We need to move now. They will be back." Noah said. Peter followed him up the embankment and then over the crest of the hill.

"That was a close call but we are safe now," Noah said. "It's almost as if they knew you were coming."

The two men slowly walked down the hill. Peter explained to Noah what the group had decided.

"It sounds like a good plan. Are you going to be able to get the women here on time? They won't be able to move as quickly as you and me and you will have to travel by road."

"I hope so," Peter replied, "I promised Jesse I would do my best, and that's all I can do."

"How are you going to get back?"

"The same way I got here. Ride the rail cars."

The two men went to the café and ordered breakfast. "We need men like you to help us I want you to think about that while you are away. There are many people who need our help and we are only able to do so much." Noah said.

"I will," Peter replied. "When I return, I plan on making this land my home."

When Peter was ready to leave Noah shook his hand. "Until we meet again." he said. "I will have my people watch for you."

The two men separated. Peter walked toward the rail yard and Noah went in the opposite direction.

TWENTY-TWO

Peter was anxious to get back to Maria and Marika. Time was short, and the longer he was away, the less they would have to travel. What he didn't realize was that fewer freight trains travelled north. The wall was making a difference.

Although it took him four days this time, it seemed like forever. Foremost on his mind was the question could Maria and Marika travel and would they go with him? Late in the afternoon of the fifth day he knocked on Mark's office door at the hospital.

Mark was tired. For the second time in a week, he had been up all-night caring for the wounded shot trying to get over the wall. This time it was a family of four. All had been shot by the border guards, the father most seriously. He wondered if the guards were playing a game. Just when the people thought they were safe, the guards used them for target practice.

"Come in." he called out and when he looked up was shocked to see Peter standing in the doorway. "Peter, what a surprise. Where have you been? We didn't know what to think after you left and we didn't hear from you. Did you make it to the Promise Land?"

"I did," Peter replied. "I want to talk to you before I speak with Maria and Marika. How are they?"

"They will be pleased to see you. Marika and the baby are doing well. Maria is the one I am concerned about. She is not recovering as much as I would like. She is not well and Elizabeth is quite concerned, as any daughter would be. I am sure it is her heart."

"Do you think she is well enough for a long journey?"

"Probably not, but will insist on going anyway. Why do you ask?"

Peter sat down on the chair in front of Mark's desk. He was exhausted.

"You don't look so well yourself," Mark said.

"Nothing, that a good meal and decent night's sleep won't cure. I came back to take Maria and Marika to the Promise Land if they will go."

For the next half hour Peter told Mark about his journey and what he had found out. "I have made arrangements for them to travel by ship but we must be in the city of Ludlow by the morning of the twenty first."

"That is less than three weeks away. How do you plan on getting them there? Unlike you, they can't get on a freight train nor can they walk that far."

"I don't know, I haven't figured that part out yet. The best thing would be to buy a vehicle and drive then we can stop and rest when they got tired."

"Ludlow is over eight hundred miles away."

"I am well aware of that, plus I would need a couple of days to make sure the arrangements have been made. How soon do you think it will be until Marika has her baby?"

"That is where the problem lies. Two months, maybe six weeks providing she is accurate about when she conceived. If not, it could be sooner."

"That soon? I thought we would have more time than that."

Mark stood up. "let's go to the house. You can eat and get cleaned up and tomorrow, when you are rested, we will talk to Maria and Marika. Tonight, they will be happy to see you and you can tell us about your adventures. We won't accomplish much, if anything, tonight."

"You are right as usual," Peter agreed.

"Peter," Marika cried out when she saw him walk through the door with Mark. "You are back." She ran to him and threw her arms around his neck.

Although still thin Marika looked healthy, but he was shocked when he saw Maria. She looked frail, her color pasty and her hair had turned white. She shuffled as she walked.

Now I understand what Mark was trying to tell me. This long journey will be too much for her.

He scooped Maria up in his arms and twirled her around. "I am glad to see you too," he said.

"Put me down before you hurt yourself." Maria said

Peter chuckled, and twirled her again, "Nothing is going to happen because you are as light as a feather."

Elizabeth had supper ready but gave Peter time to tidy up first. Around the table he told them of his trip to the Promise Land. "I didn't see much of the country but it is a beautiful place. The biggest hurdle was getting across the border and avoiding the British patrols. I was told the Believers get you identification papers and a place to stay. All newcomers are encouraged to live In a Kibbutz or common community at first, but isn't necessary."

"Are the British the same as the Brown Shirts?"

"I don't think so. No, I would have heard stories if they were. They are more interested in preventing refugees from entering and settling in the country. From what I understand once you are asked to show your papers you are safe. If you don't, you are taken to a prison camp and deported out of the country. Many wait a short period of time and then try again. There are networks of people who help the refugees as much as possible.

Then Mark spoke up. "It's getting late and I promised Peter a good night's sleep. We can talk more in the morning. I am going back to the hospital to check on my patients before I settle down for the night."

Peter was grateful. He had already decided to take Marika aside in the morning to see what she wanted to do. Maria was too frail to make the journey and would be better spending her time here, with Mark and Elizabeth.

Peter awoke the next morning to the smell of fresh coffee and bacon frying. When he went into the kitchen Maria was standing by the stove, deep in thought.

"Good morning, Peter," she said when she heard him enter the room. "Did you sleep well?" She reached into the cupboard, took out a cup and filled it with coffee.

"I did, and feel well rested this morning, and you?"

"No. I was thinking about everything you told us and I wonder why you came back."

This is the question Peter had been dreading. "I want to take Marika and the baby to the Promise Land. Their lives are still in danger here if the authorities find out she was Jesse's wife and carrying his child. Although it is quiet here some places are not."

"What about me? Am I to stay here?"

"Maria, please try to understand. You are not well. I think the trip will be too much for you. First of all, the travel to Ludlow and then the voyage on the ship…"

Maria stared at him, her face flushed, her hands curled into fists at her side. "Who do you think you are to judge me and tell me what I am capable of. You have no right.to assume you know what is best for me. You know nothing about my health or what I am capable of doing or not doing."

Peter didn't know what to say. "I am sorry Maria. I didn't mean to upset you."

Maria looked at him, "besides it's not your choice to make. "

She turned her back to Peter and continued cooking as if he wasn't there. She   didn't want him to see the tears in her eyes or how much his words hurt her. *He is right. I don't know if I can make the trip but if Marika goes, I am not staying here. I want to be with my grandchild.*

A few minutes later Marika came into the kitchen. Peter studied her. "If all goes as planned you will have Jesse's baby in the Promise Land."

Maria handed Marika a cup of coffee and then sat down on a chair beside her.

"Before you say any more Peter, Maria and I discussed this last night. I know you want to take me to the Promise Land"

"Yes, you are not safe here." he reminded her.

"I will go on one condition."

"What's that?" He already knew the answer but had to ask anyway.

"Maria comes with me. If she doesn't go, I'm not going."

A thousand reasons why Maria should stay home ran through his head but he said nothing. He knew when he was defeated.

"Are you sure this is what you want?"

Both women nodded. Then Maria quietly added, "Marika and her baby are all I have left of Jesse. I have lost so much and I want to be with my grandchild when it is born."

"I couldn't agree more." Peter replied," but what do Elizabeth and Mark have to say?"

"They agree with me," Maria said. "They are planning to come visit as soon as we are settled."

Peter knew that nothing he could say was going to change their minds. Maria was right and he felt in his heart that this is what Jesse would want too.

"Pack only what is necessary and be ready to leave in the morning. I will find a way to get us there."

Peter suddenly realized that he hadn't thought far enough ahead. He didn't have any idea how the three of them would travel. Walking long distances was out of the question.

Later he walked over to the hospital to visit Mark. "Maria is insisting on coming with us, but there is a problem?"

"What's that?" Mark asked. "You don't think she is well enough to travel. I'm not going to be the one to tell her to stay behind. Better you than me."

"Yes, I thought that but I'm not going to argue. In my haste I didn't stop to think about how we would travel. The train is very expensive and very public. That would be the fastest but not the safest."

Mark looked at Peter, "do you really believe they are in danger?"

"Yes, I have heard many things. Their escape across the wall hasn't gone unnoticed. The Brussian government wants Marika returned. Then there is the rumor among the Believers that Jesse will rise again."

"I haven't heard any of this," Mark replied. "Take my car. It is old and not that reliable but should get you there."

"I can't do that. What will you use?"

"I have means to buy a new one. Actually, I have been thinking about doing just that for some time. I need something more reliable and my car has seen better days. I'm sure it will get you where you need to go then you can sell it and use the money for your expenses."

"Thank you. I've already told Maria and Marika to be ready to leave in the morning."

"Good I am glad you agree with me. Now I will have an easier time now convincing Elizabeth to let me buy a different one,"

The two men chuckled, both of them knowing that Mark had finally won his argument with his wife.

TWENTY-THREE

Two days later they were finally able to leave. One other thing Peter hadn't thought about was the need for identification papers. Maria and Marika were forced to leave theirs behind the wall and Peter never felt the need for them. The mayor stepped in and was able to procure what they needed. No one asked whether they were forgeries or not but they looked real enough to pass.

Mark insisted that a patient of his, who was a mechanic, inspect the car. No major problems were found except for a small hole in the radiator. He advised Peter to make sure he had extra water with him, and to add water every time he fueled up.

As each day Peter became more concerned. Each one meant that the day the ship was leaving was getting closer and they had yet to begin their journey. Finally, they were able to leave but saying good bye was more difficult and emotional than Peter thought it would be.

He hugged Elizabeth and kissed her tear-stained cheek. "As soon as we arrive in Ludlow, I will send word to you. I will find a way from the Promise land but that may be more difficult."

"You are a brave man Peter to set out on such a journey with a young pregnant girl and an older woman in failing health. Why are you so willing to take this risk?"

"Because I promised Jesse. I can't let him down again."

"Please watch over them. They are the only family I have left in this world."

"I will do my best," Peter promised.

Peter hugged Mark. "Thank you, my friend, for all you have done for the them, for me and the Believers."

"Take care of them Peter. I gave Maria extra medication in case she becomes ill on the trip. If Marika goes in labor and has the baby before you leave bring them back here and we will find another way, at a later time, to get them to the Promise Land.

"I will." Peter agreed "We have come a long way from freezing in the alley in Bern to here, haven't we? There has been far too much pain and sorrow for all of us. I truly hope this is the right thing to do. I hope they find the peace they deserve at the end of our journey."

"Here take this," Mark said, "handing Peter some money. "You may need this along the way.

'No, I can't take your money. I have some and if we are cautious, it should be enough."

"Take it anyway and if you don't use it then divide it between Maria and Marika when they arrive. They will need some spending money."

Marika and Maria each walked over and hugged Mark and Elizabeth one more time before they got into the car. Marika sat in the front seat; Maria climbed into the back.

With tears in their eyes Mark and Elizabeth watched the car leave. "I have a feeling this is the last time I will see them. Do you think they will make it to the Promise Land?" She asked.

Mark put his arm around her shoulder and pulled her close. "I do. Peter is very determined and I sense Jesse's spirit travelling with them. Come, we better get to the hospital our patients will be looking for us."

TWENTY-FOUR

Peter was relieved when he saw a sign on the edge of the road which read Ludlow five miles. They were tired, especially Maria, who was exhausted. The banging in the motor of the car and the black smoke rolling out of the exhaust was getting worse. He caught glimpses of the water in the distance. *Thank goodness we are finally here. If we have to walk the rest of the way we can do it.*

"What now Peter?" Marika whispered. Maria was asleep between the two of them, her head resting on Marika's shoulder.

"Don't worry so much Marika. I can see the water from here and I'm sure every road will eventually lead there. I'll find us a place to stay tonight as you both need some rest. In the morning, I'll find the ship and speak with the captain."

"Have you been here before? Do you know the way?"

"No but I am sure I will figure it out."

Peter was right. Once they entered the town there were signs directing them to the harbor. Peter watched for a decent place to stay. He presumed those closest to the harbor would be noisy and probably unfit for the two women.

He stopped in front of a sign which read Empire Hotel. The outside looked better than most he had seen. He was surprised when he entered the lobby. Although shabby, the place was bright and clean. Feeling better about his surroundings he secured a room. The clerk was surprised when he paid for two nights

"Our usual clientele usually rents by the hour or by the night."

Peter laughed. "I have my mother and wife with me."

The clerk, looking embarrassed, handed Peter the key. "Room 120 at the end of the hall. It should be quiet there."

"That will be fine." Peter replied. He went back to the car and got Maria and Marika.

The room was shabby but clean. There was a double bed, a sofa, a desk and two chairs. The bathroom was directly across the hall.

"Where will you sleep?" Maria asked.

"On the sofa. I want to stay close to you. This isn't exactly the best part of town."

Peter went back to the car and got their suitcases, the food that was left and locked the car. *Tomorrow I will have to look for some place to sell it.*

When he returned to the room Maria was across the hall and Marika was alone. "I am worried about her," she said. "This trip has been hard on her but she isn't complaining."

"May be a couple of good night's sleep will bring her strength back." He replied. He was deeply concerned about Maria too but didn't want to alarm Marika any more than she was.

"You go to bed," he said. "I'm going to go back and talk to the desk clerk to see what I can learn about our ship and where to find the captain."

The two women were still sleeping when he left the next morning. He drove to the harbor and when he located the ship, he was shocked. The boat was an old beat-up freighter. The paint was peeling from the sides and the hull was rusty. He felt sick to his stomach *This is not what I expected.*

He got out of the car and walked toward the boat. Up close it looked even worse.

"Are you looking for someone?" a raspy voice asked. Peter hadn't noticed the man standing in the shadows.

"I am Peter and I am hoping to meet with the captain."

"Follow me," the man said flicking his cigarette into the water. Peter followed him up the gang plank and up a steep ladder to the bridge.

Knocking on the frame of the door he said, "Captain Marsden, Peter has arrived. He wishes to speak with you."

An older gray-haired man turned to Peter. "We were getting worried that you weren't coming. Andy, go get our friend a cup of coffee, then make sure we aren't disturbed.".

From this vantage point Peter realized that ship was in better condition than he first thought.

Almost as if he could read Peter's mind the captain said, "she doesn't look like much but I assure you she is fast and in perfect condition. The outside keeps the port authorities from looking too closely."

Andy arrived back with the coffee and the captain and Peter sat down on the two chairs located against the back wall.

"I understand you are bringing two women with you; one is Jesse's mother and the other his wife. I set aside a small cabin for them but I'm afraid you will have to sleep with the crew."

"That's no problem," Peter replied. "How long will this voyage take?".

"Three days if all goes well. First, we have to go into international waters and when we get closer hope the British don't try to stop us. If they do, we will be turned around and escorted us back to the closest port. There I will be arrested and my ship seized. I would very much hate to see that happen. By necessity our landing will be at night. Also, just so you know, there will be three hundred people crowded on here."

"Three hundred? In this small space?"

"Yes, maybe more. I take whoever can afford the passage. We begin loading later tonight and leave before sun up in the morning. The dock crew during that time are our men. We need to leave early before the port authorities arrive in the morning."

"We will be here early," Peter replied.

The captain looked Peter in the eye. "I have a feeling you don't trust me or my crew?"

"I do," Peter replied, "it's just that this isn't exactly what I expected."

The captain laughed. "That's exactly how it is supposed to look."

On his way back to the hotel Peter regretted that he had paid for the room for two nights, but then as he thought more about it, he decided it was better this way. They could sneak out and the hotel staff won't realize they are gone. *A person doesn't know who they can trust these days.*

TWENTY-FIVE

Even though Captain Marsden had faith in his ship and his crew Peter still had misgivings. *Three hundred people crowded into that small space. Maria is sick and Marika is close to having her baby – maybe I should find another way to get them into the Promise Land.*

Then he thought about his journey and the danger he faced. *They can't do that either. The best solution is to turn around and go back to Mark's.*

When Pete returned to their room the women were anxiously waiting for him. Maria had color in her cheeks once again and Marika was excited.

"Well," she asked, "what do you think? When do we leave?"

Peter looked at them. "I think we would be better off going back to Mark's. I thought we were getting on a regular ship but this is an old rusty freighter which has seen better days. The captain assures me it is seaworthy, but I have my doubts."

"Marika replied, "If he has confidence then we should too. I'm sure he knows what he's doing. He wouldn't risk his own life and that of his crew if he didn't."

"I also wasn't aware there was going to be three hundred or more people on there as well. It will be crowded and smelly and I don't want to risk your lives. What if something happens?"

Maria looked at him. "That is not your decision to make. We have come this far and we are not turning back. I am willing to take the chance. What about you Marika? What do you think?"

"I want Jesse's baby to live in peace and security with people who will know and respect him."

"Are both of you sure about this. Once we get on the ship there is no turning back." Peter asked.

"Yes," both women replied in unison.

Resigned he said. "Okay, but remember you have until we leave port to change your mind."

"What do we do now Peter to prepare for the journey.?"

"Take what money we have and buy food enough for at least three days. I am going to see if I can sell the car some place. If I can't find a buyer, I'll leave it sitting on the street. I don't imagine it will sit there very long."

Later that evening Peter, Maria and Marika arrived on the dock. They had smuggled their belongings out of the hotel making sure nobody noticed them leave. Peter had been unable to sell the car. Once they removed their belongings he drove to a side street, parked the car, left the keys in the ignition and walked back to the dock.

Marika and Maria stared at the rusty freighter. This was not what they expected either. Suddenly Marika thought she heard Jesse's voice. "Go, I will protect you."

"Everything will be all right, Jesse is with us," she said.

The captain saw them standing on the dock and was waiting as the three of them walked up the gang plank. "Ladies, come with me and I will show you to your cabin. It isn't much but will be considerably quieter and more comfortable than being on the deck with the others."

The cabin was small. There were two bunk beds along one wall, and barely enough room for both to stand at the same time. A small closet was located at the end of the beds and a chair and desk along the other wall.

"This will be just fine," Maria said, "all we need is a place to sleep. Thank you for being so considerate. Please thank your crew members who gave up their beds for us."

"The galley, where the crew eats, is down the hall. If you wish to prepare any meals for yourself, I will make special arrangements with the cook. If not, you can eat when the crew does. As a rule, passengers are not allowed down here but I am making an exception for you. Once the other passengers begin to board, I suggest you stay in your cabin until we leave."

"What about the others? Where do they stay?'

"Where ever they can find a spot – usually on the deck or in the salon. It's very crowded. Unfortunately, we don't offer all of the comforts of home. Peter, come to the bridge with me so we can talk."

Later in the evening, until the small hours of the morning, Marika heard the sounds of many voices and footsteps. Maria was asleep on the top bunk. They had decided upon this arrangement so Marika would be more comfortable. Then she felt the ship begin to move.

"Thy will be done," she prayed.

As the ship moved into the harbor Peter said to the captain, "I see you don't have any lights on to show you the way."

The captain laughed. "I know where I am going and it's still dark enough that nobody will see us leave. I assure you we will be okay. I know these waters like the back of my hand. Once we are away from port, I will turn them on"

"What are our chances?"

"Very good, as long as the British don't stop us. As long as we remain in international waters they can't do anything except follow us. The danger comes when we begin moving toward the shore. They have been known to be waiting on the beach and will try to stop us before we actually land. The Believers radioed that they will have a convoy of trucks to meet us and move the passengers to safety. They are watching the movements of the British carefully and will warn us if they see a problem."

The next morning Maria and Marika were surprised when they walked out onto the deck. Where ever they looked groups of people huddled together. The children were quiet. Some of the men stood in small groups talking quietly. Mothers sat nursing their babies.

Maria saw the fear and uncertainty written on their faces. "You go ahead and find Peter," she said to Marika. "I am going to stay here and reassure the people."

Maria turned and walked to the first group. Marika couldn't hear what she was saying but she noticed the women begin to relax and smile.

TWENTY-SIX

Several hours after leaving the harbor the captain announced "we are entering international waters and the closest land is twelve miles away. I expect to arrive at the Promise Land within three days." The people cheered. For some, this was their first sign of hope.

Everyone quickly fell into a routine. Some erected blankets to ward off the hot sun and provide some degree of privacy. In the evenings there was music, laughter and storytelling.

Trouble reared its angry head on the final day of their voyage. The captain took Peter aside "I need to talk to you. We have company. There are two British gun ships off our port side within striking distance. They can't approach us, but can prevent us from going ashore."

"What are you going to do?" Peter asked.

"For now, we wait. Tonight, we will have a meeting with the men and decide on a course of action."

After supper the men crowded into the galley. Some sat, the rest stood two and three deep along the walls.

The captain spoke to them "Many of you were aware this was a dangerous journey. Two British gun ships are waiting for us to leave international waters and head inland. We may be forced to turn around and go back or they could commandeer the ship. I will be arrested and my ship will be seized. You and your families would be interred in a prison camp. Eventually you will be returned back to where you came from."

"Is there an alternative?" somebody shouted out.

"Yes, we can stay where we are and wait for those on shore to come up with a plan. You must decide what is best for you and your families. I can't make that decision for you."

Peter and the captain left the room to give the men freedom to talk among themselves. "I am worried," the captain said. "If they choose to wait, we will run out of food and fresh water within a couple of days, I wasn't expecting such a delay. The last two times we got in and out before the British knew we were there.

If they decide to stay, we will need to gather all of the food and water supplies and begin rationing them out immediately. Our ship stores will also be added. Once we know how much food and water we have, we will be able to determine how much to allot each person every day. As long as we remain outside the twelve-mile limit we are safe.

I am putting you in charge of that and I suggest you get two or three of the passengers to help you. The passengers will relate easier to one of their own. I have to figure out how much fuel we have and how long it will last."

A few minutes later they were beckoned back to the galley. A spokesman for the group said. "We will take our chances here. Many of us spent the last of their money to secure our passage and some have no home to return to. Being in a British internment camp won't be any better than sleeping in an alley and eating out of garbage cans."

Peter's heart broke to hear what the spokesman said. He knew it was true because at one time, he lived the same way.

He spoke up. "Okay, here is what we are going to do. We need to gather all of the food and water and bring it to a central location. Water and food will be rationed out each morning. The children and elderly will receive a bit more. We also need to appoint a committee to work with us to address any complaints that may arise. We all need to be together to make this work."

Within hours of this decision Maria was called to the side of a sick child with a high fever and covered in large red spots. She had seen this before – measles and they were contagious.

She pulled Peter aside and together they went to the captain. Peter said, "I have more bad news for you. Maria was called to attend a child who probably has a case of measles. Because of the close quarters I expect there will be more."

"What do you need us to do Maria?" the captain asked.

"We need to set aside a place to quarantine those who are sick."

"How much room do you need?"

"I would like to use half of the salon. Also, those families whose children are affected should move to the other side of the ship. I don't know if that will help but we can try to keep them quarantined. I am afraid this is just the beginning, there are sure to be more cases."

"What about my crew?"

"Tell them to be careful and if they begin running a fever to come to me. We may have to set up a separate area if any become ill."

For nine days the ship stayed in international waters. The number of measles cases grew, especially among the children. Some died. Unable to conduct proper funerals the bodies were wrapped in a shroud; prayers were said and they were tipped overboard. The grief was palpable but still those on board refused to give up.

Maria and Marika spent their days nursing the sick. At night they fell into bed exhausted. Instead of eating and drinking they shared their rations with the sickest.

Peter was worried. Although they never complained, he saw what was happening to them. An exhausted Maria looked more fragile than ever. Each day her eyes sunk further into her face. Her lips had a bluish tinge and her hands trembled. Peter knew that she had taken all of the medicine Mark had sent with her. Marika was getting closer to her due date but was losing weight.

I was wrong to subject them to this trip. Instead of taking them to a better life I have put their lives at risk. Jesse, can you ever forgive me for my foolishness. I wonder if I will ever learn?

On the sixth day the food ran out and the daily ration was less than a quarter cup of water. The ship reeked of unwashed bodies and human waste. The captain was frantic. He contacted the British and explained the situation on board. He begged for food and water but was refused. He asked for permission to land but was refused because of the measles outbreak. Each message the captain received said the same thing. They would gladly provide food, water and medical assistance if he returned to Ludlow and turned himself in. Of course, he refused.

Talking to Peter he asked, "What can I do? The Believers are willing to attempt a rescue but the logistics are against them."

With calmness he didn't feel Peter replied, "we will find a way."

Peter had barely fallen asleep when he was roused by somebody shaking his shoulder. "Peter you must come immediately," Maria whispered.

Instantly he was awake. "What's wrong?" he asked.

"Marika is having her baby."

He jumped off his cot, pulled on his pants and shoved his feet into his boots. "Where is she?"

"In our cabin. It is too early and the baby is small."

Peter followed Maria to their cabin. Marika was lying on the bottom bunk in the throes of a contraction. When it eased off Peter asked, "what can I do?"

"Find out if there is a midwife among the people. I have had babies but I have never been on the receiving end.".

Peter laughed. "I guess that is one way to put it."

"We will need scissors, string, clean towels if there are any and some boiled water also."

Peter went out on the deck and looked around. *How do I find a midwife? Do I wake up every woman and ask if she knows of one?*

Then he noticed an elderly woman standing at the railing staring out over the water. He approached her. "Forgive me for intruding, but do you know of any woman on the ship who is a midwife? Marika is having her baby."

"I am not a trained midwife but I delivered many babies in the camp under worse conditions than these. I can help if you wish."

There was something about this woman that gave Peter confidence in her ability. "Go to her then, she is in her cabin. I need to find the supplies Maria asked for."

The woman put her hand on Peter's arm. "I will bring what I have but she will need some water to sip. Give her my ration for tomorrow. Go back to her and I will follow in a few minutes."

Peter's excited voice had awakened others close by. Word that Marika was having her baby quickly spread. Many other women volunteered to also give up their daily water ration for her.

Peter returned to the cabin. Maria had moved one of the chairs and was sitting beside Marika holding her hand and talking to her in a soothing voice.

"How is she?" he asked.

"She is resting between contractions. Did you find somebody?"

"Yes." He replied. Before he could say any more the woman entered the room and pushed him aside. "I am Eva Schultz and I delivered many babies in the camps" she told Maria.

To Peter she said," go and bring me some hot water from the galley. When that is done go up to the deck and wait."

"I would rather stay here."

"You will not," she said, "besides there isn't enough room in here for all of us. This is woman's business and the last thing we need is a man getting in the way. Now go do what I told you."

Peter did as he was told. When he got back on the deck it was unusually quiet.

"Has she had the baby yet?" a voice asked.

"No and I was sent to wait up here." he pouted.

The men laughed. "That's what usually happens," one said.

Peter paced up and down the deck. *Jesse, if the baby survives, I promise you I will always be at his side as I was with you. I will make sure nothing happens to the three of them again.*

Several hours later Maria came up on the deck, walked over to him and whispered "Jesse's son has arrived."

Caught up in the excitement of the moment Peter shouted "It's a boy. Jesse's son is here."

The people instantly became silent. "The son of our beloved Jesse?" they whispered among themselves.

"Yes." Peter continued. "Maria is his mother and Marika his wife. I am taking them to the Promise Land to keep them safe and allow the baby to grow up in the footsteps of his father."

Turning to Maria he said, "I must see this miracle for myself."

Marika looked radiant lying on the bunk holding the baby at her breast. "Come see Peter, he looks just like his father. Do you want to hold him?"

Maria took the baby from Marika and placed him in Peter's arms. "Do you have a name for him?"

"Yes, Jessie Joseph, after his father and grandfather but we will call him JJ for short."

"That is a good name," Peter said. He looked at the baby sleeping in his arms and said softly "your father would be proud of you."

Eva took the baby from him. "Go away. They are both tired and need to rest. Maria, you need to rest too. You look exhausted."

Peter went back on deck. The people crowded around him asking if this was truly the son of their leader Jesse.

By now Peter realized he had made a mistake but it was too late to correct it.

"Yes, this is Jesse's son but I beg you to forget what took place here today. Agents from Brussia are searching for Maria and Marika and, if the British find out, they will be deported and held up as an example. Nobody needs to know about this momentous occasion until Marika is prepared to share his birth with the world. We must protect them at all cost."

A silent nod of agreement passed through the crowd. They were all aware of what Peter was talking about and what the consequences could be. Each swore to himself to keep Marika's secret safe.

TWENTY-SEVEN

Conditions on the ship continued to deteriorate. Children cried because they were hungry and thirsty, the men became increasingly disgruntled because of their inability to do anything for their families. Several more children died from the Measles even though the total number of infections continued to fall.

An aura of helplessness hung in the air. To complicate matters the ship was running low on fuel. The captain couldn't turn around and go back if he wanted to. Some of the women feared they would all perish.

A few believers attempted the dangerous journey of bringing supplies in the middle of the night but couldn't bring the amount needed. The weather was cooling off and the seas becoming rougher. More of the passengers who escaped the Measles outbreak were now getting seasick.

Peter went to the captain. "I understand you received a weather warning from the Believers? What did it say?"

"I am getting reports of a storm approaching which will either benefit or sink us. The British will go to the nearest port and wait it out and this could be our one and only chance to make a run for the coast, but it will be dangerous. Anything could happen."

"What if we try to ride it out here?"

"There isn't enough fuel to battle the waves. Some of those on the deck could be washed away if the waves get high. There isn't enough room to put them all in the salon."

Peter thought about this for a while then said "we don't have much choice, do we?"

"No, we don't. I can use the power of the storm to head for shore but, depending upon where we land, we could be smashed against the rocks."

Peter took the decision out of the captain's hands. "You prepare the crew and I'll prepare the passengers."

The passengers secured their belongings as best they could. The women and children crowded into the salon and the men tied themselves to the railing and anything else available. A deathly quiet settled over the ship, except for the sound of murmured prayers. Even the children, sensing the danger, were quiet.

The storm hit sooner and harder than expected. The captain fought with the wheel to keep the bow pointed toward the shore. Huge waves washed over the railings and deck dragging anything loose. into the ocean. Most lost everything they owned.

For several hours rain poured down and the ship rose and fell with the waves. Then, as suddenly as the storm hit, it was over. The ship came to rest upon a pile of rocks about a hundred feet from the shore.

"Do you know where we are," Peter asked the captain.

"I have no idea," he replied. "We can't waste any time. We need to get everybody off as fast as we can. Women and children first, every available man is to help them ashore."

It was a slow process. Some of the men helped the people off the ship into the water, others formed a chain of helping hands. Those who could, swam toward the shore until there was a firm footing and walked the rest of the way. The young and elderly had to be carried to the shore. When one man became exhausted, another stepped in to take his place.

Peter and the crew members stood in water up to their knees and helped the people the last few steps. The wind was cold and the wet survivors huddled together to keep warm.

Finally, Peter saw Maria and Marika wading toward him. Marika held the baby tight to her chest in one arm, the other supported Maria. He ran toward them and picked Maria up in his arms carrying her to the shore.

"Peter, put me down," she whispered to him. "I need to feel the sand of the Promise Land beneath my feet." Peter did as he was asked,

Maria took several steps and then fell. Marika rushed to her side. Maria looked up at her and said "I am very tired. I want to rest here for a few minutes."

At that moment Peter was called away to help a mother and her children. "I'll be right back" he said and turned toward the water.

Marika sat down behind Maaria, cradled her head in her lap and laid Jessie on her chest, both oblivious to what was happening around them.

Maria opened her eyes and looked at Marika. "Your son will be a great man, but not in the path of his father. Protect him from those who try to make him into what he is not. I love you Marika and feel blessed to have had you un my life," She sighed, closing her eyes for the final time.

Later, when Peter came back to the two women, Maria was lying in the sand where she fell. Marika, still cradling Maria's head, was sobbing. "What is it?" he asked.

"She is dead," Marika whispered. "She should have stayed with Mark and this wouldn't have happened. I begged her not to come, that she wasn't strong enough, but she insisted. Now she is dead and will never see her grandson grow up."

"Don't blame yourself Marika. Maria made her choice knowing the odds were against her. Now she is with Jesse, Joseph and her other children. Come, you are wet and shivering and it's not good for you or for the baby. I will tend to Maria."

He bent down and kissed Maria on the lips. Then he helped Marika stand up, guiding her to a small group who somehow managed to get a fire started. Several more dotted the shore line. Instead of excited voices it was eerily quiet. His heart was breaking, but this was not the time to be overcome by his emotions, there was still much to do.

"Did we get everyone ashore?" Peter asked the captain.

"We lost two men who were swept overboard. I checked before I left the ship and didn't see anybody."

"Maria died," Peter said, his voice choked with grief.

"I am sorry my friend. I know she was special to you." The captain patted Peter on the shoulder. "Come we are not finished yet. Now we need to move these people inland before the British arrive."

They stood there discussing what to do next when they heard the sound of engines approaching.

"Do you think it is the British?" Peter asked.

"I hope not. It would be a shame after what these people have gone through to be returned home."

They watched the lights approach, "Peter look," the captain exclaimed, "trucks, dozens of them and they are not British. The Believers have come to rescue us. Before I left the ship, I sent out a distress signal trying to describe where we were. They must have heard and been able to figure it out."

"Thank God," Peter replied.

When the trucks arrived, the survivors were wrapped in blankets and given water to drink. One by one the back of the trucks left filled with the sick and the survivors.

"Where are they taking them?" Peter asked.

"To the various Kibbutz's in the area.

"Marika and the baby…?"

"I'm not sure but we will find them."

Peter walked back to Maria's body and stood looking down at her tears streaming down his face. *She was a wonderful person and I will miss her."*

.   "Come Peter." The captain said gently. "These men want to move Maria's body and take it to a better place."

The men reverently wrapped Maria's body in a blanket and Peter carried her to a waiting truck then he and the captain climbed in the back with her. He lifted her head and put it on his lap, "She was one of the best people I have known."

Seeing his grief the captain said, "Tomorrow we will return and try to salvage what we can."

"And your ship, what about that?"

"I am sure she can be salvaged and with just a few minor repairs will be sea worthy again. I told you she was a tough old girl."

TWENTY-EIGHT

Marika felt as though nothing around her was real or made any sense. Maria was the closest person she had known as a mother and her dying was leaving a wound so deep she didn't know if she would ever heal. *First Jesse, now Maria. I feel lost and alone.*

Somebody wrapped a blanket around her and clutching Jessie to her chest she climbed into the open back of a truck with the other survivors. Although the air was warm, she shivered uncontrollably.

She stared straight ahead until the truck stopped. Hearing voices and she looked around to see she was in a brightly lit compound along with three other trucks carrying survivors. They were being helped down and led toward a long low building. She smelled fresh bread but, for all the activity and people it was quiet.

A young girl climbed into the truck bed and squatted down in front of her. "Come with me," she said gently "I will take you to a warm place, get you something to eat and a bed for the night. You are safe here."

She reached to take the baby from Marika's arms but, when she saw the look on Marika's face she stopped. "Is it a little boy or girl.?" She asked.

"A boy," Marika answered.

"He is very small, how old is he?"

"Just about two weeks."

She helped Marika out of the truck and led her toward a long building. Once inside she heard   the murmur of soft voices.

"First we will get you registered, and while you are doing that, I will find you something to eat."

The registration process was quick. They asked her name, age, where she was from and the age of her baby. They also asked if she had relatives travelling on the ship with her.

Marika looked up, "There was but, she died shortly after we came ashore. There is only me and my son. I have no other family."

When the process was finished, the young girl led Marika to a table. On it sat a tray with a bowl of soup, a slice of bread, a chunk of cheese, a glass of milk and a cup of hot coffee.

"Where am I?" Marika asked. The fog in her head was beginning to clear. Looking around the room, she recognized other faces from the ship.

"You are at the Freedom Kibbutz in the Promise land. One of our trucks rescued you from the beach and brought you here. Eat. The food will help keep your strength up so you can feed your baby."

"Do you know where they took my mother-in-law's body? Peter promised she would be taken care of." Tears filled her eyes, but she held them back.

"I don't know but I will find out for you. There were several bodies removed from the beach but with all the confusion, it's hard to say. Our first priority is going to be finding out where people are and reuniting those separated from their families."

Just then Jessie let out a thin wail. "He is hungry," Marika said. "I don't have much milk for him."

"Are you finished eating.? Do you wish to have more?"

"No, not right now. This is more than I have eaten in quite a few days."

"Come, I will take you to the area we set aside for mother and children's. We are quarantining everybody for several days because of the measles on the ship."

Marika was led to another building. A cacophony of noise hit her, babies were crying, and squealing children were running around. She led Marika down the hall to a small room. Eight cots had been set up each containing a pillow, blankets, and a robe to change into. On one there was a stack of diapers and fresh clothes for the baby.

"You can stay here tonight. When you are done feeding the baby, it is probably a good idea to get some rest. You must feel overwhelmed."

Marika took the cot closest to the window and looked out. Although it was still the same day she felt as though a month had passed.

"Is it okay if I take this one?" She asked.

"Yes of course. I'll see if I can find a something for the baby to sleep in for tonight. We didn't realize he was so young. "

Jessie began crying again. Marika sat down on the cot and putting the baby to her breast, allowed the tears she was holding back to flow. She was in the Promise land but the price of entry had been steep.

She looked down at Jessie. "I will miss Maria very much but I am glad she lived long enough to see you and reach this place."

After Jessie finished nursing, she stripped off her damp clothes, put on the robe, laid down tucking the baby into her side and promptly fell into an exhausted sleep.

TWENTY -NINE

The sound of military music blasting over loud speakers woke Marika up. At first, she wasn't sure where she was. then remembered the escape from the ship, dragging Maria through the water and her death on the beach. Jessie fussed once in the night but she barely remembered feeding or changing his wet diaper.

He stirred and she felt him rooting against her chest. Taking out her breast she began nursing him. After the days at sea, she didn't have much milk and he always seemed to be hungry.

There was a knock on the door and the young girl from the previous evening came in carrying a tray. "I brought you some breakfast. There are eggs, bread and jam, fruit. coffee and a large glass of milk.

By the way my name is Allie. While you are eating, I will take the baby to the nursery and have the doctor check him out."

"No," Marika practically shouted, "He stays with me."

Allie got a funny look on her face. "I assure you it's perfectly safe. I will bring him back as soon as the doctor is done."

"No," Marika said again.

"I'll tell you what," Allie said, "You finish your breakfast, have a shower and then we will both take him. I brought you some clean clothes, I hope they fit."

Marika finished eating and went into the small bathroom leaving the door ajar in case Jessie cried. She was afraid to let him out her sight in case something happened.

Allie must have sensed her anxiety. "Don't worry we'll both be here when you get back,"

The warm water felt like being in heaven. Weeks had passed since she had been able to bathe properly. She washed her hair and her body and was shocked at how thin she was. Although she wanted to stand there and let the warm water wash over her, reluctantly she got out. It wasn't that she didn't trust Allie, she simply didn't want to be away from Jessie for very long.

When she returned Allie had changed and bathed the baby, put him in clean clothes and wrapped him snuggly in a soft blue blanket. "I brought these with me this morning. I hope you don't mind me going ahead and dressing him," she said.

"No, I don't mind," Marika replied.

The clothes Allie brought her were simple, a set of clean white undergarments, a pair of Khaki colored pants and a white T-shirt, exactly the same as Allie was wearing.

"What is the plan" Marika asked as they went outside and walked across the court yard. In the distance she saw groups of young people marching, still others doing calisthenics

"You told me the name of this place last night but I can't remember."

"This is Freedom Kibbutz." Allie replied.

"I don't know what that means." Marika said.

Allie looked at her strangely and then it dawned on her. "Of course, you wouldn't. A kibbutz is a form of communal farm. Most refugees, when they arrive, have no place to go. They come here and stay with us but are free to leave any time. We work together for the common good. We are self-sufficient producing our own food and meat and selling what is left.

See those long buildings over there? They are the boys and girls dormitories. Many who arrive here are alone and scarred from what they have seen and experienced. We give them a place to heal. There are few rules and regulations except that you are required to do your share."

"I noticed a group marching and another exercising, what is that about?"

Allie looked at her. "Although everything seems peaceful, war is being waged around us. The British don't want us here and the local Arabs claim we stole their land. This land is our birth right, given to us in the ancient scriptures, and we are not leaving. If necessary, we will fight."

Marika didn't know what to say. Some of the Believers on the ship talked about places such as this but didn't seem to be aware they would still be fighting for a home to call their own."

Allie continued, "From the age of twelve all boys and girls are required to take military training. We all have jobs. Some work with the animals, others farm, others cook, each person does what they are best suited for. We are here," Allie announced.

They entered a brightly lit building and Marika heard the sound of children singing. Allie led her down a short hall way, past an office and through a set of double doors. "This is the day clinic. If people are sick or hurt, they come here. Please sit down and I'll let the receptionist know you are here."

Marika sat on a wooden chair and looked around. Clearly, she was in a waiting area of some sort. Jessie began to fuss. She unwrapped him, put the blanket over her shoulder and tucking the baby underneath began feeding him. *This seems too good to be true. When something looks this good there is usually a catch. I wish Maria or Peter were here to tell me what to do.*

As she was wrapping him up again a nurse in a white uniform approached "I see you are finished. I didn't want to disturb you. Come Dr. Lemieux will see you now."

THIRTY

Marika was led to a small examination room. "Please undress the baby and lay him on the table. The doctor will be with you in a minute."

Seconds later an older, rotund, white-haired man came into the room. "Now let's see what we have here," he said, walking over to the baby. "How old is he?"

"Almost two weeks. He was born on the ship."

The Doctor looked in his ears, listened to his chest and heart, prodded his belly and weighed him. "He seems to be healthy enough, except for being small and slightly malnourished. Do you have enough milk for him?

"He always seems to be hungry" she replied.

"Now let's take a look at you." The doctor did the same to her and checked her breasts. He asked a lot of questions and she answered as best she could.

"No wonder you are having trouble feeding him. You are too thin and under nourished yourself but I am sure with proper food and rest you will be fine. Does it hurt when he nurses?"

Marika nodded her head, "Yes, sometimes."

"I will have the nurse give you a salve which should help. This isn't unusual in new nursing mothers, Is the baby's father with you today? Perhaps I should examine him too."

"He died," Marika said bluntly. "Heinrich Mollen executed him."

Suddenly it was as though all of the air was sucked out of the room. The doctor took her hand. "I know, I was there and watched Heinrich kill our beloved Jesse. I remember seeing an older woman and young girl standing with Peter away from the rest of the crowd. She was struggling to go to Jesse but Peter was forcibly holding her back. It was you, wasn't it?"

Marika nodded her head yes, the horror of that day suddenly overwhelming her senses. She felt dizzy and collapsed on the nearest chair.

The doctor pushed her head between her knees. "Take deep breaths, this will pass in a minute."

When she felt more composed, she answered him. "Yes, I am Jesse's wife and the other woman was his mother, Maria."

"We weren't aware there was a child"

"I didn't know myself until much later."

"Your secret is safe with me," he said. Then he added "You may think this is a strange thing to say but you must never tell anyone who his father is. If the British find out they will try to make an example of you and see that you are deported. Knowing Jesse's son is here would be too big a lure for the Believers and the refugee numbers would increase dramatically. Not only that, if the Believers find out, they will make your life a living hell. The best chance you and your son have is to keep his father's name a secret. Someday, when he is older, you can explain the reasons to him.

There is a small problem but I think we can handle it. When your baby was born Peter announced to those on the ship the baby was Jesse's son. If we neither confirm nor deny him, the rumors should disappear."

Abruptly he smiled and changed the subject. "I am going to call Allie to come and take you back. I will also have the nurse take you to the dispensary for some vitamins and that salve I told you about. Get some rest, drink lots of milk and come back in a week so we can be sure the baby is gaining."

Putting his hand on her arm he said "you are safe here. We will protect you and Jesse's son with our lives."

"Thank you," Marika replied.

When Allie returned a short time later, she said. "That didn't 'take long. All is well?'

" The doctor said we both have to be fattened up."

"I agree with him. You are much to thin but we will change that while you are here. I was told to take you to the Administration office when you were finished here. They have a few questions for you. "

Then Allie noticed the terrified look on her face. Touching Marika's arm she said, "There is nothing to worry about. They want a record of your family so you can be reunited with them if possible. If not now, for later."

"Or the dead can be accounted for," Marika replied bitterly.

"There is that too. The British make incessant demands wanting to know how many are here and where they came from. Our purpose is to unite as many families as possible. Still others are going to use this information to keep our heritage alive. This will put names to some of those who died in the camps, provide a more accurate total and provide some closure to those who need it. The same thing is being done at all the other kibbutz's and then the information is sent to a central registry. I guess you can say we are now trying to rebuild what is left of some family trees."

Jessie began to fuss again. "All he wants to do is eat," Marika said.

"We are nearly there. You can feed him while answering their question. When you are finished, we will go to the dining hall for lunch. We eat all of our meals together."

When they arrived, Marika was surprised to see Peter waiting for her. He looked terrible. His face was etched with pain, his eyes were red and he was in desperate need of clean clothes and a shave.

He walked over and hugged her' "It is good to see you again," he said. "I heard you had an appointment with the doctor. How did that go?"

"Good. He told me we are both healthy but under nourished. We need to be fattened up."

Peter laughed. "I am sure that will happen here. For the first time in a long time, you will have good food and lots of sunshine. I think you will do well here Marika.

Come, we will go into the office. The baby sounds like he is getting impatient. He definitely has a good set of lungs on him."

"Oh yes, he makes sure we don't forget about him," Marika replied with a grin.

She followed Peter into a small office. Once again, she sat down and began nursing Jessie. A dark-haired woman came into the room and spoke to Peter first and then turned to Marika. "I have a few questions for you. What is your full name?"

Marika didn't know how to answer her. Quickly Peter interjected "Marika Gustavson, age nineteen years, born in Bern."

She sighed with relief. Slowly, and as truthfully as possible, she answered the rest of the questions – her mother was dead, she did not know where her father was. He had abandoned her when she was eleven. She did not have any brothers or sisters, only one sister-in-law and her husband.

Peter answered the questions about Jessies' heritage. "His father is also dead and all of his family except his aunt had died in the Massacre of Norenburg. His grandmother died shortly after setting foot on the soil of the Promise Land."

"Now we must get him registered" the woman said. "What do you call him.?"

Marika looked at Peter and replied, "His name is Jessie after the leader of the believers but I call him JJ."

The woman wrote down Jessie Gustavson on the registration form. "You have no idea how many little Jessies we have here. Many mothers must have thought the same thing."

"Wait," Marika said "I want to register the initial J. as his middle name." The woman changed the form to read Jessie J Gustavson."

"I have one more question and then you may go," the woman said. "Everybody here is designated a job. What do you think you would be best at?"

"I don't know. I have few skills, if any. I like working with people and know first-hand how traumatizing the journey and all that led up to it can be. Maybe I can help in that way?"

"I'll see what I can do. Because we are the largest Kibbutz in this area, we took in nearly one hundred and fifty people between last night and this morning. Some will know you from the ship and be reassured by your presence. Later today we are going to start reuniting families who got split up in the confusion."

Handing Marika several pieces of paper she added. "This is our daily schedule and where the activities take place. This should help you become familiar with our routine."

Looking at her watch she said "it is nearly lunch time. Let's walk over to the dining room and I will try to answer any questions you may have."

Peter stood up, "go with her Marika. I have several things to do and will meet you there."

"Wait Peter, Maria – where have they taken her? I would like to see her one more time to say goodbye. Have you been able to get a message to Mark and Elizabeth? They need to be told of Jessie's birth and Maria's death."

"That's among the things I have to do. We lost several more older people last night and I want to see what arrangements are being made. As soon as I know something I'll find you."

Marika's eyes flooded with tears. "I miss her. I would have died if it weren't for her."

Peter's eyes glistened with tears also. "I miss her too. We can take comfort in the fact she died in the Promise land, not in some ghetto behind a fence. Now she is reunited with her husband Joe and other children."

"You are right Peter." Looking down at the sleeping baby in her arms she said, "I will do my best to make sure her legacy is never forgotten."

Peter put a finger under Marika's chin and lifted her face toward his. "And I will do everything in my power to be there for you and Jesse's baby. I made a promise and intend to keep it until my dying day."

THIRTY-ONE

Allie and Marika entered the dining hall, which was a large room with several dozen tables with chairs scattered throughout, four of which were occupied. Along one wall long tables were setup. At the beginning were trays, dishes, cutlery and napkins. Next were trays of sandwiches and fresh vegetables. Two women stood behind another table, ladle in hand, ready to dish out the choice of soup or lamb stew.

Next in line were trays of fresh buns and small loaves of bread. Along a side wall several pitchers of fresh milk, urns of coffee and hot water for tea, cups, glasses and a choice of two desserts or fresh fruit.

"Is it always this quiet?" Marika asked.

"We are early," Allie replied. "Most of the people pick up their lunch in the morning to eat while working but supper time is a different story."

Allie walked over and picked up two trays from the large stack. "Tell me what you would like to eat."

"I'm not very hungry," Marika said.

"May be so, but you need to remember you are eating for two. Didn't the doctor say we had to fatten you up?"

"He did," Marika laughed, "but not all in one day."

In the end she asked Allie to get her a bowl of soup, some cheese and a small loaf of bread. JJ slept on the table top while they ate.

When they were finished Allie led Marika to yet another long building and to a room which would be hers for as long as she was there. The room was sparse containing a bed, dresser, a crib for J J and a small closet.

"It's not much", Allie said looking around, "but at least you will some degree of privacy. Now that all of the people have been rescued the workers are attempting to salvage personal belongings from the ship. It's taking on water and they fear it is going to sink. The British haven't interfered, but are watching closely."

"What about the captain and the crew…?"

"They are safe, and on their way back home. We look after our own."

Tears welled up in her eyes. "There is nothing to salvage. Maria and I only had several changes of clothes. I miss her and still getting used to the idea that she isn't here to talk to. Do you know where they have taken her body? I would like to see her one more time."

"I'll find out what I can but, in the meantime. why don't you try and get some rest while the baby is sleeping. The bed is freshly made up. There are clean diapers and blankets for JJ and I will bring you back your clothes as soon as they are laundered."

Almost as if he knew they were talking about him J.J. woke up. Marika changed and fed him again. He went right back to sleep.

She laid him in the crib covering him with a blanket then laid down on her bed. The tears she had been holding back began to flow. She felt overwhelmed by all that happened in the last twenty-four hours. *Too much to try and understand in such a short period of time.*

She dreamed of Jesse holding her and JJ in his arms. He held her close against his chest and said," you will be happy here and our baby will grow up to be a good man. He will not be like me because he has a different path to follow."

Someone knocking on her door woke her up several hours later. When she answered the door Allie was standing there.

"I am sorry to wake you but Peter wants to see you. I'll stay here while you talk to him, He is waiting for you in the small room at the end of the hall."

Peter still had not changed. If anything, he looked even more tired, sadder and more disheveled than before.

"How are you holding up Marika?" He asked. "All of this must seem very strange to you."

"It is, but in time I will get used to being here. Were you able to get any information about Maria?"

"That is why I came. There will be a service for her and the others who died at seven o'clock this evening."

"Can I see her before then?"

"I'm afraid not, that isn't the custom here. Her body has already been washed, dressed in a white shroud and placed in a wooden coffin. Because it's hot and the bodies are not embalmed, funerals are held within twenty-four hours, then they follow a custom that allows for seven days of mourning for family and friends."

Reaching into his pocket he pulled out and handed her a gold chain with a simple gold cross hanging on the end. "They found this in her pocket. I am sure she wanted you to have it. Turn around and I will do the clasp up for you."

"I wonder where she got this? I haven't seen it before."

"I don't know, I haven't seen it either. Maybe she bought it on our journey here?"

"We did go into a couple of shops but I don't remember seeing her buy anything."

"Maybe she brought the necklace with her."

"I guess that is a possibility. Have you been able to send a message to Mark and Elizabeth?"

"Yes. I told them of Maria's passing, that you are well and they have a new nephew. There is something else you need to know Marika. Other than the camp commander, no one is aware of who you are and who J J's father is. We are worried about your safety if the truth comes out."

"I agree. The doctor recognized me from Bern and gave me the same message. What about the people on the ship? What if they tell others?"

"I have a feeling we won't need to worry about them. If someone does say something we will handle it at that time.

There is still one more thing I have to tell you. I have been thinking about doing what I can to help smuggle people here. If you ask me not to, I won't. You and Jessie will always be my first priority, but in good conscience I feel I must do what I can. Our Believers have suffered so much. They deserve to be in a country they can call their own. I promise you, if it is the last thing I do, I will find Eli, if he is still alive, and bring him to justice for betraying Jesse."

Marika walked over to Peter and took his face in her hands. "I agree you must help where you can. Jesse would want you to carry on with his work, but I don't think it is necessary for you to find Eli to punish him. That is the past. He has to live with his conscience the rest of his life."

"Thank you. I am leaving tonight and I don't know when I will see you again. If you need me tell the commander and he will get word to me. I will come and see you and the baby as often as I can."

"Promise me you will stay safe. I have lost enough people that I love in my life, I can't lose you too."

"I will do my best," Peter replied.

There was a knock on the door and Allie entered with a crying baby.

"I'll see you later," he said. "It sounds like somebody needs his mother right now."

Marika watched as Peter walked away. Once again somebody she cared for was leaving her behind. She took the crying baby from Allie's arms and whispered to him "I will build a good life for us."

At six-thirty Peter came for Marika and together they walked to the cemetery. He had shaved and donned clean clothes. As they got closer, she saw a large hole scarring the earth and several wooden coffins were lined up along the side. One had a small bouquet of flowers on top.

"That is Maria" he said. "I had Allie pick some flowers so you would know which one was hers."

"Have the others been identified?"

"Most had some form of identification on their person. We are still unsure of the name of one man. Tomorrow I am going to visit the other camps to see if I can get a list of who survived and who is missing and then compare those names against the captain's log. I am sure he had the names of everyone on board. I volunteered for the task of informing relatives their loved one didn't survive. Maybe knowing more about their last hours will relieve the pain."

"You are a good man, Peter. You don't have to take that upon yourself."

She looked around. There were few people other than Peter and herself. "Everything is so confusing right now," she said.

They watched a man in flowing black robes take his place at the head of the grave. Several other men stood on either side of him and the service began.

Marika stood quietly, JJ cradled in her arms, Peter's arm around her. As though in a movie their time together passed through her mind – meeting Maria outside Jesse's room at the inn, huddling together in the cave, watching Jesse die, living behind the border wall and how happy she was the day J J was born.

She leaned her head against Peter's shoulder. "She was the mother I never had. I am going to miss her for a very long time."

The minister said the final prayer. Other men in work clothes appeared and lowered the coffins into the grave. When they finished, each person picked up a handful of dirt and tossed it on top of the coffins.

Marika and Peter were last. Marika picked up an extra handful of dirt and dropped it on top of Maria's. "Thank you for accepting me and loving me. I will do my best to raise J.J. to be a man you will be proud of."

Peter walked her back to where she was staying. "Are you going to be okay? Do you want me to stay another day?"

"No Peter, you go and do what you have to. I need some time to myself to adjust to all that has happened and where I am."

Peter kissed her on the cheek, turned and walked away. Marika went inside, fed and bathed JJ and climbed into bed. Her heart was broken and, despite all of her bravado, she had no idea what to expect now.

THIRTY-TWO

Peter was sitting on the sand staring at the ship listing heavily in the water. Despite his best effort he was unable to find out the name of the man he watched being buried. *His family will never know what happened to him.*

He felt overcome with a profound sense of loss. *Jesse and Maria are dead. Marika and the baby are in a safe place. So much has changed in a short period of time and I don't know where to go from here or what to do.*

He felt a presence then someone sat down beside him. "We meet again," Noah said. "Were you able to rescue the two women?"

"Yes, but one died shortly after her feet touched the sand on the beach. I'm still not sure I did the right thing bringing them here. Maybe they would have been better off if I had left them alone."

"No use worrying about that now. What's done is done. Look at all of the others you protected and have given a better life."

"I guess when you put it that way. This definitely was an experience I wouldn't want to go through again. Once was enough."

"What are you going to do now Peter?"

"I don't know. I wish there was more I could do to help those who want to come here."

"Would you consider working with us? We need more men like you, men we know we can trust."

"I don't know. I will need to know more about what you want me to do and where I would fit in."

"That's what I thought you would say. Meet me in town on Thursday morning at nine at the café down from the tailor shop and we will talk." Peter agreed and Noah slipped away as quietly as he came.

For the next few hours Peter thought long and hard about Noah's proposition. *Marika and J J are safe for now, but I feel like there is more for me to do. The Believers have suffered and lost so much. I will meet with Noah and then make my decision.*

Thursday morning Peter was at the café waiting. Noah arrived a few minutes later and sat down across from him.

"I hope this means you are going to join us. I heard the British are upset that so many refugees are getting past them and arriving at one time. Are you free to leave today?"

"Yes. Maria's funeral is over and I told Marika I won't be around for awhile.in case the British come looking for me."

"Good idea."

"The refugees…"

"Were questioned, but they are safe. As soon as they stepped ashore, they became citizens of the Promise land. It is you and the ship's captain they want to talk to. Fortunately, the captain and his crew were taken out of the country that very day. By now they are far away. Now let's eat while I explain what you can do to help us."

THIRTY-THREE

A teenaged boy, probably the owner's son, took their orders for fried eggs and fresh bread and poured them each a cup of coffee.

When he was out of hearing range Noah said, "while we eat, I'll explain what we would like you to do. What do you know about the current history of the Promise land?"

"Not much, why do you ask?"

"The past still influences today. I will give you the condensed version. This land was once part of a great Arab nation that stood for thousands of years. After the great war the World League broke this area up into territories and gave each one self-governing power. The League mandated, the British occupy the territory where the Believers were beginning to settle and govern them until they could stand on their own.

Throughout the years more Believers moved here, believing this land was rightfully theirs and given to them in biblical times. Their faith waxed and waned over the years but it wasn't until Jesse became their leader and Heinrich's determination to destroy their faith that, for many, their beliefs became important. Since Heinrich's death thousands of survivors look upon this as a place where they could live according to their faith, traditions and finally a place to call home.

Under the British mandate the territory was divided into two areas one for the Arabs and the other for the Believers. The original plan was for them to work together to become one self-governing nation.

Of course, the Arabs objected. They negotiated with the British to set low quotas for the number of immigrants allowed each year. They were worried about losing some of the land they were given and becoming the minority.

That's where it stands today. The World League was incorporated into the National Union of Countries which is now responsible for supervising the British mandate."

"So much for history Noah. What has that got to do with today?"

"Relax, I'm getting to it. After Heinrich's death the quota was relaxed to take in the thousands of the refugees clamoring to move here. As the numbers increased the Arabs became worried about the British annexing more of their land and skirmishes began along the border.

As a peace offering the British slashed the quota to half of what it previously was, but the wave had started. Hundreds of Believers were already on the move. As the population swelled, some began demanding independence from the British. These demands resulted in certain factions of the Believers and British clashing. Wasn't long before the British were fighting the Believers, the Arabs were fighting the British, and the Believers and Arabs were fighting each other. That's where we stand today."

"So, what do you want from me?" Peter asked.

"To join the resistance and fight with us – to be willing to do whatever is necessary to keep from being overrun by the Arabs and get rid of the British. We want our own country," Noah answered.

Peter didn't know what to think. "Are you asking me to pick up a gun and kill for you?"

"I guess if you put it that way then the answer is yes."

Peter stood up so fast his chair fell backwards to the floor. His hands balled into fists and he stared at Noah. The other patrons in the café stopped talking.

"You are asking too much of me this time," he growled. "I am a true Believer of Jesse's teachings – forgive each other, treat others as you want to be treated, not kill as many as I can to accomplish somebody else's goals."

Noa stood up, walked over and stood Peter's chair up. Putting one hand on his shoulder he said, "sit down, you are making a scene."

Peter sat back down, put his elbows on the table and stared at Noah. Through gritted teeth he said, "I have made many mistakes in my life but I have not, nor will I, deliberately take the life of another man. To become part of your movement would become my biggest mistake of all."

He stood again and threw some money on the table. "No," he said, "I can't do what you are asking."

"Sit down Peter There is another way you can help us which doesn't involve loss of life."

Peter sat down, "I'm listening," he said.

"First of all, I apologize. I am sorry Peter. I didn't realize how strong your feelings were or I wouldn't have asked. Forgive me, I didn't mean to insult you."

"Fine, but that doesn't answer my question."

"As I told you the British cut the immigration quota to bare minimum, but hundreds of people are waiting in the refugee camps across the border for a chance to come here, by any means possible. Many suffered greatly under Heinrich.

You came here as a refugee. You know how hard it was, yet you made it and brought Marika and Maria with you. We need people with your experience who are willing to guide these people safely across the border."

"You mean smuggle them in?"

"Yes."

Peter sat and thought for several minutes. Noah knew enough not to say anything that might upset him again.

"Yes, I am willing to help you that way."

Noah was surprised; he was expecting Peter to refuse. "Let's pay for our lunch and go for a walk so we can talk freely."

Noah picked up Peter's money from the table, walked over to the counter and paid for their lunch.

As they walked out the door the owner said to his son," that's a relief. I thought for a minute we were going to have to break up a fight."

When Peter joined forces with Noah, he wasn't prepared for the problems in entering the Promise land.

"Where are the refugees living?" Peter asked.

"Outside Joshua city where huge camps have been built, but they are only slightly better than what Heinrich provided. Many want to emigrate either to the Promise land or another country. The problem is nobody wants to take them in. Those who fit the 'criteria for acceptance' don't have the required papers or financial means. Some are lucky enough to be have families in other countries willing to sponsor them but even that is a long-drawn-out procedure."

"Where would I fit in? How can I be of any use to you?"

"Let me explain more. The British have been overseeing the Promise land for years and the Arabs are becoming more vocal about the them allowing so many refugees in. In order to keep peace, instead of opening the borders the British are becoming more restrictive about the number who can enter. Those who enter illegally are imprisoned.

We need your expertise and experience. You personally witnessed the tragedy of the Believers. You travelled with Jesse. You smuggled his wife and mother into the country and you know first-hand the challenges we are facing.

Outside each camp there is a group called the Believer's Brigade who work with the resistance to move people to the camps. Then there is another group inside the camps working to move them across the border.

The British are getting smarter at seizing the ships then moving the refugees to heavily guarded prison camps. At last count there were over ten thousand confined there, including women and children. "

Peter was shocked. "As if they haven't suffered enough already."

"We have managed to open several overland routes but the numbers we can bring are limited. You can help by coordinating what we are doing and making it as efficient as possible. The British know where we cross but not when. We need to open more routes and find ways to move larger groups.

You would also work with resistance groups to create diversions at one place while a group crosses at another. Some of the British patrol members are sympathetic to our cause and look the other way but others are determined to make a name for themselves."

Peter looked at him. "Me? Are you sure? I don't have the best track record for success."

"You are the most experienced person we know of."

Peter thought for a few minutes then said, "okay count me in but I have one question. What happens if I get caught?"

"The British will interrogate you and either put you in a prison camp or exile you. I promise we will do what we can to rescue you but that may take some time. If you are in a camp, you could be there for weeks, even months before we get you out. Do you think you could handle that?"

"If I had to I could."

Noah looked at him. "You do understand this is a huge commitment on your part."

"Yes." Peter replied. "Jesse asked me to do what I can to help the Believers after he was gone. This is one way I can fulfill the promise I made to him."

"Good, meet me back here at nine tomorrow evening and I will introduce you to the others you will be working with."

The two men shook hands. Noah left first. Peter waited five more minutes, then left walking in the opposite direction.

Peter built a network of people to assist him and soon two or three crossings were occurring each night. The British always seemed to be at the wrong place at the wrong time. Only on rare occasions did he conduct the actual crossings. He seemed to be everywhere at the same time. His uncanny ability to blend into any crowd protected him from being captured and soon his exploits became legendary. Soon the British referred to him as 'Peter the Fox" because of his ability to elude them.

THIRTY-FOUR

Marika adjusted well to communal living. For the first time since Jesse death she felt as though her life had purpose. Although the stream of Believers slowed, they kept coming.

The British began taking heavier handed action against the rescuers. Her task was to provide identification papers for the newcomers and help move them to a safer place.

The Kibbutz become a transit station, always trying to stay one step ahead of the British. A silent army had risen up and taken the fight to the British attacking their communication and supply routes. The battles were bitter, independence their end goal.

Each day she left JJ in the nursery with the other babies and picked him up in the evening. He was growing into a healthy, but inquisitive child.

As the British mandate became more entrenched. the camp became more militarized as a means of protection and survival. Calls for an independent country were becoming louder. Rhetoric and emotions ran high on both sides, each determined not to give into the other.

Although Marika had heard of raids and arrests at another Kibbutz, she wasn't prepared for what happened at her own. During the night a group of twenty men, women and children had arrived tired, dirty and hungry. The most important task was to get them settled, provide papers and medical help and prepare them for transit to another camp further inland.

The evenings and nights Marika was required to work late JJ stayed in the children's dormitory.

She was locking her office door when the camp sirens began blaring and she heard shouting. Going to the nearest window she looked out and saw a convoy of British trucks filled with soldiers driving into the yard.

Quickly she went back into her office and hastily began gathering up the blank passports, list of names and any other incriminating evidence from the top of her desk. Shoving them into a black metal box she lifted the concealed trap door under her desk and placed the box inside. Then, for good measure, she pushed her desk further to one side to cover the trap door.

She had no sooner finished when her office door burst open and a British soldier with a gun in his hand walked in. "Leave this building at once and join the others in the parade square. What room is this?"

"An Administration office, it's of no importance," she replied.

"We will decide that". He pointing his pistol at her, "Hurry up."

Marika was shocked when she stepped outside. The people of the camp, most in their bed clothes, were moving toward the square. Many appeared to be in shock. Mothers held hands with their children. The men walked silently, hands clenched into fists, fierce determined looks on their faces.

Is this how it was for them before, forced to march to a central place and then stand to await their fate. They must be so frightened wondering what is going to happen now?

Most of the people living in the camp were not involved with the refugees. They were farmers, cooks, nurses, teachers, people grateful for a place to call home. Marika wasn't positive but she thought most were aware of the clandestine activities taking place, but said nothing, their silence offering acceptance.

The square, surrounded with British soldiers, quickly filled with people. Off to one side she heard the sound of children crying.

"Attention," a large man, with a narrow skinny black mustache hollered through a bull horn. David, the assistant camp leader stood beside him. The crowd became silent.

"My name is General Alan Smythe. We know a group of refugees arrived this evening and are here country illegally. I want these people to come forward and identify themselves."

Somebody shouted "Every person becomes a citizen of the Promise Land the minute their feet touch our soil."

People looked around at each other. Those who arrived earlier in the evening blended into the crowd. Nobody moved.

A young soldier walked up to the man and whispered something. They had a brief conversation and the soldier left. Within minutes he returned with several rifles in his arms.

"Why do you have so many guns here?" General Smythe asked David.

Marika heard somebody behind her whisper, "Oh no, they've found the store room."

David answered him clearly, "For protection and for food. Animals prey upon our cattle and chickens. We use them to keep our livestock safe."

"And what else, "the General demanded to know. "Could it be you are using them to attack our patrols?"

David laughed. "What you see before you are people who want to live and let live. You can see for yourself they are not soldiers. They are men, women and children who suffered greatly under Heinrich's rule. All they want to do is live in peace. The only thing you have accomplished tonight is destroy their trust and scare the hell out of them."

The General looked around. Clearly, he was losing any advantage he had. He began to walk away, and then turned back.

"There is a rumor that Jesse's wife and child are hiding in this camp. Is it true? Is she here?"

Marika felt as though she was going to faint. Instead of panicking she took a dep breath and looked around. Nobody was staring at her or pointing fingers. She felt like running but knew if she moved, she would draw attention to herself. A question ran through her mind. *How did he know or is he guessing? I can't run because that would mean leaving JJ behind. What would happen to him if they find us?*

David laughed again. "Are you serious? Is that the real reason you came here tonight? We too have heard the rumor that Jesse had a wife and baby, but that's all it is. Nobody has seen or met this phantom woman. If she were here, we would all be talking about it."

The General scowled at David "if she shows up, I demand you come and tell me immediately. All we need is a new leader for the Believers." He added sarcastically.

Then he looked at the people standing in the square. "Don't move. Stay where you are until we are gone."

The General turned and walked toward the nearest jeep. There was a collective sigh of relief/ and people began talking amongst themselves.

David watched until the last of the convoy drove through the gates. "Go back to your rooms. I will have the cooks prepare breakfast early then you can report for your normal duties. They are lying to us, seeding doubt and we are not afraid of them. We have nothing to hide. I need all Administration staff to report to my office as soon as possible."

Marika went back to her office and found it had been ransacked. Papers were scattered all over the floor, the filing cabinet had been pushed over and dumped, curtains were ripped down and pictures were slashed. She breathed a sigh of relief when she saw that her desk had not been moved and the metal box was safe although the desk drawers had been opened and the contents spilled on to the floor.

She closed the door locking it from the inside. She was terrified, her body was shaking. *Now mare than ever, I must protect JJ. I am afraid of what will happen if they find him.*

An hour later she walked calmly into David's office. "How did you find your office?" he asked.

"In a mess," she replied.

"Do you think they found anything?"

"No, I was able to hide everything before the soldier charged into my office. They tore it apart but I am sure they never found what they were looking for. Do you think there is somebody in this camp who is Jesse's wife?" She needed to know and asked for the benefit of the others in the room.

He laughed. "There is no such person here and, if there was, no one would know what she looked like. It is simply, a rumor."

David looked into Marika's eyes. "But if she were here, she would be perfectly safe and so would her child, if there is one, Many Believers want to believe the rumor, but it isn't true."

Marika looked back at David and mouthed the word "Thank you."

'Marika, I know this has unnerved you. Why don't you find your son and hold him. After all of this excitement he most likely needs to see his mother."

And this mother needs to hold her son.

THIRTY-FIVE

The hairs on the back of Peter's neck stood on end, something felt off about crossing the border tonight. Although he had made this crossing dozens of times this was the first time he felt uneasy.

He was approaching the rocks and safety when suddenly a bright light shone in his eyes and a clipped British voice said "Move and I will shoot you. Put your hands on top of your head where I can see them."

"I heard you," Peter replied, putting both hands on his head, one on top of the other.

"Yes, that's him," a muffled voice said.

Peter was stunned. Somebody with inside knowledge had betrayed him and possibly the whole organization.

"Turn around and start walking. We have finally captured the human smuggler, Peter the fox. He doesn't look so sly and cunning now."

Someone stepped behind him, grabbed his arms and forced them behind his back. He heard the click of the handcuffs as they locked around his wrists.

He began to protest, "You have the wrong person. I am not who you think I am," but he was cut off.

"Shut up and get into the jeep."

He heard a vehicle start and then pull up alongside of them and he was roughly pushed into the back seat of an open-air jeep.

When I fail to arrive at the check point people would begin asking questions. I have no doubt there is someone hiding in the rocks watching and listening to this exchange taking place.

"Where are you taking me?" he asked loudly. *Voices carry a long way in the desert. I hope if someone is there they will hear where they are taking me.*

"To the garrison commander at Zada and then hopefully to prison for a very long time. Smuggling illegals into the country is going to earn you a long prison sentence."

Peter was aware he would eventually get caught, but he didn't know what to expect after that. He hoped somebody higher up in their organization would get word to him. He knew one thing for sure, as soon as soon as he was able, he would find a way to get word to Noah that there was a traitor in their midst.

The jeep travelled through the desert and then entered a well-guarded British compound stopping in front of a white building with a tin roof.

"Don't even think about trying to escape. If you do, I will shoot you."

Nudged from behind at gun point into the building he was immediately put into a small square cell. "You are going to be our guest until we figure out what to do with you. As you can see, you have all the comforts of home."

Peter looked around. There was a cot with a blanket and pillow and a toilet located in one corner. The cell was hot, and smelled of urine and stale body odor.

"I demand to speak to your commander immediately." Peter said. "What are you charging me with and what proof do you have that I was doing something illegal? I wasn't doing anything wrong, simply walking along the edge of the rocks."

"What were you doing there in the middle of the night?"

"I happen to like to walk in the desert at night. It's quiet and I have a clear view of the stars in the sky."

Peter knew they wouldn't believe him but that was all he could think of on the spur of the moment.

"You might as well get some rest. When the base commander wakes up in the morning, we will tell him you are here. He'll want to ask you a few questions."

From his cell Peter could watch the front door. Another man walked over to them, "I see you had good hunting. Who did you bring us this time?"

"Peter the Fox."

"Well, I would say you had a very productive night."

The two men walked away. He couldn't hear what they were saying, but every once in a while, one looked over at him and grinned.

For Peter the bigger question was who betrayed him and what did they hope to gain?

THIRTY-SIX

. Peter was lying on the smelly cot staring at the ceiling when one of the guards approached his cell. A full day had passed since anyone had spoken to him. His meals were pushed through a slot in the door.

"Why is it taking so long before I get to talk to someone. I have rights you know. Either charge me with something or let me go." he declared

"You have to wait until you meet the Commander." the guard replied

"How long is that going to take?"

"When he gets around to it. What's the matter, you don't like your accommodations?"

"I've had better," Peter replied, turning his face to the wall.

A short time later the guard returned and dragged his baton across the bars. "Get up, the Commander is ready for you."

He unlocked the cell door, put handcuffs on Peter's wrists and shackles around his ankles.

"Worried I'll run away?" Peter asked sarcastically.

"Shut your mouth and start walking."

The guard led Peter out of the cell block and into a court yard. He was led across the court yard to an office building shuffling as he walked because larger steps forced the shackles to rub against his ankles.

Knocking on the first office door on the right the guard announced "Here he is Commander, Peter the Fox. He doesn't look so wily now," then laughed at his own joke.

"Come in, come in" the Commander said. He was a tall, skinny, bald man with a handle bar mustache that nearly covered his lower face.

"I am British Commander John Anderson," he said to Peter. Turning to the guard he said. "Remove the shackles but leave the handcuffs on."

When the guard left the room he asked Peter, "Can I get you something to drink? Perhaps a cup of tea?"

"I am fine," Peter replied.

Commander Anderson sat down on a chair behind a large mahogany desk and studied Pete "What were you doing in the desert?"

"Often when I can't sleep, I like to go there and look at the stars. They are easier to see when there is no light."

"We know who you are and what you do. Everybody knows who Peter the Fox is and that he aids in smuggling the Believers into the country. Now tell me truthfully what were you doing there?"

"I told you, looking at the stars."

"Who were you supposed to meet?"

"I wasn't there to meet anybody. I like places that are peaceful and quiet."

"How many refugees were you planning on moving?"

Peter looked at him, "I don't know what you are talking about."

"How dare you lie to me." The Commandeer was losing patience. He came around the side of his desk and slapped Peter across the face.

Peter laughed. "Is that the best you can do? I went toe to toe with Heinrich Mueller and lived to tell the tale. You don't scare me. Is there a special permit I need to go star gazing?"

"Who do you report to?" The Commander demanded.

"I have no idea what you are talking about. I don't report to anyone. Why would I have to?"

The Commander was becoming more and more agitated. "I have a place where you can think your answers over and I can make sure you stay there until you change your mind."

"Do what you want with me. "Peter replied calmly, "but know that as soon as I have the opportunity, I am going to report you for holding me without just cause."

"I know you were there to meet with refugee's and were going to smuggle them into the country," The Commander shouted, his face close to Peter's. "Tell me the truth and I will go easy on you."

Peter stared back at him. "What proof do you have?"

Peter chuckled. *I am sure the others waited until I was taken away and then moved the group through safely. At least that's what I would have done. If the British had arrived ten minutes later, they would have had us all.*

The Commander was silent. He walked over to the door, opened it and shouted at the guard waiting outside, "take him back to his cell. In the morning, we will move him to Exeter. He can rot there until he answers my questions."

Turning back to Peter he said," I'm going to make sure you never set foot in this so-called Promise Land again."

Peter had heard of Exeter prison but was unprepared for what he saw. The compound was heavily guarded, surrounded by a ten-foot-high wire fence, in the middle of the desert. There were watch towers along the perimeter and one road in and out. He counted ten long buildings and noticed men lounging in the small amount of shade available. The hot sun was beating down, and the air was dry.

The truck drove through the prison gates and stopped in front of a metal building with a sign which read Wardens Office.

"Get out" the driver commanded him. His handcuffs and shackles were taken off and he was shoved forward by the baton in the guard's hands. A short, over weight man greeted him inside, his shirt dark wet under the armpits from sweat.

"Peter the Fox for you sir," the guard announced.

"Aaah yes, we were expecting him today," the man replied.

A young man, who was also in the office, handed Peter a set of bright blue clothing, a pair of sandals and a tin plate and cup.

"Change over there, then give me your clothes." Peter did as he was told.

"You won't be needing these any time soon, if ever" he chuckled rolling them into a bundle.

"Take him to hut nine Lt. Crombie, we'll see how tough he is."

Peter hadn't said a word. He followed the Lt. until they came to a long hut with the number nine above the door. When he entered the room, the air was stifling hot and reeked of body odor.

"That's your bunk over there; we thought you would be more comfortable on the top." He said pointing to one in the corner as far away as possible from a window. "Stand there until I return."

Minutes later the Lt. returned with a sheet, pillow and a blanket. "Meals are served at six a.m., noon and 6 p.m. Lights out at nine. You will be assigned your duties later. Everybody does their share around here. Any attempt to escape will earn you a stay in solitary."

As he moved toward the door he said to Peter," tell them what they want to know. This place is truly hell on earth."

THIRTY-SEVEN

Every morning Peter was taken to the Warden's office and interrogated. The questions were always the same. "Who is your leader? What were you doing there? Who are you working with? Tell us what we want to know and we will let you go."

The shouting, screaming and threatening continued for several hours then he was returned to his hut. Sometimes he was beaten with a baton, other times deprived of food and water for days at a time but never changed his story.

At his hut he was forced to sit in the hot sun. other times he wasn't allowed to sleep for days at a time. Other prisoners were forbidden to approach him. He kept asking himself *how can I get out of here? I thought Noah would have found a way to rescue me by now.*

Three times a week a series of trucks arrived at the prison. One brought new prisoners and took others away. Another brought food and provisions, and in the third were new men to replace the guards.

Following one of the guard changes, a man Peter had never seen before. approached him. "Get up," he snarled.

When Peter refused to get to his feet the guard hit him on the back of the head with a baton. "I said, get up now,"

Reluctantly Peter got to his feet. The guard grabbed his arm and forced it behind his back. "Start walking."

By this point Peter no longer cared what they did to him. He began walking slowly in front of the guard.

"Listen to me carefully Peter." The guard whispered. "I am here to get you out of this hell hole and we don't have much time. Do what I tell you and don't ask any questions."

Peter tried to turn around but the guard applied more pressure to his arm.

"Shut up," the guard said louder than necessary. "I talk. You listen."

Whispering again he said, "two days from now a truck will be coming with provisions. Go to the store room when you see it coming and wait inside. Don't let anyone see you."

Suddenly the guard pushed Peter and he fell face first in the sand.

"That's what you get for talking back to me. Next time it will be ten times as bad."

The guard stalked away and Peter picked himself up. His shoulder hurt and he knew there was a bump on his forehead. He walked back to his usual spot and sat down. *It's about time. I don't know who this guy is but my only choice is to trust him This maybe a trap from the British, an easy way to make me disappear for good.*

"What was all that about?" The man sitting beside him asked.

"A new bullying tactic meant to frighten me into talking." Peter replied.

Two days later the scheduled convoy of trucks drove into the yard. Peter casually got to his feet and stepped away. When he was sure he wasn't being watched he slipped into the store room.

Along one wall stood barrels of flour, sugar and coffee. From the shadows he watched as the new barrels were rolled in and the empty ones returned to the truck. Off to one side he noticed a larger unmarked empty barrel which was different than the others.

The new guard came out of the shadows. "I hope you aren't claustrophobic. Get in quickly, they are nearly finished."

Peter climbed onto the barrel tucking his arms and legs around him the best he could then the guard placed the lid on top and tamped it down. "There are plenty of air holes so you should be able to breathe."

Now I know how Maria and Marika must have felt in those coffins.

He nearly cried out when the barrel was dropped on its side and began rolling. He felt the barrel being lifted up into the back of the truck and then stood up right. He heard people talking and then a guard saying "you're good to go."

He breathed a sigh of relief when the truck finally started to move. He thought whoever was driving would stop soon and he would be let out, but the truck kept going. He was hot, thirsty and his arms and legs were cramping from the position he was in. After what felt like hours the truck slowed down and come to a stop. He heard voices again and then someone lifted the lid off the barrel. The fresh air felt good and he took several deep breaths.

"Let me help you out," Noah said. He gently laid the barrel on its side and helped him crawl out, then stand.

"We would have come sooner but didn't know where they had taken you," he added.

Peter was in pain. The feeling returning to his arms and legs burned like pins and needles stabbing him.

"The guard…?" he asked.

"Is one of us," Noah replied. "After this he will be replaced and nobody will be any wiser.

"Where am I?"

"In a warehouse on Chelsey Street. After dark we will move you to a safe house in the city. The British will be looking for you so you need to remain out of sight for a period of time. You have done an excellent job for us and because of your efforts hundreds have been rescued, but now it is too dangerous for you. The British will put a price on your head with orders to shoot on sight."

"Am I really that dangerous to them," Peter laughed.

"To us you have been a blessing, but to them you are now public enemy Number One. There are others trained and willing to take your place. Your work will continue in the city as we need your knowledge and expertise there now more than ever. Changes are coming."

At supper time the guard pounded on the warden's door. "Peter didn't show up for supper and he is missing," he shouted.

"What so you mean missing? He has to be here some place. He didn't just walk away."

"We have searched the whole compound and questioned each person in his hut but nobody has seen him since this afternoon."

"Search again," the warden said.

An hour later the guard returned, "He's not here,"

"Was anybody here today that shouldn't have been."

"No, only the provisions truck and I personally supervised its loading and unloading." Then he paused, "Come to think about it, there was a different truck and crew today. I've never seen. them before."

"You didn't stop and question them?"

"No. I didn't see any reason to. They seemed to know what they were doing."

The warden was furious. "You stupid man. All I have around here is a bunch of idiots. Get out of here."

The guard smiled as he walked away. *They didn't call him Peter the Fox for nothing.*

THIRTY-EIGHT

"Mother, guess what?" JJ called out as he ran through the front door of their apartment. "I got to fire a real gun today. It was awesome. Now I know for sure that when I grow up, I am going to be a soldier."

She smiled at his enthusiastic entrance. "I didn't think they allowed that in your age group."

"Usually they don't, but a couple of us begged the instructor to let us try. He told us we should learn how because, if we are attacked by the Arabs, we will know what to do. I can hardly wait until tomorrow to do it again."

"I don't think that is such a good idea J J, you are too young."

"I knew you were going to say that, but our instructor will be with us."

Marika felt disturbed. Ever since he was a small child, he was fixated on the idea of being a soldier and she didn't know how to change his mind.

Now they are teaching babies how to shoot. When will this ever end? I don't want my son to be a soldier and neither would his father. I want him to be more than that. I hoped he would follow more in his father's footsteps.

They had lived in the Kibbutz for thirteen years and the one thing she hated was the military aspect. In the last few years, the Arabs were becoming more intent on regaining the land they insisted was stolen from them.

JJ was an excellent student, always at the top of his class but the other students didn't hold that against him. Even at the tender age of six he began showing the same leadership qualities his father possessed.

Marika didn't want him going into the Army. She knew he would rise quickly through the ranks, but could also be killed in one of the many skirmishes which took place. Life in the Kibbutz was perilous at the best of times and the raids were becoming more frequent.

The next morning, when she arrived at work, she marched unannounced into the Commander's office. "Since when have you started giving guns to babies?" she asked.

Chuckling he replied, "Oh, I see. JJ told you about yesterday."

"Well, I don't like it. You need to let them be children. Living here they learn enough about guns and death and dying"

"Marika, you and I both know that as long as they are living here there will always be a danger. Besides there was only J J and one other boy and I decided to indulge their pleas this time."

"Don't do it again until he is old enough. I don't want him in the army. I want him to go to university and get an education. He is smart and will be able to do so much more for our people that way."

"I agree with you, but this is also part of his education. Every child has to learn eventually."

"I know," Marika answered softly," but he could also be killed."

The Commander came around his desk and put his arm around her shoulders. "Marika, we have not forgotten who JJ is and what his purpose is, but he has to be treated the same as the other boys. You must understand, he has to learn how to protect himself if the need arises. Allow him his fantasy for now. Most children at his age change their minds a dozen times about what they want to do when they grow up."

"JJ won't. From the time he learned to walk and talk that's all he's wanted. He is waiting for the day he turns sixteen and can join the camp militia."

"How about you quit worrying for now. Yesterday was a one-time thing and he will have to learn to wait like all of the other children. You're fretting about nothing."

Marika knew he was placating her but arguing wasn't going to change his mind. Policy was policy and she couldn't change it. That same policy had been in effect when she arrived and would be in effect after she left.

"Thank you for hearing me out," Marika said. "I wish there was some other way and we could finally live in peace."

"I agree with you but I don't foresee that in the near future, if ever."

* * *

The Commander was right. Between British raids on the Kibbutz's looking for guns and the Arab incursions life changed for Marika. The Kibbutz gradually changed from a family community to a paramilitary base. Boys and girls from the age of thirteen were trained to fight. They rotated their duties between staying in the Kibbutz and going to school and some unknown place learning to defend their country.

Each time she voiced her objections to the Commander, he told her the same thing, "We will always have to fight to keep our land and, when the British leave, we need to know how to defend ourselves."

There wasn't much Marika could do. This was the life they lived on a daily basis, never quite knowing what the day would bring.

Unexpectedly one day JJ came running into their apartment. "What's your hurry young man?" she called out, "You forgot to take off your shoes."

"I have to hurry. I need to pack some clothes and be in the square ready to leave in thirty minutes."

"Leave? Where, if I may ask, do you think you are going? You just started your rotation at home and in school. You need to get your education JJ that will be more useful than being in the military. Our people need people who can lead as well as fight."

He looked at her. "I really don't have time for this lecture mom. Last night the British raided Kibbutz Atlita and found the cache of weapons the Brigade was storing. They forced every one out of their homes and burned everything to the ground. Two hundred and fifty people were left without food, water or shelter and nothing except the clothes on their back. Luckily a man travelling to the Kibbutz saw what happened and got word out."

"So, what exactly has this to do with you?"

"The Brigade put out a call for help and we are going to help rebuild it stronger. "

"JJ I wish you wouldn't go. There is going to be nothing but trouble over this."

"I have to. My group has been assigned to rebuild the fences around the perimeter. I am their leader and I need to be there."

"You are thirteen years old, not even old enough to be called to military duty. You don't have to do anything."

JJ. looked into her eyes. "I am going whether you like it or not. I promised and I can't go back on my word."

At the moment Marika realized how much he sounded like his father. They had the same zeal for doing what was right and the same look of determination.

"Okay go, but promise me you will be careful."

"Mom, you worry too much. I'll be fine. Nothing will happen."

Fifteen minutes later he left, dressed in his junior paramilitary uniform, a heavy black duffle bag resting on his shoulder.

Marika felt physically ill watching him walk away. *What is it going to take to get him to realize this is not his calling? Like his father he is meant to lead the Believers, not get himself killed.*

THIRTY-NINE

The sound of a wailing siren echoed over the country side catching everyone by surprise. Those working in the fields and gardens climbed into the back of trucks and hung on as best they could. Those inside the Kibbutz stopped what they were doing and made their way to the center square.

People talked quietly among themselves. "The siren usually means trouble. I wonder what's wrong?"

Men put their arms around their wives; mothers held their children close. Marika looked around and spotted JJ off to one side standing with a group of boys.

Someone moved a truck to the front of the Commanders building. An eerie calm settled over the crowd as they waited.

Soon the Commander and his two highest ranking officers came out and climbed into the back of the truck. Speaking into a megaphone he said," As of midnight last night the World Tribunal unilaterally divided our country into two sections. The southern half was given to the Arabs and is now under their control. The northern half stays under British control. Even as I speak construction is beginning on a border division.

Citizens living outside their designated areas have seventy-two hours to return to their side of the border if they so choose. After that, the border crossings will be guarded and a special permit will be required to travel from one side to the other."

Murmuring and anxious looks spread amongst the people. Marika felt sick to her stomach. This was a repeat of what had occurred when she and Maria were caught on the wrong side of the border in Brussia.

The Commander began to speak again. "There are rumors of rioting in the cities and that beatings and killings have taken place. I advise you not to travel unless absolutely necessary.

The Arabs are angry because their most holy city of Medina is now in the hands of the British. The British are incensed about not being consulted and are not prepared for the influx of Believers who will arrive."

"How does that affect us?" a man shouted out from the crowd.

"In several ways. Trade for goods and services with the Arabs will probably cease unless we reach an agreement with them. We must also prepare for an influx of refugees as we are closest to the border. There will be fighting and innocent people on both sides will be killed."

When he said that the young soldiers cheered and pumped their fists into the air. "Bring it on," one shouted.

The Commander ignored the outburst. "By the end of today I want a full inventory of what we have. This includes the cows, sheep chickens, guns, ammunition and vehicles. We must prepare for the worst and hope for the best. All group leaders to meet in my office in fifteen minutes."

* * *

Panic ensued among the Believers forced to relocate within the seventy-two-hour time frame. Rich Arabs quietly bought up their businesses, homes and property at rock bottom prices. Others simply packed what they could carry and walked away.

Long lines of Believers heading north chocked the highway. Soon they were joined by large groups of Arabs heading south. The effect on them was less traumatic and many had family to welcome them home.

The kibbutz welcomed all who entered their gates, Believers and Arabs were treated the same. After being given a meal and a chance to rest, most continued on their way.

Many of the travelers were in shock. Once again, they were being uprooted because of actions beyond their control. Tent cities flourished outside the larger centers. Many of the young men chose to stay and fight if necessary.

On the morning of the fourth day most of the refugees had moved onto their destination. The Arab camp which had grown alongside the highway was dismantled and British patrols drove up and down the roads.

Within days border skirmishes broke out. The Arabs were determined to regain their holy city and the Believers were not prepared to lose any of the land they were given. Casualties mounted on both sides.

Then tensions increased because, for some unexplained reason, the British began raiding the Kibbutz's closer to the border. Several were burned to the ground and the citizens herded into the desert like cattle, guns and ammunition were taken and the Commanders and group leaders arrested. Rumor had it that they were smuggling guns to the Arabs to fight the British.

In case of a raid at Marika's kibbutz, the guns and ammunition were hidden in a variety of places. Only the Commanders knew where and the army was instructed to stand down.

A small resistance movement of Believers lurked in the background. More joined as the Believers rights were slowly eroded. The words "The Promise land belongs to us" became their rallying cry.

Railway tracks were bombed. Gasoline storage areas went up in flames. British detachments were attacked, their guns and ammunition stolen. Fires of unknown origin occurred in office buildings. Now the British were waging war on two fronts, one against the Arabs, the other the Believers. Forward thinking Believers formed a shadow government and openly encouraged the citizens to demand independence.

Once again, the nation endured another shock. One wing of the prestigious hotel, the King Abraham, was blown up. Four people died, thirty-four were injured. Important people often stayed there but that specific wing housed the headquarters of the British Army. The resistance was blamed for this act, but the Arabs were also under suspicion.

As more information was released the Believers heard that half an hour before the explosion the British General in command received a phone call warning him, but he chose to ignore it.

The resistance prepared for swift and hard reprisals but nothing happened. Rumors began to circulate that the British, tired of the expense and loss of equipment and life, were leaving. Although unspoken, the truth was the British had decided to let the Believers and Arabs fight out who would eventually be in control.

Concerned about this new development the Kibbutz Commanders and Army leaders met in secret to formulate a plan. There was no doubt fighting the Arabas would escalate and they needed to be prepared. They backed the newly formed government plan in declaring an independent state hoping this would deter further Arab action.

Within days convoys of trucks filled with soldiers were seen on the highway travelling toward the ocean. Observers notice a large number of troop transport ships anchored off shore. The soldiers were ferried in small boats to the ships leaving their vehicles behind. A few were disabled but most were in running condition. Some had keys left in the ignition.

The ever-vigilant observers watched and waited. When the last of the ships disappeared from view they came out of the hills and spirited the vehicles away. Within hours of the last ship leaving the beach was empty.

Once again, the siren wailed early in the morning before the workers left for work. People hurried to the square, some still in their night clothes. A truck rolled up in front of the Commander's office and he climbed into the back.

Mega phone in hand he shouted, "As of three o'clock this afternoon the British will formally cease governing our state. At that time our government will take control and declare that we are now the independent state of Yisrael."

People cheered, hugged and kissed each other, soldiers fired their guns into the air. Spontaneously some joined hands and began singing the national anthem. Finally, after all the years of turmoil and hardship the Believers had a place to call home.

The Commander climbed down from the truck. To no one in particular he said "Today we celebrate, tomorrow we begin the fight to keep what is ours."

FORTY

At the age of sixteen two years of military service was compulsory. When JJ turned sixteen, based upon his outstanding service, he received an officer's commission.

Instead of becoming more secure after the British left life became more dangerous. The largest city of the Arab faith was in occupied territory and they demanded free access to worship. Instead, travel was restricted and the border was manned with armed guards. Later a barbed wire fence with check points was scattered along the border.

In many ways Marika understood the situation because she remembered how helpless she felt when she and Maria were trapped behind fences and walls.

One evening she tried to explain this to JJ. "It is a feeling like no other. Your freedom is curtailed by the very fact you are not free to come and go. Families are divided. You have to show papers in order to cross from one side to the other and you are dependent upon the whim of whoever is there that day. They decide who crosses or not. This isn't even considering the differences in religion."

"Mother," JJ said patiently, "you don't understand. This land was promised to our people in biblical times. Rightfully it is ours."

"Perhaps so, but the Believers are trying to impose their rule on a way of life that has survived thousands of years. In many ways that makes them no different than the British."

"We will fight to keep what is ours." He declared.

"Yes, you will and the Arabs will continue to fight for what is theirs. This is a no-win situation for everybody."

Marika never knew when Peter would appear. There would be a knock on the door and there he stood.

The next time he came she asked," is the situation getting any better? JJ doesn't say much because he knows I get upset."

"To tell you the truth Marika, it's getting worse. There is a power struggle within the Believers There will be a war between the Arabs and the Believers. We must try to get JJ to resign his commission before this happens."

"Where did you get that information?"

Peter looked at her as if to say "really Marika," instead he said, "I am aware of plans being made and it's only a matter of time until there is an incident that blows up like a powder keg. You must insist he resign. If he won't voluntarily then you need to go to the camp commander and ask for an exemption."

"You know he will never forgive me if I do."

"A bullet doesn't care who or what it hits."

Marika thought about this, "you are absolutely right. I'll talk to the commander as soon as you leave,"

"You have to understand how important this is. Yes, he will be upset, but he is of more value to the Believers. I don't want him to become another casualty of a war that neither side can win. Each side is fighting to prove they own the land, but they would be better off trying to find a way to work together. That will probably never happen in our lifetime because there is too much anger and bitterness on both sides."

That evening when JJ came home for supper Marika told him of the discussion she had with Peter.

He was incensed. "Don't you dare. Neither one of you have any right to interfere in my life. The next time Peter comes you tell him to mind his own business. My future is in the military; in fact, I am expecting a promotion any day. If there is going to be a war, I can hardly wait to be part of it. There is no doubt in my mind that we will prevail, .and you and Peter will have been fretting over nothing. You need to have some faith in us and our leaders. They know what they are doing."

During the night Marika dreamed of Jesse. "Help me stop him," she begged. "He cannot lead the Believers this way,"

"No Marika, you must let him be. His story is already written. He must experience what is to come to make him the man he is meant to be. He is part of the true path to peace."

"Why?" Marika cried out into the darkness, but Jesse was gone.

FORTY-ONE

Just as Peter predicted the triggering incident was minor. Two young boys were playing with their dog along the border. The dog ran ahead and wouldn't come back when he was called. Not thinking, the boys ran to get him and entered a mine field. A small explosion followed. The two boys were more scared than hurt and the dog suffered a slight injury to its paw.

The Believers pointed out that DO NOT ENTER signs were posted warning of the danger. The Arabs insinuated they were being held captive because of to the location of the mine field.

The word war travelled quickly through the Kibbutz. Despite negotiations between the Arabs and the government of the Promise land the troop incursions by both sides led to the inevitable conclusion.

JJ's unit was among the first to be called into action. He was excited when he came home to get his uniforms and duffle bag. His face was flushed. He was giddy with laughter, and his words clipped and short.

"It's happening. Finally, we get to fight for what is ours. We have a chance to drive them out of the country just as they are trying to do to us."

"JJ stop and listen to me for a minute."

Gathering him in her arms she held him close. JJ kissed her on the forehead, "I love you too. Now I must go before they leave without me."

Marika watched her son, duffle bag in his shoulder trot down the sidewalk. At the end he turned and waved.

When he was out of sight, she wrapped her arms around her middle and began to pray. *Please Jesse, watch over him. Bring him home safely. We both know his destiny is to take your place with the Believers.*

FORTY-TWO

Days passed and Marika waited to hear word of JJ. She knew his unit was in the active zone but wasn't exactly sure where that was. Each day, at noon, the radio announced the names of those who died as heroes for their country. Each time she breathed a sigh of relief when the announcement was over and she didn't hear his name. Unfortunately, several young men from their Kibbutz were among the dead. She grieved their deaths as much as their mothers.

At supper time on the sixth day of the war there was a knock on her door. Marika felt as though her heart stopped. She didn't need to be told something had happened to JJ.

When she answered Peter was standing there. "Oh, it's only you," she said, "come in."

"Were you expecting somebody else?"

"No, simply praying it wasn't bad news about JJ ."

"Marika, actually that's why I am here. There is something I need to tell you"

Instantly the color drained from her face. She staggered and fell against the door frame "Please don't tell me he is dead."

"No, not dead but injured. He is in the field hospital at Goa and I've come to take you there."

"How bad is he hurt?"

"I'm not sure."

She stood in the middle of the room not knowing what to do. She couldn't think. Peter got her coat and purse from the closet and handed them to her. Putting his hand under her elbow he closed the door and guided her to a car outside.

The trip to Goa took about an hour and a half and neither said a word. Marika stared out the window, silent tears running down her face. *I shouldn't have let him go. I knew he was too young. What if he dies? I don't think I can survive losing him too.*

Peter's thoughts travelled in the same direction. *I let Jesse down again. I should have been here to put a stop to this military fascination a long time ago.*

When they arrived at the hospital, the receptionist gave them directions to JJ's room. Marika was shocked when she saw him. A white bandage was wrapped around his head and covered one eye. What she was able to see of his face was swollen and bruised. She also noticed a fresh line of stitches running from his shoulder down his left arm and his body was covered in cuts and bruises. He was sleeping.

Marika looked at Peter.

"Go to him" he urged.

She approached the bed and quietly spoke. "JJ I am here. Everything will be okay now."

After her third attempt he opened his eyes and smiled at her. "I'm happy you came. I told you I would be fine." then drifted back to sleep.

Peter briefly left then came back. "I talked to the Doctor. He has cuts on his head, under his eyes and a severe concussion. His shoulder and arm were broken and they operated as soon as he was stable. Physically he will recover, but emotionally and mentally may take much longer."

"Why is that? Do you know what happened Peter?"

"JJ and three of his men were in a jeep and drove over a mine buried in the road. All four were ejected and the jeep landed a hundred feet away. He is the only survivor."

"Oh no," Marika exclaimed, "who was driving? Please don't tell me it was him."

"Yes."

"Oh Peter, we both know he will never forgive himself."

"Two were his close friends, Chaim and Henry from our Kibbutz."

Tears filled her eyes. "Oh, their poor mothers. I'm going to stay with him until he wakes up. He will need me here when he is told."

Peter left Marika sitting by JJ's side. She watched him sleep, wondering how to tell him such tragic news and how he would react.

Several hours later she heard him call her name. "Mother, are you still here?'

"Yes, I'm here. I have been waiting for you to wake up."

"I thought I was dreaming. Where am I?"

"Goa field hospital."

"How did you get here?"

"Peter brought me. Do you remember what happened?"

"Not really. I have been awake off and on trying to remember. I was driving down the road. there was a bright flash and the next thing I knew I was flying through the air."

"Yes, that's what I was told too, that you were thrown out of the jeep."

He laid there quietly then asked, "Chaim and Henry were with me. How are they?"

Marika swallowed and tears fill her eyes. "You are the only survivor."

At first, he didn't say a word. "This is my fault."

"No JJ, it was accident."

"I was driving and should have seen the mine on the road. We were laughing and fooling around and I wasn't paying close enough attention. I killed them."

"No, that's not true. You didn't know the road was mined."

"Mother, you don't understand. They were in my unit and I was responsible for them. I should have been paying more attention."

He turned his face away from here but not before she saw the tears flowing down his cheeks. After a while his breathing became regular and Marika knew he had gone back to sleep.

She sat beside the bed holding his hand. *What is going to happen to him now? Will he ever forgive himself? The responsibility lies on the shoulders of those who wanted this war. As usual our young men and women end up paying the price to fulfill the wishes of the old.*

FORTY-THREE

Marika was concerned because JJ was quiet and withdrawn. He spoke if asked a direct question, but. mostly ignored her. Several times she tried to convince him the accident was not his fault but he didn't want to believe her.

After the fourth attempt he snapped at her. "Mother stop. I don't want to talk about what happened. Nothing will change the fact my friends are dead. All I want to do is forget."

After that, no matter what she tried to talk about he ignored her. She stayed with him until late that first night and returned early the next morning. The second evening she dozed off in the chair and was wakened by him thrashing around in his bed, sweating profusely and moaning.

At first, she wasn't sure what to do so she held his hand and talked quietly to him. "You are dreaming JJ. Everything is okay, Try and relax and go back to sleep."

After several minutes he quieted down. Several hours later he cried out again but this time he didn't wake up and fell back into a deep sleep.

When Peter arrived next morning, she told him about the nightmares. "I'm not surprised. He has been through a very traumatic event. His sub-conscious is trying to find a way to deal with the situation."

"Do you think he will ever be himself again?"

"Yes, but not for a long time. He is young and resilient and will recover, but won't ever forget. I think the best thing to do is take him back home. I'm sure he will be more comfortable there."

Three days later JJ was allowed to go home. The cuts around his eye healed well and the concussion symptoms lessened. The bruises were turning yellow and green and his swollen face was nearly back to normal.

But instead of things improving once he got home, they got worse. He spent all his time in his room with the blinds closed and the lights off. When Marika tried to talk to him, he screamed at her to get out. At night she listened to him cry out from his dreams. As a mother she felt helpless.

Several days later when Peter stopped by to check on them, she burst into tears. "He won't let me in his room, and screams at me to leave him alone. He isn't eating and at night relives his accident over and over. I don't know what to do for him anymore. Do you think you could try to talk to him?"

Shrugging his shoulders Peter replied. "I guess I can try, I'm not sure that will do any good though."

He walked over to the door of JJ's room and knocked twice. "It's me. Peter. Can I come in?"

After several seconds JJ replied, "Yes, but don't bring her with you."

Without hesitation Peter walked in and Marika heard him say, "why is it so dark in here and it stinks to high heaven? When was the last time you had a shower?" The door closed and Marika heard no more.

Peter walked over to the window and pulled up the blind. "Why are you hurting your mother? She is only trying to help. Now tell me what's going on."

Marika made herself a cup of tea and sat at the kitchen table waiting. *If Peter can't get through to him, I don't know who can.*

At times she heard them yelling at each other. There was a crash and then she heard JJ's deep sobs. After that it was quiet.

Two hours later Peter came out. His eyes red rimmed from tears and he looked exhausted.

"He is going to come out, clean himself up and asked if you would make him something to eat. A word of caution, don't ask any questions. He will talk when he is ready. He needs to make some decisions about what he wants to do with the rest of his life."

"I don't understand Peter."

"Marika, he left here a boy and returned a man. He knows what he doesn't want but needs to figure out what he does. Have you ever told him Jesse was his father?"

"No, I've been meaning to, but keep putting it off. It never seems like the right time."

"Well, don't tell him now. He has enough to think about."

* * *

They spent the next few days in companionable silence. JJ went for long walks and Marika worried the whole time he was gone. Both avoided talking about the war.

One day when he returned, he said to her," Mother I've made a decision. I am going to resign my military commission. I think the time has come for us to leave all of this," he said sweeping his hand around the room. "This is the past. If we stay here there is no future, just more of the same. How old are you mother?"

"I'm thirty-three. Why do you ask?"

"You are young yet. You need to get away from here and experience life."

"JJ I have experienced "life" as you call it and most of it, I never want to relive again."

JJ looked and saw the pain in her eyes. "Why don't you ever talk about it?"

Instead of answering his question she replied, "I have a good life here. I am happy. I am grateful to still have you and that's all I ask for."

"No. All you are doing is existing. Don't you want more than living in a Kibbutz until you die. Don't you want to get married again?"

"No, I don't. Your father was the best man I could have known."

As he spoke Marika realized that she had never considered leaving the Kibbutz, moving away and doing something different.

"What are you thinking about." She asked.

"I want to go to university. I am a good student and I want to get as far away from the military as I can. I have bled for this country surely, they can't ask more of me. I don't know what my purpose in life is, but I know it's not getting shot at and seeing my friends killed in front of my eyes."

"If you go to University, what would you take."

"I haven't thought that far yet. One thing I know for certain is if I go, I want you to come with me."

Marika stopped and thought for several seconds. *If he leaves there is nothing for me here. Maybe he has the right idea.*

"Yes, I can do that but I don't know where I will find a job. I can't sit around and do nothing."

JJ leaned over and hugged her. "We will worry about that when the time comes."

Leaving the Kibbutz wasn't as difficult as she thought it would be. *I will miss the people I work and live with but there is nothing holding me here. I hate to leave Maria but I know she is reunited with Jesse and her family.*

Living in the city was a new experience for JJ. The city was noisy, smelly and people were always in a hurry. He longed for the quiet open spaces and regimen of the Kibbutz.

When he mentioned moving him and his mother to the city and his reasons why Peter had encouraged him and gone so far as to locate an apartment and arranged for their few belongings to be shipped to them.

He spent his first few days at the university trying.to find his way around. The campus was bigger than the Kibbutz he was raised in. He got lost several times, first trying to register and then looking for the book store. Locating and attending his first classes were the easiest part. In the Kibbutz class sizes were small and he knew each person, but here some of his classes contained as many as one hundred people.

Within a short period of time, he noticed people staring at him, and whispering as he passed. Complete strangers were stopping him to talk about the Believers. Others simply walked up to him and touched his arm.

Each day, he passed an old lady, dressed in rags, begging on the same street corner. When he was able, he put a coin into the cup on the sidewalk beside her. Each time he walked away, he felt her eyes boring into his back. She was always mumbling in a language he didn't understand.

He got into the habit of meeting his new friends at a coffee shop before class but this time as he approached the corner, she began staring at him. She got to her feet and began walking toward him. He began to feel uncomfortable.

"Is it you Jesse?"

JJ ignored her and kept walking. She stepped in front of him, fell to her knees, grabbed his hand and began kissing it. "Hallelujah, you have returned to save us."

He pulled his hand back. He didn't know what to do and a crowd was beginning to gather around them.

"Get up. I have no idea what you are talking about."

"It's him," she cried out. "Look at his face. I am telling you it's him. Jesse has returned."

The crowd edged closer. "Is it true? Has our Jesse come back to us?"

"No, you are mistaken," he called out. "I am not Jesse, nor am I related to him. This is all a big mistake. How can I be? Jesse was murdered more than nineteen years ago?"

That seemed to get their attention. He heard a man say "He is right, how can that be him? The old lady is crazy."

"I know who I am looking at. I cooked for his followers for many years." She cried out.

Another walked over and stared at him. "It is uncanny how much you look like him though,".

"I am not him," he exclaimed and hurriedly walked away.

He was still troubled when he returned home that evening. *What was that old lady talking about? Surely, she must out of her mind if she thinks I am Jesse.*

Marika noticed the troubled look on his face. "You look upset, did something happen at the University today?"

"Yes, the strangest thing," he replied, and proceeded to tell her about the incident.

Marika was stunned. Her deepest fear was becoming a reality. *What have I done? I should have told him a long time ago, now he will never forgive me for keeping this secret from him. I wish Peter were here so I could ask his advice.*

"People stare at me as if I am some kind of celebrity and this is not the first time, stranger things have happened. What do I do mother?"

"What did you say to them?"

"I reminded them Jesse has been dead for over nineteen years, and they were mistaken. I tell them I am not him."

"Continue your life as you have been. Eventually people will get used to the idea that, although you look like Jesse, he is dead. They will stop after a while.

Rumors have persisted for years that Jesse had a son who would become the new leader of the Believers, but that is all they are. No one has ever been able to prove he fathered a child.

Personally, I think it is possible that woman was deeply traumatized at some point and her belief in Jesse is what keeps her going. Many people suffered greatly, especially those in the comps. They were beaten, starved and lived in horrible conditions. and all because Jesse would not bow to Heinrich's wishes.

If she keeps this up gently keep reminding her that you are not him. Maybe one day she will recognize that fact. Be kind to her."

After that experience JJ and the old woman reached an unspoken agreement. Each day she would look at him and say "I know it is you" and each day he patted her on the shoulder and repeated the phrase. "I am not Him."

Then one day she was gone. He often wondered who she was and where she went, but didn't make any effort to find out. *Best to leave things the way they are.*

FORTY -FOUR

"You know that you don't need to ask Marika, you are welcome any time. I'll have tea waiting when you get here. How long do you think you will be? "

That was a stupid question he chided himself. *I wonder why she sounds so upset. Has something happened with JJ.?*

The words of their argument echoed in Marika's mind as she knocked on Peter's door. When he opened it, she stood there crying. He took her hand, led her into the living room and helped her off with her coat.

"Sit here, the tea is ready. I have some of that poppy seed cake you are so fond of."

Marika sat on one of the chairs, her hands clenched tightly in her lap, struggling to get her emotions under control.

"To what do I owe this pleasure?" he asked, placing the tea tray on a coffee table and handing her a cup.

"Do you remember I told you that JJ had a girlfriend, somebody he cares deeply for?'

"Yes," Peter replied.

"He brought her home for supper this evening so I could meet her." She swallowed and once again her eyes filled with tears. "I think she is Heinrich's daughter. No wait, I don't think, I know she is."

Peter was shocked. "I didn't know Heinrich was married. At least I never heard he was."

"I don't know either, but he could still have a child. From what she told me her parents never married and she doesn't know her father's name."

Marika stood up and began pacing back and forth across the room. "When I asked, she said her mother was alive and her father was dead. JJ took her back to the university and when he returned home, I forbade him to see her again. We argued and he stormed out and I don't know where he is."

"What did you hope to accomplish by telling him that? All you have done is given him one more reason to continue seeing her. The forbidden fruit is always the sweetest."

Marika turned on Peter practically shouting. "You tell me what I'm supposed to do? You were there. You watched Heinrich kill Jesse in cold blood. Do you think I want my son to be associated with the daughter of a man like that? What am I supposed to do, turn a blind eye?"

Peter patted the cushion on the couch beside him. "Come and sit down."

"I'm not going to change my mind. You know as well as I do there is no way I can allow this to continue."

"You may not have a choice. JJ is a grown man and capable of making his own decisions. Now tell me more about this young lady."

"I don't know much. She is an exchange student from Bern University. He father is dead and she was raised by her mother. All I know is that she lived in Strausberg before moving to Bern."

"How did they meet?"

"At the University – they are both studying history so I assume they are in the same classes."

Peter let Marika talk. Finally, he interrupted her. "Do you think she knows Heinrich is her father?"

"I don't know? I doubt if either one of them knows much about the other or what went on before they were born. I know I haven't said much to JJ. I didn't think he needed to know how bad it was for all of us."

"I don't imagine her mother was shouting from the roof tops that Sophya was Heinrich's daughter. I know I would keep that secret from mine if I had one.

We came to the promised land to start a new life and you have given JJ everything you possible could. I am sure her mother did the same. She is not responsible for who her father is. She didn't ask to be born into that situation."

Marika looked at him, "what are you trying to tell me?"

"Marika, Sophya is not responsible for the sins of her father. Put yourself in her shoes. If she knew Heinrich was her father she would be devastated. When she learns the truth, she will need all the love and support she can get from others. Isn't that what Jesse tried to teach us? Didn't he tell us to forgive those who have hurt us and treat others as we would want to be treated?"

"Yes, but…"

"You need to understand that this child is not the one responsible for your pain. At some point both she and JJ will need to be told, but forbidding him to see her is not the way to go. You need to tell him, and then let him make his own decision. We can't hold the children responsible for what the parents did, or didn't do."

Marika sighed. "You are right as usual. I was so upset when I saw her, I couldn't help myself. I will explain this to JJ when the time is right – just not yet."

Marika laid her head on Peter's shoulder. "What would I do wit out you my old friend? We have been through so much together."

Suddenly Peter under stood Jean's words. *This is still part of the journey of protecting Marika. I am doing exactly what Jesse asked of me. In my own way I am still fulfilling my promise to him. Sometimes I wonder if he knew what was going to happen after he was gone, but I guess we will never know.*

FORTY-FIVE

After moving to the city and getting settled Marika felt restless. In the Kibbutz she was busy either in the office or helping where she was needed, now her days felt long and empty.

One evening, during supper she said to JJ. "I have decided that tomorrow I am going to start looking for a job."

"Why? You should be using this time to relax and enjoy life. There is no need to rush into anything. Do you have any idea what kind of a job you want to look for?"

"I don't know what's out there. The only real work I have done was at the Kibbutz. Once, a long time ago, I tried to be a waitress but, which, if I remember correctly, didn't go very well. Do you think there are any openings at the university for cleaning staff?"

"No way. I won't allow you to do that. I will not have my mother reduced to sweeping floors or cleaning toilets."

"It is honest job, not hard work and will give me something to do."

"I do have one request though," JJ said, "find a job that isn't dealing with what happened in the past. You need to put that behind you. You've lived too long with the sorrow."

"JJ in this country people will always be haunted by the past. Many suffered, lost family members and have been unrooted from their homes and all they held dear. You can't expect them not to remember. Some will never recover, but there are those determined to never allow such a thing to happen again."

"What about the Believer code, treat others as you want to be treated? Forgive those who hurt you. How does that fit in?" he scoffed.

Marika looked at her son. "You really do have a problem accepting those teachings, don't you?"

"I do after seeing my friends killed. How do I forgive the person who put the mine on the road? How can thousands of people forgive what was done to them? I wonder what Jesse would think now?"

"Why are you so angry? The only way forward is to learn from the mistakes of the past and not repeat them."

"I know you are right but where does that thinking get anyone? We will always be fighting to hold the land we were promised. My friends will have died for nothing."

Marika realized how much he was still hurting from the war. She went over to him and put her arms around him and held him tightly. He hugged her back.

He smiled at her. "If you are determined to get a job you could check the Help Wanted ads in the newspaper and I will see if there are any at the university. Just promise me it won't be scrubbing floors."

"Agreed."

The next morning Marika left home, purchased a newspaper at a vendor, went to an outdoor cafe to see what, if any, jobs were available. Several small ads caught her eye.

Volunteers Needed

The Believer's Museum is seeking volunteers to work as a receptionists three to four hours a week. Duties may vary. No experience necessary. Apply in person.

Refuge Settlement Committee

Seeking part time help. Experience not necessary but would be an asset. Applications are being accepted each afternoon between 2 and 4 p.m. Apply in person only.

"I can do that," she exclaimed. Looking at her watch, she said, "If I hurry, I still have time today."

That evening when JJ returned home Marika was excited. "I found a job today."

"That was fast," he said. "Where may I ask?"

"At the Refugee Resettlement Center. When I explained what I did at the Kibbutz they hired me on the spot."

He sighed. "I was hoping you would find something different, not get involved with the same old stuff."

"Stop worrying about me. I'll be fine. I am used to helping others this way. I am going to be more involved with locating families and providing identification documents."

"If that's what makes you happy but promise me one thing, you will quit if the job becomes too much."

"I promise," she answered.

The ad for volunteering at the Believers Museum intrigued her. The more she thought about going the more she felt as though she was being called to apply.

Finally, gathering her nerve she phoned the museum. "I saw an ad in the newspaper that you are looking for volunteers. Is the position still open?"

"We are always looking. Volunteers are in short supply. Are you interested?"

"Yes, but I would have to find a way to work around my current Job."

"No problem. Are you able to come by on Thursday at 2:00?"

"Yes."

"Good I will see you then."

Marika was apprehensive as she approached the museum. *I wonder how much this will have to do with Jesse? I miss him terribly and this might bring back too many memories.*

The building, made of stone, was old and dated. Chips appearing to come from bullets marred the stone work. There was talk of building a new museum in the future and she could see why.

She was surprised when she walked through the front door. Great care had been taken to make the entrance bright and cheery. An elderly lady was sitting at the reception desk. Racks filled with books and pamphlets stood along one wall.

She walked over and introduced herself, "My name is Marika. I have an interview to volunteer here."

The lady studied a piece of paper. "Yes, I see your name. Have you visited us before?"

"No, we just moved to the city and my son is attending the university."

"First, I think you need to see what you are volunteering for. Some find it too hard to be around the memories."

The two women walked down a short hallway. "The Believers as a faith has been around for centuries. In this annex we have begun a collection of ancient weapons, scrolls and first-hand accounts of our people through the ages."

Marika would like to have stopped and spent more time at each display. As it was, she had to hurry to catch up.

"Annex B is the more recent times, the last two hundred years. Life remained relatively calm until the first great war. After that there was a renewed interest in our beliefs and more young people became interested in their history.

During the second war the "youth movement" as we call it, began flocking to our faith. Life was hard and our faith offered a renewed sense of hope."

They stopped in front of a large display of photographs, including several of Jesse and his followers. "There were two new dynamic leaders Jean Baptiste and Jesse who people chose to follow…"

Maria gasped. Unconsciously she moved to the one which showed a close up of Jesse's face and ran her fingers down his cheek. Tears filled her eyes. She remembered clearly the day this was taken. Quickly she scanned the picture to see if she was in it, then breathed a sigh of relief when she wasn't.

"Did you know Jesse?" the woman asked.

"Yes," Marika replied, reaching into her purse for a handkerchief. "He was a close friend of mine."

The lady gave her several seconds to get her emotions under control then said, "shall we continue? Annex C recalls the last years of Heinrich's rule and the British mandate."

Although every attempt had been made to make the room appear bright and feel peaceful Marika wasn't prepared for the starkness of the displays. There was a large glass box filled with thousands of shoes of all sizes, another packed with suitcases. Framed newspaper clippings screamed out from every available inch of wall space. There was a picture of Jesse hanging on the cross and two of Heinrich and Rotter's bodies swinging from the lamp post.

Further down was a picture of refugees coming ashore, most alone, broken and emaciated. The last display was of the British leaving with accompanying newspaper articles.

As they re-entered the reception area Marika was trembling. The last half hour had been a voyage into the memories of her past.

"Are you okay my dear? You are as white as a ghost. Can I get you something – a glass of water? Do you need to sit down?"

"I am fine"," Marika replied. "I just need a minute. I am one of those who arrived by boat and lived in a Kibbutz while raising my son." *This is where I need to be no matter what JJ says.*

"Still interested in the job," the old lady asked. "At this point some say they can't be here and leave."

"Yes, I am, now more than ever. I would like to volunteer here."

"Can you start tomorrow, the eleven to three shift. That is our busiest time of the day, and there are usually two of us. If a school tour is coming, we have others who volunteer for that."

The lady showed her where the museum guides and few souvenirs for sale were kept. A display of books from local authors was being set up along one wall.

"Oh, I forgot to mention, there is a small room behind the reception desk we call the quiet room for those who feel overwhelmed. There is a recording device and pen and paper for those who wish to recount their stories. Some find this brings them a degree of closure."

"I am looking forward to being here," Marika said as a group of people came through the door.

Before she left Marika signed the guest book and read some of the comments. "Government propaganda." Variations of "we know this never really happened" were several of the others. Another read, "what a waste of time".

A new resolve filled her. *I will do whatever I can to make sure this madness never happens again.*

That evening at supper Marika told JJ "I took. a volunteer position at the Believers Museum today."

He stopped eating. "Do you think that's a good idea?"

Marika smiled at him. "Yes, it's the perfect place for me." *I feel closer to Jesse when I am there. I don't know if I will ever stop missing him.*

FORTY- SIX

JJ 's last economics class, comparing a enterprise system to a state-owned system, was loud and conflict filled. Students were vocal about which would work best in the Promise Land. One girl was louder than the rest. Afterwards JJ went to the library to do more research to try and understand the differences.

"Just who do you think you are?" a pretty blond woman, about his age, was pointing her finger at him as she marched toward his table.

He looked around. He was the only person in the library. "Me? I have no idea what you are talking about."

"You made me look like a fool in our Economics class."

He grinned. "You managed to do that to yourself. I wasn't the one so upset I was banging my fist on the table."

Hands on her hips she continued to glare at him.

He stuck out his hand, "My name is JJ and you are?"

Shaking hands with him she replied "my name is Sophya Benoit, an exchange student from Bern university."

JJ pulled out a chair. "Please sit-down Sophya Benoit from Bern University and we will discuss this like civilized people."

Sophya blushed. "I do tend to come on a little strong at times."

"Yes, you do. Are you always that vocal about what you believe in. How did you end up here as an exchange student?"

She didn't answer his question and instead said, "My mother and I live in Strausberg and I earned a full scholarship to Bern University. All I ever heard was how badly the Believers had been treated and how wonderful this man Jesse was. When I challenged my professor to prove what he was teaching he couldn't. Stupid people caught up in a propagandas machine spewing nothing but lies.".

"If I may ask, how have you come to that conclusion?"

"That's what we were taught in school."

"Where is Strausberg? I don't remember hearing that name before."

"It's a small town in the mountains just outside the Brussian border."

"What are you studying?"

"History, the same as you. In fact, we have several classes together."

"Oh, I wasn't aware of that. I don't remember seeing you. So how did you end up here?"

"I wanted to see for myself if there was any truth to the lies and propaganda. An older woman, a survivor of one the camps spoke to our class and something about the way she talked made me curious. When the opportunity arose, I applied to come as an exchange student."

"Have you found what you are looking for?"

"I believe something happened, that is a fact, but there is so much hysteria around this Jesse person I'm not sure. He was probably a charlatan of the worst kind."

J J looked at his watch, then began gathering his books. "I must go; my mother is expecting me for supper."

"Do you come here to study often?" Sophya asked.

"Nearly every day. It is quiet and I can think. See you around." He said walking away leaving her sitting there.

She is something else. How can she not believe when the evidence is all around her? Does the world not believe the truth? If she lived in the Kibbutz and listened to the survivor's stories, she would know what is true and what isn't.

Several days later Sophya again appeared at J J's table.in the library.

"May I sit with you?" she asked.

"Of course." He rose and pulled out a chair for her and noticed she had been crying.

"Has something happened? You look upset."

"As part of an assignment several of us toured the Believer's Museum today. There was a picture that bothered me. I suddenly realized there is more to the Believers story than I was led to believe. I am such a fool."

"Here, sit down. You are not a fool Sophya. The biggest problem in this country is that people need to stop reliving the past and move on with their lives. Do you want to tell me about this picture.? To be honest I haven't been there myself."

"There was a picture of Heinrich pointing a gun at a man who was bleeding and badly beaten. The caption told of Heinrich executing Jesse the leader of the Believers. There was something about that picture that filled me with horror. I can't explain what I felt. What a terrible way to die."

J J stood up, picked up his jacket from the back of the chair. "Come. Let's get out of here and go for a walk. There is a little coffee shop not far from here that serves the best coffee I have tasted."

They sat and talked for hours. Sophya told him about her life in Strasberg and he told her about his life growing up in the Kibbutz.

After that, they met at the coffee shop every day. Sometimes they took their coffee outside and walked in the park across the street. Other times they studied together in the library.

One evening after supper J J said to Marika," I met someone at the university and I would like you to meet her."

Marika was surprised but didn't say anything. JJ was an attractive man and it was inevitable that he would meet somebody.

"Tell me about her."

As he spoke Marika became aware of his feelings for her. "I would like to meet this girl. Why don't you invite her here for supper on Sunday?"

"I must warn you first, she can be very outspoken at times. She says what she thinks but is a good person."

FORTY-SEVEN

When she heard the front door open Marika turned away from the stove, removed her apron and patted down her hair. JJ was bringing his girlfriend home for supper and she was anxious to meet the girl who captured his heart.

"Hey mom, we're here," he called out.

"I am in the kitchen, supper is ready."

She heard footsteps and then the words, "Mom, I would like you to meet Sophya Benoit. Sophya this is my mother."

Marika turned to look at the young lady and froze. In front of her stood a person closely resembling Heinrich Mollen, the man who killed her husband She dropped the plate she was holding in her hand.

"Mom, are you alright?" J J asked. "You are as pale as a ghost. Here, sit down," he said pulling out a chair from the table.

"I am sorry," Marika replied. Then she said to Sophya, "you remind me of somebody who died a long time ago." she added, her voice flat, devoid of emotion.

JJ handed her a glass of water. "Here drink this."

To Sophya he said, "My mother lived through the persecution of the Believers before we moved here."

Sophya smiled, "I am very pleased to meet you," she said putting out her hand. Marika reached out and shook hands with her.

"Forgive me," Marika said, "I don't know what came over me."

Is it possible that she is some relation to Heinrich? Oh God I hope not. If she is, I can't allow JJ to be involved with her any longer.

J J was concerned. He had never seen his mother act like this. "Should I set the table for you?" he asked.

Reaching into the cupboard he removed three plates and three wine glasses. "Sophya maybe you could put these on the dining room table for me. I'll bring the silverware."

When she left the room JJ looked at his mom. "You are acting strange. Is everything okay?"

"Yes, I am fine. There is nothing to worry about."

"Who does she remind you of?"

"It doesn't' matter. He is dead, and it was a long time ago."

While JJ and Sophya were out of the room Marika took a few moments to compose herself.

Several days ago, a group of students had come into the museum for a school project. One voice particularly stood out. "Can you believe this crap? That Jesse was a man who took advantage of people at their lowest point in life. He probably made a fortune off them. I can't understand why so many thought he was the answer to their prayers. I guess their expectations were low."

"Do you really believe that," another commented. "Those who knew him will argue with you"

"Are you telling me you believe all of this?"

"Yes, actually I do. His teaching was based upon forgiving those who hurt us."

"Not me. I don't forgive anybody. I would rather find a way to get even."

The voice she heard disparaging of Jesse was the same as the girl JJ brought home. She busied herself putting the food into bowls and carrying them into the dining room. When she entered the room, she heard them laughing and teasing each other.

Marika was quiet during the meal. JJ did all the talking, telling her about a new project at school he was excited about.

When the opportunity arose, she asked Sophya. "Where do your parents live?"

"There is only my mother and she lives in Strausberg." A shadow crossed her face. "I don't know who my father is. My parents never married and mother refuses to tell me his name."

"I am sorry to hear that. J J tells me you are an exchange student at the University."

"Yes, from the University of Bern. I am studying history."

The more Sophya talked about herself the more concerned Marika became. She looked at her son. *Oh, JJ what have you done. This is an impossible situation.*

JJ left to take Sophya back to the University leaving Marika to tidy up the kitchen and wash the dishes.

"Your mother doesn't like me," Sophya said to him.

"What is there not to like?" he replied.

"I could see it in her eyes."

"I asked her and she said you reminded her of someone she knew a long time ago. She suffered greatly under Heinrich's rule, that is probably what you saw."

Pulling Sophya into his arms he kissed her. "I will talk to her. I'm sure you are mistaken. My mother is very accepting of the people she meets."

When he returned home, he was upset. Confronting Marika he asked "What was with the third degree? Your questions made Sophya uncomfortable. She thinks you hate her."

Marika took a deep breath. "I don't want you to see her any more. She's not the right girl for you."

"What is going on? This isn't like you."

Marika knew what she was going to say would upset him. "Stay away from her JJ, she will break your heart. Nothing good will come of the two of you being together."

Marika turned and walked away from her son. Her head was pounding and she felt nauseous.

What do I do now. She will destroy us both.

"How can you say that? This is the first time you met her. You don't know anything about her." JJ called after her.

Turning around and facing him she replied "I know what I need to know and that's enough. She isn't who she says she is and I am asking you not to see her anymore."

Minutes later she heard the front door slam. *What a mess. I never thought something like this would be possible, but here we are.*

FORTY-EIGHT

After JJ stormed out Marika paced the floor. *How could this happen? Of all people for JJ to meet and care for is the daughter of the man who murdered his father and made our lives a living hell.*

Without hesitation she picked up the phone and dialed Peter's number. When he answered she said Can I come over? I need to talk to you."

"You know you don't need to ask, you are welcome here any time. I'll have tea waiting when you get here. How long do you think you will be?"

That was a stupid question he chided himself. *I wonder why she sounds so upset. Has something happened to JJ.*

The words of their argument echoed in her head as she knocked on Peter's door. When he opened the door, she began to cry. He took her hand, led her to the living room and helped her off with her coat.

"Wait here, the tea is ready. I have some of the poppy cake you are so fond of."

Marika sat on one of the chairs, her hands clenched tightly in her lap and struggled to get her emotions under control.

"To what do I owe this pleasure?" he asked, placing a tray on the short table in front of him he handed her a cup. He offered her a piece of cake but she refused it.

"Do you remember I told you JJ had a girlfriend – someone he deeply cared for."

"Yes," Peter replied.

"He brought her home for supper this evening so I could meet her." She swallowed and once again her eyes filled with tears. "I think she is Heinrich's daughter. No wait, I don't think, I know she is. She looks just like him."

Peter was shocked. "I didn't know Heinrich was married. At least I never heard he was."

"I didn't know either but he could still have fathered a child. From what she told me her parents never married and she doesn't know her father's name."

She stood up and began pacing back and forth across the room. "When I asked, she said her mother was alive and her father was dead."

After we finished eating JJ took her back to the university and, when he returned, I forbid him to see her again. We argued, he stormed off and I don't know where he is."

"What did you hope to accomplish by telling him that? All you have done is give him another reason to continue seeing her. The forbidden fruit is always the sweetest."

Marika turned to Peter practically shouting. "You tell me what I am supposed to do? You were there. You saw Heinrich kill Jesse in cold blood. Do you think I want my son to be associated with the daughter of a man like that? What do I do, turn a blind eye?"

Peter patted the cushion on the sofa beside him. "Come and sit down?"

"I'm not going to change my mind. You know as well as I do there is no way I can allow this to continue."

Taking her hands in his he said, "you may not have much choice. JJ is a grown man and more than capable of making his own decision. Now, tell me more about this young lady."

"I don't know much except she is an exchange student from Bern university. Her father is dead .and she was raised by her mother. All I know is that she lived in Strausberg before moving to Bern."

"How did they meet?"

"At the university. They are both studying history so I assume they are in the same classes."

He let Marika talk. Finally, he interrupted her."Do you think she knows Heinrich is her father?"

"I don't know. I doubt if either one knows much about the other or what went on before they were born. I know I haven't told JJ much. I didn't think he needed to know how bad life was for all of us."

"I don't imagine her mother is exactly shouting from the roof tops either that Sophya is Heinrich's daughter. I know I would keep her a secret if she were mine.

We came to the promise land to start a new life and you have given JJ everything you possibly could and I am sure her mother did the same. You can't hold her responsible for who her father is. She didn't ask to be born into that situation."

Marika looked at him, "what are you trying to tell me?"

"You must understand Sophya is not responsible for the actions of her father. Put yourself in her shoes. If she finds out Heinrich is her father she will be devastated. When she learns the truth, and she will one day, she is going to need all of the love and support she can get.

Isn't this what Jesse tried to teach us? Didn't he tell us to forgive those who have hurt us and to treat others as you want to be treated?"

"Yes, but...."

"There are no buts Marika. You need to understand this child is not the one responsible for your pain. At some point both she and JJ need to be told, but forbidding him is not the way to go. You need to tell him then let him make his own decision. We can't hold children responsible for what their parents did, or didn't do."

Marika sighed. "You are right as usual. I was so upset when I saw her, I couldn't help myself. I will explain this to JJ, but not right now."

She laid her head on Peter's shoulder. "What would I do without you my old friend? We have been through so much together."

Suddenly Jean's words came back to him. *This is still part of my journey to protect Marika. I am doing exactly what Jesse asked of me. In my own way I am fulfilling my promise to him. Sometimes I wonder if he knew what was going to happen after he was gone. I guess we will never know for sure.*

FORTY-NINE

The conflict between JJ and Marika continued to escalate after Marika tried to stop him from seeing Sophya. One evening, several weeks later, she was resting when he came into her room and sat down on the side of the bed.

"Mother please, we need to talk about Sophya."

"No JJ we don't. I'm not going to change my mind. The sooner you break this off with her the better it will be for both of us.

"Mother you don't seem to understand. I love Sophya and she loves me. Are you ever going to tell me why you are acting this way?"

"No, I'm not. You are the one who doesn't understand. I have nothing against her. She seems like a decent, personable young woman."

"Then what's your problem?"

"This goes back to the time before Jesse died."

"Of course it does. I am sick about hearing what happened a long time ago. This country is built on ghosts. People live in the past. Look at you, - a perfect example. All you do is focus on what happened, you act like you are ashamed to be alive."

"That's enough young man. You have no idea what we went through. I had it easy compared to many. Jesse for one. He lost all of his family in a massacre except his mother and sister. Six hundred people were killed in a single day and only a few survived. He was a great man and in the end that's what got him killed."

"I am sick and tired of hearing about Jesse. Jesse this, Jesse that. I don't want to be like him. For your sake I follow our religion but I do not believe in everything he said. I don't want to be compared to him. – ever."

Marika was stunned. "How can you say those things? He was a great man. He wanted us to live by his teachings."

"What? Teach people to be meek and mild and forgive every person who ever hurt them. No thank you. Let me ask you one thing? Have you ever forgiven Heinrich for killing Jesse?"

Marika stared at him. Nobody had ever asked her this question before.

"No, I have not."

"Then you are as big a hypocrite as everybody else. You all talk about forgiveness but that is all it is – talk. If you did, you wouldn't always be living in the past, but be looking forward to the future. I am done."

"But many people, including you father gave their lives for him," she stated.

"I don't care what my father believed or died for. That man Jesse you all looked up to was the cause of the death and destruction that took place. Because of him thousands of people died, and for what?"

He got off the bed and moved toward the door.

"JJ wait", Marika called out "I didn't know you felt like that. Maybe we can talk this over."

"No, I've had enough. I am going to find Sophya. Maybe her country has the right idea – a government that controls everything."

Marika had never seen him so angry before. "Please don't leave. We can go to Peter..."

"No. there is no working this out. No talking with Peter. I am so done with all of that Believer crap."

Marika sat there in shock. She heard the door open and JJ leave the apartment. *He is so much like his father.* She wiped the tears from her eyes.

"Help me, Jesse. I don't know what to do. This is not what you wanted for our son."

* * *

JJ was still angry when he arrived at Sophya's dormitory door.

"What's wrong," she asked when she saw the look on his face.

"That woman drives me crazy."

"Who, your mother?"

"Who else? I told her in no uncertain terms that I am done with the Believers and everything they stand for."

"How did she take that? I don't imagine she was very happy."

"I am so done with hearing about the past. Why can't she see this is a different world and times have changed?"

"You are right JJ. She shouldn't expect you to feel the same as she does. We have our own lives to live. When we are married, we will leave here – go back to Bern, away from what she expects of you."

JJ pulled her to him and put his arms around her. "One more year and then I will graduate and move to Bern with you."

"We can go next term. You can finish your degree there."

"No. As much as I would like to, I need to stay with my mother for now. I'm all she has."

As he held Sophya, he couldn't help but wonder *Am I making the right decision?*

FIFTY

The pain of fighting with his mother was almost too much to bear. One evening he found himself knocking on Peter's door looking for someone to talk to. Usually confident in his actions, this evening his shoulders were slumped, his eyes red rimmed, and his demeanor agitated.

Peter opened the door, took one look at J J and said "You look like hell. Come in, I just made a pot of coffee. My doctor tells me I shouldn't drink it in the evenings but old habits die hard."

JJ closed the door then walked over to the tall window overlooking the plaza below. Peter came back into the room carrying a tray with two cups, cream and sugar, a carafe of fresh coffee and a plate of cookies.

He watched the young man staring out the window for several moments, then asked, "why are you here JJ?"

Jesse turned around. "Mother has forbidden me to continue seeing my girlfriend, Sophya."

Peter pretended that Marika hadn't been there and talked with him. "This is the first I have heard that you had a serious girlfriend. Tell me what this is about."

"I don't really know," JJ responded, "I invited Sophya over for supper so they could meet each other and when I introduced her mother turned as white as a sheet and looked like she had seen a ghost. I wanted them to meet and get to know each other."

"Did she say anything?"

"Only that Sophya reminded her of someone she knew from back home a long time ago. She scared me Uncle Peter, I didn't know what to think. I've never seen that look on her face before. Then all through supper she gave Sophya the third degree."

"What kind of questions did she ask?"

"Who her mother was, who her father was, where was she born and raised, stuff like that. It's not like her to pry into people's affairs that way."

"Then what happened?"

"After supper I took Sophya back to the University and when I got home, she was upset and forbid me to see her again."

"Did she give you an explanation?"

"No, I didn't give her a chance. I stormed out of the house and went for a walk. I don't like to argue when she is that upset."

"Has anybody ever told you about your father and mother?"

"No, she doesn't talk about it. When I ask, she doesn't say much. I know he was one of the followers of the Believers and he was killed for his beliefs. I know you rescued her from behind the Brussian wall and brought her here."

Peter refilled their coffee cups and passed JJ the plate of cookies.

"You may need to sit down after you hear what I am about to tell you. I am going to tell you something you are not prepared to hear. Jesse was not just one of the followers of the Believers, he was their leader and your father. He was a man born for a specific purpose He was quiet, introspective, and believed in the rule, treat others as you want to be treated. He believed in forgiveness and gave us hope for a better way of life."

"Jesse is my father? The same Jesse who led the Believers? Why hasn't she told me this before? How could she keep this from me?" JJ shouted at Peter, his face as white as a ghost. "Do you really expect me to believe you?"

"Yes, because it is the truth."

JJ collapsed on the couch, his arms on his knees, his head in his hands. He looked up at Peter, "In some way, I always knew she was keeping something from me."

"Why do you say that?"

"The way she kept me hidden and protected. The way people stared at me when I started university, others who wanted to touch me and the crazy old lady who thought I was Jesse reincarnated. I remember once looking at his picture and thinking we looked somewhat similar."

"Did you tell your mother about any of this?"

"Just about the old lady. I didn't think she needed to know everything. She worries too much about me as it is."

"Believe me, she had good reason for doing what she did, but you have to talk to her and let her explain."

"Did you know my father well? Is that why you do so much for us?"

"Yes. I first met your father when he was a young man, probably not much older than you are today. He was studying to become a minister in his home town and became disillusioned when he found out the Elders were greedy and taking advantage of the people in his village. He left home and made his way to the city.

We lived in an alley and ate from a soup kitchen. At first your father was angry and went through a very hard time. He drank and fought with people and generally was miserable. One day I convinced him to go to a revival meeting being put on by my friend Jean Baptiste. Something Jean said touched him. He quit drinking and went back to his ministry of teaching others how to live a happier, more fulfilling life.

Heinrich Mollen and your father grew up in the same village and were childhood rivals. When Heinrich became leader of the country, he wanted your father to acknowledge him, not only as head of the government but also as head of the church. Your father flatly refused.

The Brown shirts destroyed the village your grandparents lived in, killing over six hundred people in a one day. His whole family was killed except for his sister Elizabeth and your grandmother Maria. I don't know how they survived the abuse they were subjected to that day.

Your mother's story is even sadder. She was turned out onto the streets as a prostitute at the age of thirteen. Her father sold her to pay a gambling debt to the man who did this. Terrible things happened to her. Rather than condemn her life style, your father fell in love with her and they were married. You are the product of their love, the child they thought they would never have.

I watched Heinrich shoot your father and leave him bleeding to death. It was a difficult time for your mother and I am not sure she has ever completely recovered from the trauma. You already know the story of how she came to be here. Maria, Jesse's mother, stayed with her but died as she came ashore. After that your mother decided keeping you safe was her sole purpose in life and that meant not letting the Believers know you were Jesse's son. She wanted you to have a normal life.

Your father died for his beliefs and because of his death – well you can see for yourself how strong the Believers have become. From the faith of one man, people all over the world live by his teachings."

The two men sat quietly, each lost in their own thoughts. The only sound was the ticking of the clock hanging on the wall.

Jesse broke the silence. "Am I anything like my father? Is my mother disappointed in me?"

"You have much of your father in you, but you're not like him at all. Your mother is proud of you, and proud of the man you have become.

She worries about you and what would happen if the believers find out who you are. She has gone to great lengths to keep her secret and keep you safe. That's why she stayed at the Kibbutz for so many years. You were safe there.

If the British had found you, she would have been jailed and you would have been taken from her. If the Believers found out, they would have taken you away and raised you as the reincarnation of Jesse. Something about meeting Sophya triggered a memory she would rather forget. She is afraid for you."

"Has she talked to you? Do you know what it is?"

"Yes, to both, but it's not my story to tell. That is something she has to do herself."

Again, the men sat quietly "When your mother does decide to tell you, you will need to be prepared. It is a sad story but happy at the same time. What she will say is going to be hard to hear. Whatever you believe will be changed forever."

"I don't understand how this relates to Sophya?"

"That is what you need to learn from your mother and I am sure she will tell you when she is ready."

"I need you to tell me the whole story. I can't wrap my head around everything you have said so far. Will you do that for me?"

"I can." said Peter. "I hope you have lots of time because it's long one."

"I have no place I would rather be right now."

Hours later Peter voice was hoarse from talking. "Do you understand now why your mother reacted the way she did?"

Tears were streaming down J J's face, "I didn't know. My God how she must have suffered – to go through all of that."

"Yes, your mother is one of the most courageous women I have ever known. That is the power of forgiveness. You don't have to walk up so someone who has hurt you and say "I forgive you. You don't have to shout it from the roof tops and tell the world."

Thumping his chest Peter said, "this is where it starts – letting go of the past and the people who hurt you. There is no need to profess undying love or to even like that person. What you are doing is giving yourself permission to move on and not allowing whoever hurt you to continue to have power over your life. Cut your mother some slack JJ., she will come around, she just needs time."

Shortly after that JJ left for home. He needed time to think, to comprehend the story Peter had told him. He knew the history of the settlement of the Promise land country and why most of the Believers had settled in the area, but this was the first time he understood his mother's story was an important part of history.

Something inside him was changing. He began to see the older people who passed him in a new way. *What is their story? Where did they come from? Have they lived in the camps or lost some body dear to them? How could one human being treat so many others in such a barbaric fashion?*

A new resolve began to fill him. *I must learn more and do what I can to make sure this never happens again.*

FIFTY-ONE

Marika was frantic. She hadn't heard from JJ since he stormed out hours ago. She had no idea where he was and became more alarmed when Sophya phoned asking if she knew where he was.

The sound of the door opening in the early hours of the morning roused her from her light sleep. She listened to the footsteps come down the hall way and her bedroom door opening.

"Are you awake," JJ whispered.

"I am now," Marika replied. "I was worried about you. Sophya contacted me and she didn't know where you were either."

"Can we talk?"

"Of course." Marika replied patting the side of the bed, "come, sit here."

JJ sat down and Marika heard a sob, then felt his body shudder.

"What is it? Has something happened? Where have you been?"

"I... I have been with Uncle Peter."

"And…"

"He told me about you and my father. I didn't know Jesse was actually my father, I thought he was a friend you and Peter had in common. I should have figured that out for myself a long time ago."

Marika moved out from under the covers, sat beside him, wrapped her arms around him and held him as he cried.

"You should have told me. Why didn't you? How could you keep something this important from me," he said angrily. "I had a right to know."

Marika took a deep breath. "Yes, you did. I wanted to tell you when you were a small child but couldn't find the right words. All I could think of was protecting you. Peter and I didn't know what would happen if those who hated the Believers found out you were Jesse's son. I felt threatened from all sides and I was afraid. I am sorry."

He looked at his mother, "how in heaven's name did you survive everything that happened to you and still be sane?"

"First, I had Jesse, then I had your grandmother Maria. Together we gave each other courage when our faith fell short. The one good thing that came out of all the darkness is that it brought us to this place. I have been blessed."

They sat quietly for a long time.

"You must be tired," he said, pulling himself out of her arms. "I'm tired. I haven't slept for more than thirty hours."

"We'll talk more when you get up in the morning," Marika said, "I have much to tell you,"

As he was leaving JJ turned to look at her. "Am I like him?"

"In some ways very much, in others you are your own person." She answered. "He would be proud of you. One thing I know for sure, is that you are as stubborn as he was."

The rest of the night JJ and Marika lay awake in their separate beds. Both asking the same question *where do I go from here*

FIFTY-TWO

Peter was surprised to hear a knock on his door. He wasn't expecting anyone and when he opened the door he was pleased to see his good friend Joe Fournier and another man standing there.

"Come in, come in," he said "What a surprise.   It's good to see you again."

The two men entered the room and stood inside the door.

"Come, sit down, can I get you something to drink, a glass of wine perhaps?"

"Not for me," Joe replied, "my wife is complaining I drink too much as it is" he said patting his belly. All three of them chuckled.

One man sat on the couch, the other on the chair and Peter got a third chair from the kitchen. "Something tells me this is more than a friendly visit. What can I do for you?" He asked.

"I want you to meet my friend Allan Tulberg. Allan works with the AFWC, the agency responsible for finding war criminals and bringing them to justice."

"I've heard of them," Peter replied. "Pleased to meet you." Both men stood and shook hands.

Joe continued, "I will get right to the point. You were there and witnessed first-hand the devastation Heinrich brought upon our country. Some of the top commanders of the indoctrination camps managed to slip away and elude us. Our job is to find them and bring them to justice.

Because of your experiences with Jesse and the Believers we would like you to join us. I do believe you were questioned yourself at Grenwald prison?"

"Yes, I was, but why me?"

"You know people and you know the country. You have resources that could be invaluable to us. We want you to work from our office and head up one of our searches."

"Who are you looking for?"

"Commander Gus Renic"

"The warden of Grenwald prison?"

"Yes. He directed the interrogation of hundreds of prisoners and was a sadistic bastard. His specialty was to personally interrogate and rape young women and then turn four or five guards loose on her until she talked. Some died in the process. Others told us he liked to watch and shout encouragement. Some we have spoken to survived their ordeal but have never been the same since. He liked to beat the men in the genitals using a board with short nails sticking out of it."

"I heard a lot of terrible things took place there." Peter replied.

Tulberg continued, "As soon as Heinrich died and before we got properly organized, many of the commanders fled to foreign countries. but we have every reason to believe he didn't go far. There are rumors he left but has since returned to Bern, hiding under an assumed name."

"What about his wife and children?"

"They disappeared too. Since then, we have learned she divorced him and took the children with her. She changed their names back to her maiden name to avoid any stigma or retaliation for her children. If that's true, there is no sense bothering her. If need be, we know where she is. She has a good life now and we don't want to disturb it. Knowing the kind of monster he was, she probably doesn't care what happens to him."

Peter looked at them and hesitated "I need time to think about this, but I do have one question. If I happen to find Eli, the Betrayer of Jesse, will you prosecute him?"

"If that is what it takes to get you say yes, I guarantee it?" Tulberg agreed.

"Then I say yes."

"Meet me at my office room 314, on the third floor of government house, around nine tomorrow morning and we'll get started."

The men shook hands and the two men departed s short time later.

There is nothing more I would like then to find Eli and punish him for betraying Jesse. He deserves whatever happens to him. Too bad we can't give him the same treatment Jesse got but murder is against the law.

* * *

Peter arrived early the next morning to find Joe Fournier and Allan Tulburg waiting for him. The three shook hands and then sat down around an old scarred wooden table.

"Can I get you anything to drink?" Tulburg asked.

"Not for me," Peter replied. "But I will admit curiosity is getting the best of me.

"We are waiting for one more person." Tulberg replied. As if on cue, there was a knock on the office door and Noah walked in.

"You old son of a gun," Peter said standing and shaking Noah's hand. "I should have known you would be up to your neck in this."

"I assume you two know each other," Tulberg commented.

"You could say that. We've worked together many times."

"Let's get started then," Tulberg said picking up a sheet of paper from his desk.

Over the course of the next two hours Peter learned how the AFWC worked. When the meeting was over Noah suggested to Peter," let's go for lunch. and catch up on what you have been doing. There is a small café around the corner that offers an excellent lunch special."

FIFTY-THREE

Before they parted at the café, Peter and Noah made arrangements for Noah to pick him up early the following morning.

When he got into the car Peter asked," do you know where we are going?"

"To the warehouse district. AFWC has a small building rented there."

"I'm still not sure what I am getting myself into. Why all the secrecy?" Peter asked. "I'm not sure I have the qualifications you need for this type of work."

Noah laughed. "You are in for a lot of watching and waiting, broken by brief periods of intense activity. Sometimes it feels like we are looking for a needle in a haystack. We don't always get our man but every lead is followed up. Other times we just get lucky. I joined this organization after the British left. I lost most of my family in the camps and I vowed to bring those killers to justice."

"I didn't know that," Peter said

"It's not something I like to talk about." Noah replied. "We are here."

Peter looked out the window and saw a small warehouse bearing the sign 'Saul's Antiquities.' They walked to the rear of the building and entered through a back door.

"First, we need to get you some identification papers and a gun. They are mainly for show but you never know when you may need them. You do know how to shoot don't you? "

"Not very well," Peter replied.

Noah laughed, "it figures. We also have to get your fingerprints and photo."

"Why?"

"In case we need to identify your body "Noah answered quite seriously.

"You have got to be kidding. You are, aren't you?"

"Yes and no, but it is a safety precaution."

They walked into a large room with a double row of three desks and a telephone on each. Two men were working; the rest were empty.

"That one is yours," Noah said pointing to one in the middle.

Peter noticed at the front of the room was a wall with dozens of photographs. Some had captured written across them with a date. Others had convicted and some read confirmed dead. Front and center were pictures of the most wanted which included Renic and Grossman with pieces of paper were taped to the wall beneath them.

"Every tip or clue is written on the papers. Sometimes one of the other units give us information and this way it is easily available to all. Alpha and Omega groups also work out of this center and others groups are scattered across different countries.

279

"Good morning gentlemen." Allen Tulberg said entering the room.

"Quite an operation you have here," Peter commented.

"That it is," Tulberg answered. "Shall we get started?"

He began to explain what they did in more detail than at their previous meeting and filled them in on the active searches.

"One is Raul Petterson. He was in charge of supplying food and feeding the prisoners in the camps. He sold most of the food on the black market, lined his pockets and that's the biggest reason most prisoners got less than seven hundred calories a day. He got rich while they starved.

The other is Otto Grossman., the sub commander at the Jawal River camp. He patrolled with two mean black dogs and, if he was displeased with a prisoner, unleashed them and watched as they tore the man or woman apart.

We know he escaped soon after Heinrich died and was spotted in Brazil. He must have thought it safe to come back because recently he was seen going into a store in a small town not far from Bern.

When he is captured your first assignment will be to bring him back. We will have a plane waiting for you. After we are done, we'll hand him over to the British. We also believe Patterson is working as a cook in one of the small restaurants in Bern. I guess he thinks if he disguises himself and changes his name, he is safe."

"The only person I am interested in is Eli. I want him to pay for what he did." Peter stated.

Tulberg looked at him. "Eli is a small fish in a big sea. If that is your sole purpose for working with us, we don't need you here. You are either all in or you can leave right now."

Peter looked down at his feet for several seconds then looked up "I'm in. Tell me what you want me to do."

A telephone rang in the background. Then somebody called out," they picked up Grossman on his way to work and want to know what to do with him?"

"Tell them I will make arrangements to have him brought here." Tulberg answered. To Noah and Peter, he said "I guess you are going to Bern tonight. Be at the airport by four o'clock. With any luck you will be home the day after tomorrow."

Hours later the they landed and went directly to the local AFWC office. There they waited for their orders and for Grossman to be turned over to them.

Noah asked one of the captors "How did you catch him? We're part of a new team and have much to learn."

The man, Edmond Rubenstein, answered.," A great many Believers live in this area. A camp survivor spotted him going into the liquor store. You might say he was hiding in plain sight. I'm sure his neighbors don't have any idea of who he is.

The camp survivor, who wishes to remain anonymous, followed him home then called our office. We can't arrest somebody without proof.

One of our teams followed him for weeks. They took pictures and showed them to other survivors. Some who worked at the camps provide us with information in order to stay out of jail, others because they wanted to see him punished. At one point we considered breaking into his house looking for incriminating evidence, but didn't need to.

Grossman has a drinking problem and one of our agents befriended him in a bar. Turns out when he is under the influence, he likes to talk about the "important work" he did for Heinrich.

When confronted his first response was "I was only following orders." You don't know how many use that excuse to justify what they did. When he realized his pleas and excuses weren't working, he offered to make a deal. That's why you are here. Tulberg wants him first before he is turned over to the British. Once they get their hands on him, we will get very little, if any information.

Listen why don't you guys get some rest. Come back in the morning and he'll be ready for you. There is a visitors' suite at the back where you can rest and freshen up"

When they returned in the morning a guard brought Grossman into the room. He was handcuffed and his legs shackled. Instead of seeing him as once proud soldier Peter saw a short bald man with beard and bulbous red nose.

"Who are you?" Grossman asked. "Maybe you can make them listen to me. I was following orders. I did nothing wrong. You must understand, this was not my fault."

Noah stepped in front of him. "Save your excuses for someone who cares."

Rubenstein walked into the room. "There is a private plane waiting to take you as far as Petroina where a car will be waiting to drive you through the pass. Someone will meet you on the other side there and take you to Tulberg's office."

Grossman started to object. Noah got right up close to him and said "shut up. We are not interested in anything you have to say unless you want to tell us where we can find more scum like you."

Grossman looked over at Peter.

"Don't look at me" he smirked, "he's my boss and I have to follow orders."

"Please I beg you, don't turn me over to the British. I will spend the rest of my life in prison."

"Not my call." Noah replied. "You should have thought of that when you watched your dog's kill and maim people. You deserve whatever they do to you and then some. It's too bad we can't give you a taste of your own medicine but our dogs would likely lick you to death."

To Peter he said. "Let's get out of here. Being around this guy makes me sick to my stomach."

As soon as they returned Grossman was turned over to Tulberg and whisked away to a secret place.

"What happens to his family now?" Peter asked.

"We are not completely heartless. They have the option of staying where they are or relocating with our help. Usually, they are shocked to discover what was taking place under their noses and disavowed their relationship. When we questioned his wife, she claimed to have no idea what his actual camp duties were."

"Do you believe her?"

"No, but as far as we can find out she stayed in Bern and visited him infrequently. When he went to Brazil, he left her and the children behind. As far as we know they haven't been in contact with each other since he returned."

Months later the newspaper headlines read "Otto Grossman sentenced to twenty-five years in prison."

Months later with the arrest of Gus Renic, Noah and Peter gained the reputation of always getting their man.

FIFTY-FOUR

Sophya was studying in her dorm room when somebody began pounding frantically on her door. Usually, she and JJ studied together at the library but this evening was an exception.

Elsa, the floor monitor called out to her. "Hurry Sophya, there is an important phone call for you."

Sophya fumed as she followed Elsa to her office. *Now everybody will be wanting to know who called and why? Sometimes Elsa needs her head examined. Phone calls are meant to be private.*

Picking up the phone she answered, "this is Sophya."

"This is Dean Schmidt from Bern University. I received a troubling call from your mother's physician a few minutes ago. She is very ill and you are to return home as quickly as possible. Her bank trustee is making travel arrangements as we speak. A ticket will be waiting at the airport for the eleven thirty flight tonight."

She looked at the clock on the desk. "that's only two hours from now. I'm not sure I can get there in time. Is that all they said? Did they give you any idea what is wrong with her?"

"I apologize for being the bearer of such distressing news, but he did empathize that you should come as soon as possible. I hope your mother's condition isn't too serious."

"Thank you for calling." She replied. She hung up the phone and turned to Elsa. "My mother is very sick. I have to go home."

"Is there anything I ca do?" Elsa asked.

"Would you please notify Professor Schultz that I will be gone for several days and that I request permission to take the exam when I return."

She picked up a pen and piece of paper, wrote down JJ's phone number handing it to Elsa. "Call JJ and tell him what's happened and I will get in touch with him later. I don't have much time and I still have to pack."

She was stunned by the turn of events. There was just the two of them and not once had her mother mentioned she wasn't well. In fact, she encouraged Sophya to take this year to study as an exchange student.

She hurried to her room, began throwing clothes into a suitcase, arriving at the airport with ten minutes to spare. Her ticket was waiting for her as planned.

Changing planes at Bern she arrived in her home town of Strasbourg eight hours after leaving the university. From the airport she took a taxi directly to the hospital.

When she entered her mother's the room she appeared to be sleeping. Sophya pulled up the lone chair to the side of the bed. Then, taking her hand, she whispered," I am here."

Her mother opened her eyes, "I have been waiting for you,"

Her mother smiled, closed her eyes and drifted back to sleep. *If she dies, I will be alone. Most of her family died in the camps.*

Throughout the rest of that night and into the next day Sophya's mother roused, spoke to her, then drift off again.

"The trustee will continue paying your expenses until you are twenty-five, then whatever is left you will receive in a lump sum payment."

"Promise me you will finish university."

"Go to the house, and bring me the wooden box on the top shelf of my closet. Get some rest while you are there. I'll still be here when you get back."

Sophya went home, showered and changed her clothes. She retrieved the box, returned to the hospital and resumed her vigil. As tempted as she was, she didn't look inside. Eventually she fell asleep, her head resting on the side of the bed, her mother's hand clutched in hers.

The next morning her mother seemed to rally. Her voice was stronger and she was awake for longer periods of time. At one point she said, "bring me the box".

Picking up the box from the bedside table she placed it into her mother's hand. Only then she did she realize tears were streaming down her mother's face.

"Don't cry." Sophya said reaching for a tissue and blotting the tears away, "Everything is going to be okay. Look you are already better than when I got here. In a day or two I will be able to take you home."

"Sophya come closer," her mother whispered. "I need to tell you about your father and don't want anyone to overhear what I am about to say. He was an up-and-coming Politian I met at a party, not yet the important man he was to become. For several years we had an intense love affair. When I became pregnant, he was the powerful leader of our country and becoming more volatile every day. The only picture I have of us together is in this box.

We frequently argued because I didn't agree with his policies and what he was doing. He didn't want people finding out about our relationship so he bought me a small house in Strausbourg and moved me there. Over the years he set up a trust fund for us but I never saw him again. When he died, I was devastated."

She stopped to rest. Sophya sat patiently waiting for her to continue. When she began speaking again Sophya had to strain to hear her words.

"Your trust fund will end when you turn twenty-five, mine ends with my death. Throughout the years I put money away for you and you will find it in the bank under your full name."

Sophya had a sick feeling in her stomach. "Why all the secrecy? Who is my father?"

She grasped Sophya's hand and squeezed. "Heinrich Mollen. I didn't know he would turn out to be such a monster. I didn't want you to find out because of all the horrible things he did. If people knew you were his daughter your life would have been a living hell."

Sophya was in shock. She sat there trying to absorb what her mother was telling her. *How can this be true? Surely, I would have known before this.*

"Did you love him?" she asked.

"Very much so and I still do. Who he became wasn't the quiet gentle man I fell in love with." She began to cry. "He was a dreamer, an artistic man with many talents, but driven by his ambition. I am so sorry. I was young, in love and very foolish."

"The Heinrich Mollen? Are you sure it's the same man?" Sophya asked, but her mother didn't answer.

She closed her eyes and over the next several hours her breathing slowed until it finally stopped. It was though once she told Sophya who her father was her conscience was clear and she could die peacefully.

Sophya opened the wooden box. Inside was her birth certificate, the father's name left blank, bank account numbers, valuable pieces of jewelry and a letter addressed to her.

There was a picture of a much younger Heinrich Mollen and her mother gazing into each other's eyes. He wore a military uniform; she wore a white flowery dress and a straw hat and obviously pregnant.

Sophya felt sick. In her hands was the proof she needed that they knew each other. When she looked at the back there was no date on the picture. She stared at it, recalling that every time she asked who her father was her mother would answer. "You don't need to know yet, but some day…." Now she understood her mother's reluctance.

She placed the picture back into the box face down and put everything else on top. For some reason she felt dirty and not worthy of being with anyone, especially a good man like JJ. She doubled over as though in pain. *How am I going to tell him? Now he will hate me.*

But, in the end, she was left with the knowledge that her father was the most hated man in the world and responsible for the deaths of thousands.

She put her face down on her mother's unmoving chest and cried. She kissed her cheek and thought *I am not angry. You did what you thought was best at the time. I love you and will miss you terribly.*

She picked up the box and walked toward the door. Taking one last look at her mother she said "I don't know how I will live without you."

The trustee made all of the arrangements and, other than herself and several of her mother's friends, few attended the simple graveside service.

After the burial she went back to the house and picked out what personal items she wanted and packed them into boxes. There wasn't much. The rest she decided to leave for the next resident. *They can do whatever they want with this stuff. I have no use for it.*

On the last evening in her home Sophya was surprised to knocking on the front door. Her plane was leaving at seven the next morning and her packed suitcase and boxes waited by the door. She went to the door and calmly asked. "Who is there?"

Then she heard a familiar voice. "it's me, JJ. Are you going to make me stand out here all night?"

She opened the door and stared at him. "What are you doing here?"

"Peter and I decided to come get you and take you back to the university. He wanted to show me where my parents met and lived so I could understand their history better. Besides I wanted to see you. I was worried about you being here alone."

Holding her at arm's length he said "You look terrible. Are you okay?"

She looked at him and sighed. "I don't think I will ever be okay again."

"What do you mean? What happened?"

Peter walked into the house. He couldn't help but notice the devastated look on Sophya's face and watched as she pushed JJ away.

"Go home," she said. "I don't want or need you here."

"Not until I find out what is going on," he replied. Putting his hand under her chin and lifting her face he said," Talk to me."

She collapsed into the closest arm chair and buried her head in her hands. Sobs wracked her body.' I didn't know. God help me, I had no idea."

"Know what?" JJ asked kneeling in front of her. "What didn't you know? Tell me Sophya."

"Heinrich Mollen was my father," she blurted out.

JJ was stunned. He looked at Peter and realized that he already knew.

"You knew?" he asked, turning to Peter.

"Yes," Pete replied, "and so does your mother."

"But how…?"

"Marika knew the day you brought her home for supper."

Sophya gripped JJ's arm and looked into his face. "Don't you understand? My father killed Jesse the leader of the Believers in cold blood and that makes me as much of a monster as he was. Can you forgive me? I didn't know until my mother told me on her deathbed. How you must hate me?"

JJ looked at Peter. "Is this true," he asked.

Once again Peter nodded yes. "Sophya's father was directly responsible for Jesse's death."

Suddenly JJ understood what Peter was trying to tell him. Her father killed his father. Without saying a word, he got to his feet, strode out the door, slamming it behind him.

Sophya looked up at Peter. "What do we do now?"

"Give him a few minutes and I'll go talk to him. This is quite a shock for him too."

JJ stood on the front porch gazing into nothing for a long time. Eventually Peter came out to join him.

"How is she?" he asked.

"She is resting. The bigger question is what are you going to do?'

"I don't know."

"She loves you."

"And I love her. What a mess this is."

"Does she know Jesse was your father?"

"Yes."

"I am going to tell you the same thing I told your mother when she came to me. These are different times. We can't hold the children responsible for the sins of their fathers. Jesse was not perfect either. He often he went out of his way to antagonize Heinrich."

"Is this why you wanted me to come with you when you heard Sophya's mother was sick?"

"Partly. I haven't been back for a long time and decided this would be an excellent opportunity to see Mark and Elizabeth again and thought this was good a time as any to show you where you came from."

"You said partly, what is the other part? Are you holding something back I need to know?"

"You know I work with a group involving capturing and bringing war criminals to justice. Before I left, we got a message Gus Renic, the notorious warden of Grenwald prison, could be in this area and I am following up on the tip. I am going to ask around and see if anybody recognizes his picture."

"I have no problem with that," JJ replied. "Don't mention that to Sophya, it will only add to her guilt."

"After hearing Sophya's devastating news, I think this trip will benefit her too. If nothing else this will give both of you a fresh perspective on what occurred so long ago."

JJ stood for a long time then said," I better go see how she is. I'll talk to her about the idea of driving back with us."

As he turned to go back into the house, he noticed Peter walking toward the road. "Where are you going?"

"I'm going to leave you two alone while I see if I can find something for supper. Maybe you two can live on love but as for me, I'm hungry."

JJ quickly found the bedroom Sophya was lying in. She was curled into a ball; a pink quilt wrapped around her shoulders. He didn't say anything. He took off his shoes, lay down beside her and wrapped her tightly in his arms.

Neither one spoke. They clung to each other grieving their losses. JJ grieved for the father he never knew. Sophya grieved for the loss of her mother and her innocence. After her mother's revelation she knew she would never be the same. The carefree life she had known was over.

* * *

Upon his return, Peter made a great deal of noise coming through the front door. "I brought supper" he announced. "The nice lady at the café packaged it up so I could bring it here. Come and eat before it gets cold."

He went int the kitchen, set the food on the table and got three bowls, knives and spoons from the cupboard.

"Did you have to make so much noise?" JJ asked walking into the kitchen. "How is a person supposed to sleep through all of that racket?"

When Peter looked at JJ he noticed how haggard he looked but sensed a difference in him. He had left a boy, not sure of what to do and returned to find as man who had made an important decision.

"Is Sophya awake?"

"Yes, she is in the bathroom."

At the sound of her name Sophya entered the kitchen. She looked worse than he did, her eyes were red and puffy from crying. But mostly Peter noticed the slump of her shoulders and defeated attitude.

"I don't know about you, but I'm starving, "he announced, as he began filling the bowls with potato soup from the container on the table. He unwrapped the cheese and fresh bread and placed them in the center. Cautiously he watched them for a sign as to what might have transpired while he was gone. They sat quietly beside each other and ate.

"When are you leaving Sophya?" he asked. "I noticed your suitcase sitting beside the door."

"My plane leaves early in the morning, and you?'

"Tomorrow morning as well."

"Since we are here, I thought this would be a good time for JJ to learn more about his family. Unfortunately, in order to learn his history, some of it will be unpleasant."

"Can't be any worse than what I told him." she stated.

Looking at Sophya he said. "I have an idea. Why don't you come with us? A break will do you both good and you can learn about your family too."

"That's a good idea," JJ added. "You need time to think. Knowing you, you will go back to the university, sit in your room and hide away from the world."

"I know all I need to know about Heinrich Mollen," Sophya snapped at them. "He was a monster. My mother hated him for who he was and I feel responsible for his legacy of cruelty and horror."

J J reached for her hand. "You are being too hard on yourself. What he did was not your fault and you have nothing to feel guilty about. Neither one of us had a choice about who our parents were."

"I agree," Peter said. "You are not responsible for his actions. In his own way he's hurt you most of all."

Sophya looked at JJ., tears filling her eyes. "Your mother won't think so. Every time she looks at me, she will be reminded of who I am and what my father did."

"My mother will get over it. She was taken by surprise that's all."

Looking into JJ's eyes she asked "Even after all you learned today, are you sure you still want to be with me?"

"More than ever. My feelings haven't changed. Beside the more we learn, the more we will understand. Isn't that right Peter?"

"I wouldn't have suggested you come with us if I didn't think it a good idea. We have to drive back anyway and there is definitely room for one more. Since we are going that way why waste money on a plane ticket?"

Sophya smiled. "You are right. I would rather be with you."

Peter reached into his shirt pocket and pulled out a crumpled road map. He spread it out on the table smoothing it as best he could. "I plotted out a route that will have us home in five days giving ourselves plenty of time to stop."

The three of them pored over the map. Peter explained his reasons for this particular route and what they would see. He noticed both begin to relax and lose the haunted looks on their faces.

Glancing at his watch, Peter said, "If we are going to leave early, we better get some rest."

"Where are you going to stay?" Sophya asked.

Peter looked at her and then tapped the side of his head. "I meant to stop at the inn and book a room but I forgot. I hope the innkeeper hasn't gone to bed yet."

"You can stay here. There is lots of room. One of you can use my mother's room, and the other the couch. Her bed isn't made up but I can get you some blankets and pillows."

"We will manage," Peter replied. "Thank you for your offer."

Sophya took Peter upstairs stopping to get a pillow and blanket from the hall closet. She showed him the room, where the bathroom was and went back downstairs.

Peter lay in the dark thinking. *I wonder where JJ will be sleeping tonight? I'll be very surprised if it's the living room.*

He heard the murmur of voices then a door close. A short time later he heard JJ exclaim. "How am I supposed to sleep on this? It is too short."

In the morning Sophya looked more relaxed. She busied herself making coffee and putting out the bread and cheese left from the night before. She folded Peter's and J J's blankets and put them back into the closet.

"I am going to find it hard to leave here," she said to Peter. "This is the only home I have ever known. My friends are here but these walls feel empty without my mother. I plan on coming back for a short period of time after the semester ends. The trustee is going to rent the house until I decide what I am going to do. Without my mother being here there is no reason to keep it."

"You are right." Peter told her. "But this is not the time to make decisions you might regret later."

Peter and JJ washed and dried the few dishes while Sophya checked the rest of the house.

"Are you ready to go?" he asked as she came down the stairs.

"Yes," she replied.

JJ carried her suitcases and two small boxes out to the car. They both got into the back seat and Peter sat alone in the front.

"We have one stop to make. I promised to return this pot in the morning?".

Turning around he grinned at them "How does it feel to have a chauffeur?" he asked

"Pretty darn good," JJ replied."

FIFTY-FIVE

As they approached the Jawal River Peter turned off on a side road and stopped. "The is where the resistance launched its first great offensive against Heinrich's forces. One group fought to capture the bridge, the other the town where the guards, camp commissioners and their families lived. After they had control of the town the inhabitants were forced, at gun point, to leave with only the clothes on their backs. and walk for miles to the next town. Then, they freed the camp.

Those still alive were brought here and protected until they were well enough to leave. The stories of their suffering and mistreatment were horrifying to hear.

"Have you been here before?" J J asked."

"No, like you, this is my first time." Peter replied.

As they drove past the derelict town the road narrowed to a faintly discernable two wheeled track which they followed until they came to a welcome sign hanging between two high steel posts.

"This is the Jawal River Indoctrination camp. Tens of thousands of people were transported here. Ovens were built to cremate the dead and undesirables. Towards the end a selection process determined who would live or who would die.

When the last of the prisoners were evacuated the resistance blew up the ovens and burned the buildings. As you can see more than half are damaged but still standing. The two left undamaged have been turned into a museum which bears testament to the horrendous living conditions. When the war was over the town's people moved away. They didn't want to be associated with this place. Do you want to go in and look around?"

"No." JJ replied. "We've seen enough. Why haven't we heard about what happened here? In all the history available I haven't seen this mentioned."

"Heinrich's puppets controlled the newspapers and radio stations and were forbidden to tell the story. To do so would admit that Heinrich could be defeated. He was still alive when this happened.

It's getting late. Should we go into the town to see if we can find a place to stay?"

"No," JJ replied. "It's too early to stop yet. Let's keep going until we find another town."

"Fine with me," Peter agreed.

He turned around back the way they had come. Sophya, who was quiet during this exchange put her head on JJ's shoulder sobbing. "I didn't know/" He put his arm around her pulling her closer.

The next morning Peter drove to the town of where Mark and Elizabeth lived and stopped in front of the hospital. "Come with me, there is someone I want you to meet," he said. The three of them walked up the sidewalk and entered through the front door.

"Have a seat, I'll be with you in a minute," a voice called out.

Several minutes later a man dressed in a white lab coat entered the waiting room. His eyes grew big and a huge smile covered his face.

"Peter, you old son of a gun, I never thought I would see you again. What are you doing here?" He walked over to Peter and threw his arms around him.

"You haven't changed a bit, Mark." Peter replied, hugging him back. "There is someone I want you to meet."

Turning to JJ he said," this is your uncle Mark. His wife, Elizabeth is Jesse's sister, your only surviving relative."

"Mark, this is Marika's son Jessie Junior but we call him JJ and his girlfriend Sophya."

Mark stared at the young man in disbelief. "You look exactly like your father," he blurted out. "I am so glad to finally meet you. Elizabeth will be surprised." He shook hands with JJ and Sophya.

Looking around the empty room he said "I'm going to close the clinic and we'll go to the house. People know where to find me if necessary. You must join us for supper and stay overnight."

They got into Peter's car and travelled the short distance to Mark's home. He jumped out of the car and ran up the steps.

"Elizabeth, we have company. You will never guess who is here."

Elizabeth came out of the kitchen drying her hands on a towel. When she saw Peter, she rushed to him and threw her arms around his neck.

"Peter, is it really you after all this time?"

Then she noticed JJ and Sophya standing off to the side. She looked at Peter with a stunned expression. "Is this who I think it is?"

"Yes. This is Marika's son JJ and his girlfriend Sophya."

She walked over to JJ, put a hand on either side of his face and stared into his eyes, her own brimming with tears. "You look just like him."

Then she looked at Sophya and froze. Sophya reached for J J's hand.

"Elizabeth you are not mistaken. This is Heinrich's daughter Sophya. She recently lost her mother and learned who her father was. Before her mother passed, she revealed to Sophya the secret that she was Heinrich's daughter. I don't need to tell you she is deeply troubled by this news."

Elizabeth shrugged her shoulders. "Come supper is ready. It's a good thing I made extra tonight."

When they finished eating Mark and Peter went to sit on the front step like old times. Elizabeth, JJ and Sophya continued to sit around the kitchen table while Elizabeth regaled them with stories of Jesse as a child.

"How is Marika?" Mark asked.

"She is doing well but extremely upset about JJ and Sophya being together."

"I can understand why," Mark replied. "This would be like having her worst nightmare come true. Now my old friend, tell me what you have been up to."

The two men sat and talked far into the night.

"So, you are telling me that JJ has also recently found out who his father was. Marika kept this from him this long?"

"Yes, and that's the reason for this trip. To him Jesse is an enigma, a name, not a real person. I felt it was important for him to see the places Jesse frequented as well as meet his aunt and uncle. This trip I want him to learn about his family and his roots. I believe Sophya will benefit too."

"How is he taking this information?"

"He is like his father that way, when he is ready, he will talk."

"How is Marika with Sophya?'

"She is still in shock but will come around when she realizes they are destined to be together. That will be her ultimate act of forgiveness."

"What about Sophya?"

"She is struggling but she and JJ are working this out. They are both learning to understand their new reality. My heart goes out to both of them; this isn't an easy situation."

After breakfast the next morning the trio bid a tearful farewell to Mark and Elizabeth.

"Tell your mother we will come see her as soon as we can" Elizabeth said hugging JJ "You are always welcome here, you know that."

Hugging Sophya she said, "go enjoy your life. You are not responsible for what your father did."

Mark and Peter shook hands and Peter hugged Elizabeth. "Until we meet again," he said.

FIFTY-SIX

Over the next several hours Peter regaled JJ and Sophya with stories of Jesse and his followers, exaggerating some of the funnier moments. He pulled over to the side of the road where they saw the blackened remains of a church spire in the distance.

"This is where the village of Norenburg once stood. Your fathers were raised here, played in the same streets, went to the same schools and worshipped in the same church. As adults they chose different paths. Jesse was a skilled carpenter like his father but chose to become a minister. He was about to be ordained and chose to leave when he learned the Elders were stealing land and money from the people.

Heinrich was raised by his bitter unhappy grandmother. His father was long gone and his mother died in childbirth.

In reality they were complete opposites. Jesse was charismatic, easy going, always cheerful. Heinrich had a dark personality and, even as children, targeted Jesse with his bullying. I believe Heinrich was envious of Jesse and felt the need to prove to himself the better of the two."

Peter drove into what was left of the town and followed the main road to the cemetery. In the center was a large mound covered in wild flowers with a white cross reaching high into the sky. Off to one side was a small unmarked mound. They got out of the car and walked toward the grave site, an intense feeling of being on sacred ground surrounded them.

"Six hundred people are buried here. The Brown shirts, under Sig Rotter's command, came into town looking for Jesse. When the people refused to give up his where abouts he ordered every man, woman and child be killed. Jesse's mother Maria and Sister Elizabeth were among the few survivors."

Peter shuddered. "It was a horrible sight that day. The bodies of men women and children lying in the streets, many still in their night clothes. Maria and Elizabeth were horrifically abused by the guards and left to die. I honestly don't know how they survived.

Jesse was devastated and we didn't know if he would ever recover. As for myself, I vowed to get revenge for these unnecessary deaths.

The saddest part is that Jesse had left town the day before and was in the cave where he often sought refuge. The last thing he wanted was to put his family and the villagers in danger."

"Do you know where Jesse is buried? Is he with his family?" Sophya asked.

"See that slightly misshapen mound on the side. After Jesse was killed, and in the middle of the night, we stole his body from under the noses of the guards, brought him here and buried him with the others. That's what he would have wanted."

"Why doesn't his grave have a marker? One that proclaims Jesse, leader of the Believers lies here."

"So, he can rest in peace with his family. Only a few of us know where his final resting spot is and Marika chose to leave his where abouts unknown. Heinrich was incensed and she didn't want his grave desecrated. This act marked the beginning of Heinrich's down fall."

"That makes a lot of sense." JJ remarked.

"How did Jesse respond?"

"If I remember correctly, he said "greater love has no man than this, to lay down his life for his friends." With these words he ignited the resistance movement which spread across the country."

JJ stood for a long time staring at the cross and mound of dirt in front of him. "I would like to be alone for a minute if you don't mind," he said.

Peter and Sophya respectfully stepped back and let him be. After a period of time Sophya went to him wrapping her arms around his waist. Peter couldn't hear what she was saying but they joined hands and walked back to him.

"I am not the man he was." JJ said.

Peter put his hand on the boy's shoulder. "No, you aren't and he didn't expect you to be. That's the reason your mother kept you in the dark for as long as she did. She wanted you to be your own person. She knew you had to follow your own path. There will only ever be one Jesse, so now you need to figure out what your path is and how to get there.

You too Sophya. You cannot change who your father was, nor can you make amends for what he did. The most important thing we can all do is make sure this never happens again."

Peter paused and looked over the grave site again. "There's not much more to see here so perhaps we should keep on going. I want to show you another place Jesse often visited."

Within minutes he pulled over and stopped along the edge of the highway. "We will walk from here."

Sophya peered into the tall grass in front of them. "Are there snakes?" she asked warily.

"I'm not really sure. If there are I haven't seen any," Peter answered.

Peter and JJ both laughed. "Only a girl would ask a question like that." JJ said. Sophya punched him in the arm.

With Peter in the lead, they followed him single file along a barely discernable path. Near the top Peter stopped at the entrance of a cave.

"This is where Jesse took refuge when he was here. He often needed a quiet place to be alone and think. We also met here when he needed to discuss important things with us."

"Can we go inside?" JJ asked.

Winking at Sophya he said, "you may want to wait out here. I can't guarantee there aren't snakes in there."

"You aren't going to let me live that down, are you?" she replied.

"Probably not," Peter laughed.

They looked around the cave but couldn't find anything left of when Jesse was there. Both were disappointed. Peter stood very still. The walls echoed the memories, laughter and solemnity of the space.

When they left the cave JJ and Sophya stood looking out over the valley. "It is beautiful and peaceful here. I can understand why this was a refuge for him."

"He was most at peace when he roamed these hills. Whenever he was upset or had a decision to make, he would disappear and walk for hours. He always came back relaxed and more focused."

Peter looked at his watch. "If we hurry, we can still make Bern today and then head home. Our time is almost up."

They arrived in Bern in the late afternoon. Sophya was excited to show JJ the university campus. Peter dropped them off there, then. filled the car with gas, and found lodging for the night

He still had a job to do. Throughout the evening, he went from café to café and into several taverns showing Renic's picture and asking for information.

"Why are you looking for him?" a man challenged at one of his stops.

"He is my second cousin. We were in the camps together and I don't know what happened to him. I was told he survived and I am trying to find him," Peter lied.

"Haven't see him but check the refugee center. They still have files of those who registered with them."

I doubt very much he registered. He would be afraid of being recognized so I am sure that is the last place he would go. He thanked the man and continued on his way.

The next morning Sophya said to Peter. "When I was at the museum, I read a newspaper clipping about a student massacre that was supposed to have taken place around here. Is it true?"

"Unfortunately, yes." he replied.

"Is it far? Can we go there? I want to see for myself. I have a hard time believing all of the stories I read."

Peter drove them to the site of the massacre. The gully had been filled with dirt and planted with grass. Hundreds of white crosses dotted the grassy area. A black marble wall declared the area as the Gully of The Dead and on it was inscribed hundreds of names of those who died that day.

"All so young and so many," Sophya said.

Peter related the story of the student resistance. "Jesse was devastated. He went to Heinrich pleading for him to stop the madness, Heinrich told Jesse he would stop if he publicly proclaimed him head of the church and turned himself into the authorities.

Jesse had no choice but to refuse, but by then most of the damage had been done. In many ways he felt responsible blamed for this too."

The three of them stood quietly paying tribute to the fallen students. Sophya was openly weeping.

"Come, I have one more place to show you," Peter said.

He drove to a decrepit part of town and stopped at the entrance of an alley. A barrel was burning and a group of men stood off to one side talking. JJ noted other men wrapped in blankets huddled along one wall.

"Looks like nothing has changed," Peter commented.

"What is this place?' JJ asked.

"This is where Jesse's movement started. He wandered in one evening bruised and bloody from being beaten and robbed and asked if he could stop and get warm. He never left.

He was a lonely, sad, disillusioned young man trying to run away from his past. For a while he struggled with his demons until I convinced him to come to a revival meeting with me. That night turned his life around.

He had a kind heart and people were drawn to him. First, he spoke with one man and then small groups. As more and more people heard his message "treat others as you want to be treated and forgive those who hurt you" his demand grew. This is where he met your mother and they began their married life. When he left to carry his message to other places, I went with him."

Up until now Sophya had been very quiet," Can you explain to me how and why my father acted the way he did?" she asked. "There had to have been a reason."

"Heinrich was an ambitious man. While in jail he wrote a Manifest of how, if given the opportunity, he would govern the country. He knew where he wanted to be politically and didn't care who he stepped on to achieve his goal. He had a vision, but his personal motive was to prove once and for all he was a better man than Jesse.

As he became more powerful, he began delegating to others, trusting them to follow his vision. Some did as was expected but others, such a Sig Rotter, had their own agenda. which was to replace Heinrich.

As Heinrich was working his way up the political ladder Jesse was becoming more popular. Even though Heinrich confronted Jesse several times, the problem continued to grow. Not only was he up against Jesse, but also his growing legion of followers.

Heinrich lost control of Sig Rotter and his Brown Shirts. Rotter quickly realized that he could do whatever he wanted and Heinrich would be blamed."

JJ and Sophya nodded in understanding. "But he still killed Jesse in cold blood. "JJ said.

"Yes, he did, but that was Heinrich's ultimate defeat. He couldn't conquer Jesse, so in a stroke of madness, got rid of him. Not only did he fail to accomplish his goal of making Jesse subservient, he made him a martyr. Killing Jesse destroyed his purpose for living. Instead of becoming the great man he wanted to be, he became the most despised person on earth

Yet Sophya, I believe there was a side of him that loved you and your mother deeply. That's why he never told anybody about you. He wanted to protect the good people in his life from the misery surrounding him."

Sophya sat looking at her hands. "Is that why you hunt war criminals?" she asked.

"Jesse was my closest friend. From the first time we met in this alley our lives became intertwined. He charged me with looking after his son and Marika. He knew from the beginning he would die for his beliefs. He could have stopped what he was doing any time but, like Heinrich, he also needed to fulfill his destiny. "

"You didn't answer my question?"

"My only reason is to find and capture Eli, the man who turned Jesse over to the Brown Shirts. I want him to pay. I will never forgive him for what he did and the pain he caused."

They walked back to the car and Peter slowly drove away. Sometimes the past was too painful to remember.

JJ was lost in thought. *After all I have seen and heard in the last few days why am I wasting my time studying History? I want to make a difference. The believers have suffered enough. They need to see that all they endured was not in vain. They deserve justice and I am going to make sure they get it. When I get back to the university I am going to transfer to law.*

Beside him Sophya stared ahead stone faced. He put his arm around her. "We can't change the past but together we can change the future so this kind of persecution never happens again. I have decided that I am going to see about changing my major from History to Law and learn more about the Believers."

Sophya reached up and squeezed his hand. "Because I am an exchange student I have no choice, but to continue as I am. All I can do for now is help you study, and work by your side."

JJ leaned over the front seat. "Peter, I believe it's time for us to go home."

FIFTY-SEVEN

The next morning Peter drove to a small village and parked the car on the main street. "We will be leaving the car nearby and from there we walk," he announced.

"Is this some kind of a joke?" JJ asked. "We are in the middle of nowhere. What about Sophya's belongings? We can't simply walk away and leave them."

"They will be safe. The car belongs to AFWC and somebody will come pick it up. Sophya, your things will be delivered to your dorm room."

"I wondered where this car came from, now I know. That was your reason for going to pick her up, wasn't it? You were working the whole time searching for war criminals. You used us. I should have known you had an ulterior motive."

JJ's face was red and his hands gathered into fists. "How could you put Sophya through this, especially knowing her mother had just died. What kind of a man are you?"

"JJ I told you about this. Don't you remember?"

Then Peter realized he was overwhelmed and filled with rage from what he had seen and heard the last few days. *I should have thought this would be too much to take in at one time. Once again, I didn't think far enough ahead to see what the consequences would be.*

Sophya reached for JJ's hand. "I am sure Peter has his own reasons for this trip and that's not the only one. He doesn't have to explain anything to you. As for me, I am grateful for this opportunity, now I understand so much more."

"How can you," JJ roared at her. "All you saw was death and destruction in your father's name. Now I know why I have no extended family and why my mother is so overprotective."

Sophya turned to Peter. "Can you give us a minute alone?"

"Of course. While you are talking, I want each of you to take one of the knapsacks in the back of the car. Pack only the essentials, your papers, and one or two items that are valuable to you. While you are doing that, I going to make arrangements for the car to be returned and get a bowl of soup at the café across the street. We'll wait here until dusk before we continue."

Through the window Peter watched JJ pace back and forth gesticulating wildly with his hands. He could feel the anger rolling off him. Finally, he saw Sophya embrace him and noticed they were both crying.

From out of nowhere Noah slid into the chair across from him, "Oh to be young and in love again." he sighed.

"As usual my intentions were good but I didn't handle this the right way," Peter confessed. "I didn't know how to make JJ understand his roots without actually showing him."

"Who's the girl?"

"That's the irony of this whole situation. She is Heinrich's daughter. She too just found out who her father was."

"How can that be?" Noah exclaimed. "Heinrich was never married and if there was a child you would have thought we would have heard. I must go and talk to her."

Noah began to rise from his chair but Peter put his hand on his arm to stop him. "Leave her alone. If you expose her, can you imagine the scorn and shame she will be subjected to? Her life would become hell which she doesn't deserve. She knows nothing. If those two young people can get over the past and still love each other then maybe there is hope for the rest of us. You will have plenty of time to talk to her later."

Noah watched the young couple set out their belongings and pack their knapsacks. As he stood to leave, he said "I've arranged for someone to pick you up on the other side. Tomorrow you will sleep in your own beds."

He slipped away as quietly as he came. JJ and Sophya were laughing as they came into the café and sat across from Peter. A sense of relief washed over him. *Maybe everything is going to be okay.*

"Try the soup," he said, "It is excellent."

While they ate Peter explained what was going to happen next. "There has been a change of plans. We are going to walk into the Promise land as hundreds of refugees were forced to do."

"Do you know where to go Peter?" JJ asked"

"Oh yes. I made this trip regularly before the British left. I was part of a group who was responsible for bringing the refugees to safety."

"Did you ever get caught?"

"Once. I was interred in a British prison camp for some time but managed to escape." He laughed out loud. "They used to call me the silver fox because I was as smart as a fox, and just as hard to catch."

Peter chuckled at the confusion on their faces. "It's a long story. Remind me to tell you some other time."

As the sun began to set, they got back into the car. Peter drove for several miles then stopped. "We walk from here. The border is on the other side of these hills."

JJ and Sophya shouldered their packs and looked at each other as if to say "we will humor him."

At first the going was easy but as the light faded into night the path became steeper.

"It's a perfect night," Peter told them. "There is no moon to give away our presence. Watch where you put your feet in case there are loose rocks that could tumble and make a noise."

As they walked behind Peter both began to feel the rising terror the refugees must have felt. Sophya whispered to JJ. "I don't know how the refugees did this, putting their trust in the complete stranger leading them and hoping they didn't get caught. I don't know if I would have been that brave."

When they reached the top Peter lay on his stomach and looked over the edge. Headlights were coming toward them.

"Stay down," Peter whispered. "I don't know if that's one of the routine patrol cars or our ride home. We will stay here until I see the pre-arranged signal."

The vehicle drove slowly along the edge of the hill using a spotlight to scan toward the top of the rocks. The three of them pulled back and waited until it drove away.

Sophya began to shiver in the cool night air and JJ put his arm around her. "Better," he asked.

"Yes."

A short time later they saw the lights of another vehicle approaching. It stopped, then the lights blinked twice.

"Let's go, our ride is here." Carefully they picked their way down the rocks.

"Stay here," Peter said, walking over to the car. He spoke to the driver, then motioned for them to follow. He got in the front seat beside the driver, JJ and Sophya climbed into the back. Peter turned around and said "won't be long and we will be home."

Sophya rested her head against JJ's shoulder and fell asleep. He looked out the window at the blackness surrounding them. *I didn't know but am beginning to comprehend why the Believers are so fierce and have such a strong bond with this country. They have paid dearly for their freedom.*

FIFTY-EIGHT

Marika awoke from a sound sleep when she heard the key in the lock and the front door open. She got out of bed and called out, "JJ is that you?"

"I'm sorry. I didn't mean to wake you." he replied.

"What time is it?" she asked, walking down the hallway.

"Three in the morning."

"Are you hungry? Should I make you something to eat?"

"No, I'm good. Go back to bed."

When Marika walked into the living room, JJ was standing in the middle of the room, his arms wrapped around himself. He was trembling.

She moved toward him, wrapping her hands around his waist her head resting on his back. They stood like that for a long time then he began to sob.

"Come and sit down," she said, leading him to the couch. "I'll make us some tea."

Marika took her time in the small kitchen. While waiting for the water to boil she made him a sandwich and added a couple cookies to a plate. *He needs time to absorb what he has learned. Maybe I should have stopped him from going with Peter.*

She fixed a tray with two cups, the sandwich and cookies and placed it on the long table in front of the couch. She sat down being careful not to touch him. He was sitting with his elbows on his knees cradling his head in his hands. She poured a cup of tea and handed it to him. He took it and smiled at her.

"How was your road trip with Peter. He certainly has a tendency to talk too much."

"You can say that again," JJ laughed.

They sat side by side without talking. Marika understood his silence and knew he would talk when he was ready.

"I am going to change my major at the university from history to law at the end of the semester. Sophya is going to do the same as soon as she can." He said.

"Do you mind if I ask what prompted this decision. I thought you were happy with your choice of studies."

"I was but now feel like it's a complete waste my time. I didn't understand about the Believers and how they were persecuted. Peter not only opened my eyes to their pain and suffering but also to their courage."

Taking her hand, he said," I need to tell you something. Heinrich Mollen is Sophya's father but she didn't find out until her mother told her on her death bed. She is shocked and upset. She is hoping that by changing to law she can make up for some of the evil he."

"I thought as much," Marika answered. "What are you two going to do about that?"

JJ looked at his mother. "About what? I don't see a problem. I love her and I am going to marry her."

"JJ you can't. What will people think? She is the daughter of a murderer, a violent crazy man."

"I thought about that too. No one knows Jesse is my father, why do they need to know who her father was? Why should she be punished for the rest of her life because of what he did? Can you imagine what that will do to her?"

"What if word gets out? The Believers will see your marriage as the ultimate betrayal."

"It doesn't have to be that way. Others may see our marriage as the ultimate act of forgiveness. Isn't that what Jesse taught?"

Jesse stood up and began pacing back and forth across the room. "Mother, I didn't understand but after visiting the places Peter showed us, I want to do whatever I can to ease their suffering."

"Are you going to be like Peter now, bent on revenge? That will get you nowhere."

"No, that's not for me, but I certainly understand his feelings. We followed the route of the refugees smuggled into the country. Even after all this time many still need our help with their citizenship documents, proper jobs and someone to turn to if they have a problem. "

"What if you are asked to prosecute a war criminal? Do you think you could do that?"

"I wouldn't want to but could if I had to. To many, justice will bring closure."

He sounds so much like his father when he talks this way. I'm not sure if this is a good idea but has to be his decision. For now, it's better to work with him than stand against him. After all he is a grown man and has to do what he thinks is right.

"Now," she said, patting the couch beside her." Tell me where you went and what you saw."

"Well, we went to visit Uncle Mark and Aunt Elizabeth. They were happy to see us and said to tell you they are coming for a visit soon. I didn't realize I still have some living relatives. I thought they were all dead."

"That's my fault. I didn't think of them that way."

They talked over the next several hours. Sometimes they laughed, other times they cried, but Marika tried to be as honest as possible when answering his questions. The sun was coming up when he asked," why didn't you tell me any of this before?"

Marika thought for a long time. "I wanted you to have a normal life. One that you decided upon to become the man you are meant to be. Your father came to me in a dream and assured me you would do great things, but not as leader of the Believers. I chose not to tell you because the memories hurt too much to talk about and, I didn't want to unduly influence you. Now I believe you have found the path you are meant to follow."

Marika looked at her watch. "You need to get some rest and I need to get ready for work. Together we will do whatever we can so this type of cruelty never happens again."

FIFTY-NINE

Sophya heard someone knocking on her dorm room door. "Go away I don't want to see anybody." The knock came again, more insistent this time.

Sophya got up from her bed and walked to the door. She was still in her clothes from the day before, her hair sticking out in all directions and her eyes red from crying.

I said," go away."

The knock was louder and longer this time. She opened the door shouting at the person on the other side. "I don't want to see you. Can't you get it through your thick head. I want to be left alone."

Then she realized Marika was standing there. "You of all people, what do you want? I suppose you've come tell me to break up with JJ. If that's the case, consider it done. If you want to tell people who I am, go ahead. I don't care what happens to me anymore."

Marika calmly asked, "may I come in?"

"Might as well. You are going to anyway."

Marika entered the room and closed the door behind her. Sophya stood in the middle of the room her back turned to her. "Say what you have to say, then leave. I have to start packing."

"Why? Where are you going?" Marika asked.

"Because I am quitting school, that's why. You hate me, JJ hates me and I know Peter hates me. He was nice enough while we were travelling but that won't last."

Marika saw standing before her a young woman broken by what she learned and experienced. *Why she is nothing more than a child who just lost her mother.*

A voice in her head whispered "go to her. She needs you."

Marika took several steps forward." Sophya, I am sorry about your mother, JJ told me you were very close. I know how hard it is to lose someone you love deeply."

Sophya turned around, tears running down her face. "She was the only person I had in this world and now she's gone. I feel so lost and alone. I don't know how I am going to live without her."

Marika opened her arms and Sophya walked into them. She held her until she stopped sobbing. "I know how you feel. I felt the same way when Jesse died but, one day at a time, we learn to move forward. We simply learn to live with our loss. Although their body is not here their presence is always with us."

"Did JJ tell you who my father was. I swear I had no idea." She began crying again.

Marika took her hand and they both sat on the side of the bed. "Sophya, I came here to tell you that you and JJ should stop seeing each other. If word gets out about who your father was you won't be safe and will drag him down with you. If these same people find out who his father is he will be seen as a traitor by the Believers. Both of your lives will be in danger.'

"I know," Sophya said, "I will tell him tomorrow."

"Now, that isn't what I want for the two of you. Jesse's message was one of forgiveness. Neither one of you bear any responsibility for your father's actions. That is the past and others, like you, are the future. We cannot change what happened because that will always be part of the history of the Believers.

My Jesse was a stubborn man driven by what he felt he needed to do. Heinrich was also driven but he had a different motive. The assassination ended their relationship the way it was meant to be. Neither of you had anything to do with it."

"Can you ever forgive me" Sophya asked.

"Oh, my dear child, I have nothing to forgive you for. JJ loves you and that's what matters." Marika responded.

They sat there in silence. "Did he tell you I am going to switch my major to law at the end of the semester. As an exchange student I have to clear the idea with my professors first."

"Yes, he did, but why, if I may ask?"

"Peter explained to us that some of the men directly under Heinrich's command had their own agenda. I'm not trying to make excuses for them. He told them what he wanted done but was not responsible for how his orders were carried out."

"I can go along with some of that but he shot and killed Jesse before my very eyes. I will never forgive him for that."

Sophya began crying again. "I'm so sorry. Now I know why you were shocked to see me that evening."

"Please try and understand. I don't hate you, but I hate what your father did to my husband.

So, to change the subject, if you go into law what are you going to specialize in?"

"Women's rights. I want to help the women recover. Men can fight back but the women and children are the real victims in any conflict. Even now they have little or no choice in what happens to them."

Once again, the two women sat in silence. Marika reached for Sophya's hand. "Get yourself cleaned up and join us for supper this evening. JJ will be glad to see you."

Marika walked to the window and pulled the curtains open. Sunlight poured into the room.

"Today is a new day. Supper is at six. I'll see you then." Marika said, letting herself out the door.

As she left the building Marika felt as though a weight had been lifted from her shoulders. For the first time in a long time, she felt happy and contented. *They will be good for each other. If I didn't know better, I would think Jesse had a hand in this.*

SIXTY

Three years later Peter knocked on the open door of JJ's office and walked in. JJ looked up from his desk "Good morning, Peter. What can I do for you today?"

"I have great news. After all of these years Eli, the man who betrayed your father, has been captured. The police arrested him last night."

JJ looked up at him. "So why are you so happy? That was twenty-five years ago, what does it matter now?"

"It matters a lot to those of us who were there that night. If he hadn't betrayed Jesse, he would still be alive. That night the Believers swore to bring Eli to justice and make him pay. You should be happy. Now you will get justice for growing up without a father."

"Why do I have a feeling there is more to this? I suppose you are going to give me the case to prosecute."

"What could be more fitting? You finally get revenge for your father's death. I had to pull a few strings to make this possible."

JJ ran his fingers through his hair then, looking at Peter, he said, "You should have consulted me first. What if I don't want to?"

"Think about it for a minute. Terrible things happened during that time and not every man has this opportunity. You will go down in history." Peter replied.

After Peter left JJ was troubled. *Is this something I really want to do? What will it accomplish? All I see is more bitterness and mistrust in the future.*

First, he phoned home to Sophya to tell her he would be late for supper, then he phoned his mother. "Do you mind if I stop on my way home from work? There is something I need to talk to you about."

"Of course, I'll be here. I don't work today. Will you have supper with me?"

No, I have already called Sophya to tell her I will be late. She usually waits to eat with me."

When Marika opened the door a deeply troubled JJ stood on the other side. "Is something wrong? Has something happened? Come in and tell me."

He entered the room and sat down on the faded green couch. Marika sat down beside him and took his hand in hers.

"I haven't seen you look this serious for a long time. What's troubling you?"

"Peter came to my office this morning. The police raided a homeless camp last night and Eli was among those arrested."

"Eli? The same one who betrayed your father?"

"Yes, the same man. Without asking, Peter called in a few favors and he wants me to be the prosecutor on his case."

"What is he being charged with besides vagrancy?"

"Murder. They are holding him responsible for Jesse's death. The Believers still want revenge."

"After all this time? How can they do that? This happened such a long time ago. Besides Heinrich was the person who shot and killed your father. I was there, I saw it happen with my own eyes."

"Some of the Believers took a vow that day. They have every intention of using this man to get justice. They hold him responsible. They claim that if he hadn't betrayed Jesse, he would have lived."

Marika sat quietly looking down at their hands. "Yes, Eli was the man who brought the Brown Shirts to him that night, but Heinrich was bent on capturing Jesse. If it wasn't him, it would have been somebody else.

The outcome was inevitable. It wasn't so much a question of if Heinrich captured Jesse, it was simply a matter of when. Your father was well aware that he had little time left to complete his mission."

"Tell me about Eli. What kind of a man was he?"

"He was one of the close followers but a very unhappy man. He drank a lot and was always complaining about being treated unfairly. The Brown Shirts heard his complaints, arrested him and took him to Duvenwald prison. Nobody knows for sure what took place, but he was badly beaten and tortured. He was a different man the next time we saw him.

After that he disappeared and nobody saw him again until the night he brought the Brown Shirts to the cave. The only thing he was guilty of was revealing where your father could be found. He disappeared and hasn't been seen or heard of again until now."

JJ was quiet. "I don't know what to do mother. I know he betrayed my father's location but it seems unfair to blame him for what Heinrich did. Do you think he knew Jesse would be killed?"

"No, I don't think so. I believe he thought Heinrich would only talk to him or put him in prison. Heinrich was like a man possessed that morning. To be honest I don't think he meant to go as far as he did. He simply wanted Jesse to acknowledge him, to prove once and for all that he was the better of the two. The blind rage he was in got the best of him."

JJ got up and walked to the door.

"What are you going to do?" Marika asked.

"I honestly don't know," he replied. "Will you testify against him?"

"No son, I will not. Some things are better left in the past."

"What would my father do?"

"Your father believed in forgiveness and treating others as you would want to be treated. He would forgive Eli."

He slept poorly that night. The only thing he knew for sure was that he wished Peter had got the case assigned to somebody else.

SIXTY-ONE

Peter and JJ were sitting at the prosecutors table in the court room when Eli was brought in. The man standing before them was gaunt, with hair too long and a white beard that fell to his chest. His clothes were practically rags and he wore no shoes.

The first thing JJ noticed was his eyes. They were like the those of a hunted animal, furtively looking for a way to escape. Every person in the court room could see life had not been kind to him.

The judge entered the room. "Stand up Eli. Do you know why you are here?"

"Not really," he replied.

"You are charged with the murder of Jesse, the leader of the Believers."

Eli swayed on his feet, clutching the railing in front of him. "I didn't know they were going to kill him. You have to believe me," he pleaded. "I thought all they wanted me to do was take the Brown shirts to where he was."

The judge cut Eli off, "How do you plead?"

Eli was crying. "I didn't know what they were going to do. You have to believe me. I loved Jesse. I believed in him."

The judge asked again," how do you plead?"

"Not guilty of murder, but guilty of doing a very stupid thing."

The judge looked over at JJ "I am setting a trial date for one month from now. Can you be ready by then?"

JJ looked at Eli. He saw a broken man, burdened with guilt from what he had done so many years ago."

He stood and faced the judge. "Your honor if I could speak for a minute?

What happened took place twenty-five years ago when our country was in the grip of a mad man. Men and women were beaten and coerced into things they would never have thought they would be capable of doing.

Jesse believed in two things. The first, forgiving those who wronged you. To him everybody was equal. I believe, if he were here today, he would forgive Eli. The second is treating others as you want to be treated.

I stand in front of this court and say "I forgive you Eli. You were not responsible for my father's death. Heinrich was the man who killed him. I believe you made an error in judgement and were unaware of Heinrich's intentions."

The crowd gasped and began talking among themselves. The judge banged his gavel on the desk in front of him.

"If I may continue," JJ said. "This morning, I reviewed the evidence against Eli and have determined that we will not be prosecuting him because there isn't enough evidence for a conviction. Many of those who witnessed that day are either dead or unable to be located. I can't find one person willing to testify against Eli, not even my own mother. Twenty-five years is a long time to carry out the revenge the Believers swore to. Therefore, I move this case be dismissed."

He sat down. The courtroom was quiet. The judged looked at JJ and then at Eli.

"Eli, stand up," he commanded.

Visibly shaking, Eli got to his feet.

"I agree with the Prosecutor. There is insufficient evidence to continue. You are free to go."

Then, as an afterthought, he added, 'You have been forgiven by those with the most invested in this case. Now the time has come for you to forgive yourself. Go, and be the man Jesse thought you were when he welcomed you as one of followers. Case dismissed."

The judge left the room. The hand cuffs were taken off Eli's wrists. He walked over to JJ and said "thank you for giving me back my life. Never a day goes by that I haven't thought about what I did, but sometimes I wonder, if it wasn't me, would somebody else have done the same thing?"

JJ nodded. "That is one thing we will never know."

ABOUT THE AUTHOR

Judy lives in northern Alberta Canada with her dog Toby. As a child she began writing and, at one time thought of becoming a journalist. When she retired from the business world, she decided there was nothing stopping her from following her dream. Since then, she has published fifteen books, five under the name of Judith Costes, the rest as J L Coates. Needless to say, there are several waiting to be finished.

She can be reached at jcoates@telusplanet.net or on her face book page.